1

On a lazy afternoon in late May, 1846, DeWitt "Dooey" Dolan was in the mood for making love. He and Sally Middlebrook were lying in tall grass on the bank of the Connecticut River, an ideal spot for what Dooey had in mind. The last thing he wanted was to be distracted by nagging questions from Sally:

"Dooey . . . ?"

"What?"

"Where were you these past two weeks?"

"Away."

"Silly! I know that!"

Sally frowned at him, and Dooey frowned right back, aping her. The grassy knoll they'd picked for this particular rendezvous was about a mile north of Wethersfield, which was home for them both. Actually, Dooey, an orphan, didn't really consider it his home; it was simply a place where he had been living for the past fifteen years. But Sally, whose parents owned a dairy farm, had lived there all her life.

"Sure is a lazy afternoon, isn't it?" Dooey said.

Sally pouted. "You're changing the subject."

As so often happened when she was with Dooey, she was torn between anger and desire. At twenty-four, he was terribly attractive. Lithe and muscular, black-haired and black-eyed, he had a rebellious air that fascinated her. But he could also get her goat.

She tried once more. "Dooey Dolan, you're so secretive sometimes you disgust me! I don't know, I can't see why John admires you so!"

"He doesn't know any better." Dooey grinned at her in that infuriating way he had. "You two should get married, Sally—you love each other. As for me, why, I've been to New York City."

Sally said, "Oh!" then, "But that doesn't help! What were you doing there?"

"Come on now, Sally, that's enough."

The truth was that Dooey was a little troubled by Sally's question. He was also a little troubled by this affair he was having with his best friend's fiancée, though not enough to keep him from enjoying it as long as it lasted. He had gone to New York to see about joining the Army, which had put out a call for volunteers after war with Mexico was declared earlier that month. But he didn't want to discuss this with Sally, not now and perhaps not ever. Sally would object to his taking part in this war; like many New Englanders, she thought the war against Mexico unjustifiable, morally indefensible. So did Dooey, for that matter, but he had private reasons for wanting to go to Mexico. They had nothing to do with fighting a war and they had nothing to do with Sally. They had a lot to do with a secret dream he had been nurturing since childhood.

He stirred, coming out of his reverie in time to see a breeze blow a ringlet of blonde hair over Sally's questioning blue eyes.

"You look awfully pretty, Sally," he said.

Sally ignored the compliment, gazing at him expectantly, still waiting for an answer to her question.

Dooey sighed and joshingly said the first thing that came to his mind. "Sally, don't you know there's a war on? President Polk just declared one. I can't talk. Some Mexican spy might come up out of the Connecticut River and—"

As soon as Dooey said it, he realized he'd made a mistake. Sally leaped on the remark.

"You've joined up! You've volunteered for the army!"

"Well, no, I haven't."

It was true, he hadn't . . . at least, not yet. Dooey looked at Sally's anxious face, saw how much she was yearning for him to tell her that it wasn't so, that he would not go away and leave her. "I did no such thing," Dooey said firmly. "Come here."

He was lying on his back on the grass now and Sally was bent over him. He reached up and pulled Sally's face closer to his. A rush of desire had come over him when he'd seen her concern. Her lips were full and red and slightly parted; the smell of mint was on them from the clover she'd been nibbling on. He wanted to banish the worried look he'd put into her eyes, which had filmed with passion now when he touched her. He wanted to taste those lips.

Dooey Dolan hungered avidly for whatever it was Sally Middlebrook was offering him at the moment.

"Dooey, not so rough."

He ignored her. He kissed her, hard and deep. "God, you're beautiful!" he muttered, and Sally, knowing herself to be short of that, suddenly rose to meet the illusion Dooey was creating for them both.

She flung herself on him. He had to wrestle with her passion, which was a young girl's and immediately demanding. As she drove her lips down hard on his, he held her off long enough to work his hand beneath her blouse. He slid his hand down her breast and cupped it, gently caressing the nipple with his fingers until it hardened. Then he removed the hand, slid it down between their stomachs to between her legs and rubbed there until his fingers were dampened through her dress. Then he tasted his fingers.

Sally, seeing the gesture, became distraught. Gluing her lips to his, she hunched her lower body, pulling down her undergarments while Dooey unbuttoned the fly of his trousers. His erection was enormous. Sally's breath caught. She had an overwhelming urge to take it in her mouth, but Dooey stopped her, pulling her directly over him.

Dress clutched wildly about her middle, Sally sat down hungrily on the whole length of his erection. Everything, all sense, seemed to leave her at that moment, except for the feeling of its penetration. Her eyes glazed and her tongue curled against her top lip. Dooey, seeing this, all but drowned in his own yearning. He made a move upward to catch her tongue in his mouth, but at the nudge of his hips, Sally shook her head frantically, bent to put her cheek against his and, not looking at him, began to move and then, quickly, to gallop against his groin.

Dooey met her movements, one tantalizing, slow thrust of his to three furious gallops of hers. Finally, with a great lurch, Dooey erupted in a sudden powerful orgasm. Now Sally moaned and buried her mouth against his shoulder. Abruptly she went limp and lay nuzzling his neck. He smelled her hair . . . the odor of honey. Her cheek was warm and flushed in the hollow of his neck.

Sally murmured, "Why is it only you can do this to me?"

Dooey chuckled. "Maybe because you never tried it with anyone else!"

"Shh!" She put a finger over his lips. "I never want to hear that from you again. Do you hear me? Never!"

After a while, they stood, fixed their clothing and started walking back to town slowly and at some sad distance from each other. Sally was thinking: *I must get over Dooey, I must. It's John I love and want to live with for the rest of my life. What I am doing with Dooey is wrong.*

Dooey was thinking: *I'll catch hell when she finds out I really am going to Mexico. I wonder why she loves me so much when I don't love her? Women are strange. . . .*

The usually articulate James Bell was reading the *Gazette*'s war news and spluttering when his son John came bounding up the porch steps after the Saturday morning ball game on the village green.

"Provoked . . . American soil . . . rot!" James peered up at his son over rimless spectacles that made him look a bit like the portrait of Ben Franklin hanging in the parlor. "Did we win?" he said. "From your beaming countenance, I'd say we did."

"Just." John, as blond and slim at twenty-two as his father had been at that age, grinned. "By one run. Dooey made a mighty throw to save the game."

James Bell grunted. "And you?"

John said modestly, "I did well enough. I hit the ball that led to our winning run."

"Baseball," James Bell remarked mildly. "In my day, it was rounders. Still, everything changes, I suppose. New games come into fashion. Were it not for my gout, I would have been at the green cheering you boys on."

John smiled. "I know that, pa." He looked at the crumpled condition of the New England weekly his father was holding. John wondered if it wasn't the war with Mexico and the statements about it coming out of Washington that was aggravating his father's gout. The Bells, father and son, were coopers in Wethersfield, an occupation the family had pursued in New England for eight generations, dating back to 1630. They had the stable values of simpler times. During the Revolution, for example, the issue had been quite clear: freedom from British political oppression was at stake, and New Englanders like John's great-grandfather Matthew Bell had fought valiantly for it. But in this war with Mexico, the issues were more perplexing, perhaps because the country had grown and changed so much in seventy years. There was no question that Americans like James Bell were sorely troubled by it.

John asked, "Is the news bad, pa? I haven't seen it yet."

"It's not that it's bad, it's that I don't understand it," James Bell said. "Perhaps, being more in tune with the spirit of these times, you can explain it to me, John. I confess I've become steadily more confused about the direction this country has taken ever since Andy Jackson was elected president in 'twenty-eight."

John smiled. "No, you haven't pa. You're as clear-headed as ever—and just as foxy."

"Well, maybe." James Bell looked up at his son, his

blue eyes twinkling behind his spectacles. "Would you like to wash up before I put my questions to you? Your mother will be serving dinner at noon sharp."

John shook his head. "Not necessary, pa. I washed up at Dooey's place after the game."

"I see. I assume DeWitt will be here promptly for dinner?"

John hesitated, "Dooey's not coming today, pa. He had some business to attend to after the game. He didn't say what."

James Bell frowned. "Well, then, I'd best tell your mother she needn't set a place for him." He half-rose from the rocker.

"Uh, pa . . ." John was shaking his head again. "Don't trouble yourself. I told ma this morning that Dooey wouldn't be here."

James sat down, glowering at him. "That's another thing. You boys keep secrets from me. DeWitt lived in this house for almost ten years and I swear I never knew what was in his head. Still don't. And," he added bluntly, "I don't think you do either, John."

John said simply, "I like Dooey. He's like an older brother to me."

James said sourly, "I see no indication that your affection is returned. However . . ."

John knew his father would never understand about him and Dooey; it was best to drop the subject. "Tell me about the war, pa."

James leaned forward, tapping the *Gazette*. "We have here, finally, a full report on the so-called border incident that led our esteemed president, Mr. Polk, to declare war on Mexico two weeks ago. It seems that a Mexican cavalry unit crossed to the north side of the Rio Grande River, where General Zachary Taylor is presently headquartered, and attacked a Captain

Seth Thornton and some sixty-five other dragoons who had been sent to see if the Mexicans were there. They obviously were. Did you ever hear of Captain Seth Thornton, son?"

"Well, you will, as it appears he will soon become a national hero. Captain Thornton himself apparently escaped the Mexicans' evil clutches, but some of his men had, according to Mr. Polk, 'spilled American blood on American soil,' thus enabling us to recognize —and these are General Taylor's words to Mr. Polk— that 'hostilities can be considered to have commenced.' Ergo, the declaration of war by Congress and the call for fifty thousand volunteers."

John nodded. "I suspect you have a sharp point to make about all this, pa."

James Bell snapped angrily, "My point is, that any young man who volunteers for this war is a fool or a knave—one or the other! This border incident is without significance except to serve as that Tennessean Polk's pretext for taking Mexican land by force and dividing it into slave states for the South! Everyone knows this! Daniel Webster knows it! Polk himself knows it, only he'd never admit it! And I know it! American soil indeed! Down where Taylor and his troops are, it's no more American soil than China is! Not even the Texans claimed a border down to the Rio Grande. They would have been satisfied with a Neuces River border, up near Corpus Christi! Both sides of the Rio Grande are in Mexico, and it's downright wicked to claim otherwise! Here, let me get my map, I'll show you. Oh! *Ow*! My foot!"

James Bell rose and sat down again abruptly, clutching his big toe. John put a hand on his father's trembling shoulder. "Pa, don't carry on so. Things will work out for the good of the country, you'll see, I'm sure of it." But he soothed his father absent-mindedly, and barely felt the familiar flesh under his fingers, so preoccupied was he with his own thoughts.

The elder Bell shook his head. "I am afraid, John. I fear that this disgraceful war of conquest may well end this nation's beginnings. As much as we here in New England oppose it, so people in the South favor it. If the issue isn't slavery—and I'm bending over backwards not to follow the abolitionists in saying that it is—at the very least it's the struggle for sectional power. Any lands we might take by force from Mexico, the South will carve states out of—with Polk's backing. They'll put slaves there as a matter of course, and they'll also have increased legislative power to remove import duties on European manufactured goods and do other things harmful to industries in the North. We will not stand for this. Things are bad enough between us as it is. I fear that if Polk gets what he wants in Mexico, it will lead to a bloody civil war here. You're only twenty-two, John. You're my son, and I don't want you to have to fight in such a war."

John blinked. His father was painting a very gloomy picture indeed. John had not been looking so far into the future; he certainly had not seen the present conflict with Mexico in so dark a light. Now, he realized, he would have to confront his father and let him know how *he* felt . . . and what he was planning to do about it.

"Pa," he said quietly, "you may as well know now that I'm thinking of volunteering for duty in Mexico."

James Bell stared speechlessly at him for a moment. When he did speak again, his voice was hoarse with emotion. "But . . . why, John? Why?"

John shook his head. "There's no one reason, pa. To

see more of the world than Connecticut. To see for myself what the war is all about. To meet fellows like me from all over the country—maybe some Mexican girls too. Just for the adventure of it, pa. If I do volunteer, I figure I'll only sign three-month papers, so I'll be back here before you know it."

James Bell shook his head slowly. "This is a disgraceful war, son. You have no business going off to fight it." He paused, then asked, "Has the trouble you've been having lately with Sally had something to do with your decision?"

"I guess it has, pa," John admitted. "Not that Sally and I have had any major argument, I just thought I'd leave her alone for a while."

"And Dooey, how does he figure in all this?" John's father asked shrewdly.

"Well, Dooey, he's volunteering—he's made up his mind about it—and he asked me if I didn't want to go along with him. I thought that might be a good idea, because if you're going to go off some place as far as Mexico, it's better to go with a friend."

"I guess that's so," James Bell said. His look was sad, reproachful, but he sensed it would be useless to argue with his son. He couldn't help saying though, "Maybe you'll change your mind, John. I hope you do."

2

"HEY, DOO—EY!"

All the loneliness in the world was in that call as John Bell spied his friend two blocks ahead of him on Wethersfield's main street and hurried to catch up with him. It was twilight, the Monday after the ball game and its aftermath. John had worked silently all day hammering up barrel staves, at odds with his equally silent father. He wanted to go to Mexico but was having trouble leaving home, trouble wrenching Wethersfield out of his heart.

Dooey Dolan turned and smiled. "Hello, John. Made up your mind yet?"

"I—I want to talk to Sally first. That's where I'm heading."

"You could have talked to her yesterday," Dooey pointed out.

John said, "Her folks came over to the house with

her. We all had Sunday dinner together. I couldn't get her alone." He didn't add that Sally hadn't given him the chance to.

Dooey made no comment. The two young men trudged along together for a while. It had been another langorous spring day. Now the descending sun seemed to add more sweetness to the aroma of the roses planted in boxes along the sidewalk by Wethersfield's Ladies Society.

Dooey said, "Sally's just a girl, John."

"But I love her. Dooey, do you have any idea why she's been avoiding me lately?"

Dooey's pulse quickened. "No, why should I?"

"Well, you talk to her sometimes, and you're more experienced with women than I am. I'm wondering—I'm wondering if maybe she didn't meet some fellow up in Litchfield last time she went to visit her aunt." He looked at his friend anxiously.

Dooey sighed with relief. He didn't want any trouble with John— not now. He was just as eager as the other, younger man was for companionship in the Mexico adventure. "If she did, she didn't tell me about it," he said.

They walked on in silence again, John breathing in the flower scents in the cool twilight. He shook his head. "It must be awfully hot in Mexico. There's nothing but scrub, thorns and snakes there, they say."

Dooey shrugged. "I suppose that's so," he said, and fell silent again.

John, after a moment, said, "Dooey, why do you want to volunteer from New York? We could do it here. Connecticut's raising a regiment of its own, you know."

"Told you," Dooey answered impatiently. "I made

arrangements in New York that will get us to Mexico faster. Besides, it's home for me."

"Home! After what happened to you there?"

What had happened to Dooey Dolan, then eight years old, was the sudden, shocking death of both of his parents. John didn't know much about them, only what his mother had told him. Dooey's mother was Catherine DeWitt, of a wealthy New York family known to the Connecticut Bells largely through contacts earlier generations of the family had had with each other. According to Abigail Bell, Catherine had been an independent young woman who had chosen to marry beneath her station in wedding an Irish immigrant by the name of Tyrone Dolan. The couple had apparently been very much in love with each other and had had Dooey as something of an afterthought. In 1830, when Dooey was eight, a nighttime fire of unknown origin had flared up in their Bowery house, consuming them both. Dooey, rescued from the fire escape onto which he had crowded, was sent briefly to stay with his uncle, Carson DeWitt, and was eventually adopted into the Bell home—Abigail's foundling, James's nemesis and John's boon companion.

John was thinking now, as he often did, how painful this all must have been for Dooey. But Dooey never wanted to talk about it and he didn't now, though John had left the door open for him.

They had reached the Bull and Bear Tavern on Main Street and Dooey stopped. "Here's where I leave you. Good luck with Sally. Good luck with making up your mind."

John hesitated, but Dooey did not ask him to join him. Instead, he said, "Don't worry about New York—that is all taken care of. Just keep thinking about the free roast beef, ice cream and three months advance pay we'll be getting, like they're saying on the recruitment posters. That is, if Sally doesn't persuade you to stay home."

"Heck, Dooey, it'll be a miracle if that happens. Still, I want to give it a try. You know . . ."

"Sure. I know. Good luck, John."

John went to the Middlebrook farm. He and Sally sat in the sideyard swing and John told her what was in his heart. She seemed nervous to him, and for a while he saw that as a sign of hope.

"You look awfully good in that dress, Sally," he said.

"Oh, do you like it?" Her blue eyes brightened and she stopped twisting her handkerchief. "I bought the material by mail from the Sears company and mother sewed it up for me."

John nodded. "It's a real nice pink."

He hesitated, then went on. "I'm thinking of going off to the war in Mexico, Sally. Dooey's going and we've been talking about it."

"I know Dooey's going. He told me so Saturday afternoon."

She looked glum and John could understand that; the three of them were good friends. Sally wouldn't want to see either of them go away.

"I'm not so sure I'd be wanting to go if I didn't feel that something's come between us these past few months," John said. "I thought maybe you'd tell me why you've been kind of avoiding me."

Sally put her hand on his. "I haven't been avoiding you, John. You mustn't think that. You are always in my mind."

John shook his head. "That's not what I mean. I just

haven't seen you much. I know I've been busy. Pa and I have barrel orders clear up to Maine now, and we have to work hard to fill them. But even on weekends . . . well, for instance, you didn't even come to the ballgame Saturday." He grinned at her shyly; not that the ball game had been all that important, but he *had* missed seeing her there.

"I—I just didn't feel like going."

John studied her. "Don't you want us to get married anymore?" he asked bluntly.

"Yes, yes, I do," she said. "But . . . but—" She kept twisting her handkerchief and there was a hint of tears in her eyes.

"Is there somebody else?" He asked it quietly, but his heart was pounding.

"No . . . no, you mustn't think that, John."

"Well, what am I supposed to think?"

Sally thought quickly. "That I need more time to think about getting married. That I've been away from you, but thinking about it all the time."

"Well, I'll think that, if that's what you want." Then he grinned, blue eyes twinkling. "You don't mind if, in the meantime, I have some fun with some hot Mexican girls, do you?"

"You run off with one of them and I'll come and shoot you, John!" Her eyes sparkled and she slapped him playfully. "Now, you sit here and I'll go get us some cider."

Sally got up and moved to the back door of the farmhouse. Closing the wooden door as well as the screen door behind her, she leaned against the kitchen wall and fell into uncontrollable weeping. She had made a terrifying discovery early Saturday morning; she was three months pregnant with Dooey Dolan's child. It must have happened when they went to his hayloft after the Washington's Birthday dance. She hadn't told Dooey; she would not tell John. How could she tell either of them?

What would she do with the baby? Ghastly thoughts flitted through her mind as she stood there, trembling, in the darkening kitchen. There would be no baby. She would kill herself. She would take a knife and thrust it up inside her, because it was not Dooey but the itch she had within her that had brought this monstrous calamity down on her. If only it had been John's child, she thought desperately, there might have been a way! But it hadn't been John she lusted for—it was Dooey. Lust and love were mixed up in her head. Most of all, in her heart, was the shame of bearing a child out of wedlock. Until she could think of what to do, they all had to go away—Dooey, John, her father, the whole town of Wethersfield, everybody! She had to be alone. She had to die. . . .

Sally stood in the kitchen and sobbed.

Outside, John sat relaxed and content, except that Sally was so slow bringing out the cider. Things had suddenly and unexpectedly come together for him. He figured if Sally could tell him she'd come and shoot him for fooling around with some Mexican girl, she must still care for him, and that was good enough for him for the time being. He'd go to Mexico with Dooey, come back with some colorful stories and maybe, by then, Sally would come around to wanting to get married again.

A firefly lit on his hair and he brushed it away. The moon was up. He glanced up at it, then down at the patterns its light made, shining through the leaves of the elm behind him and down onto the swing's seat. Simple Wethersfield sights and sounds like these mattered to John, but they weren't too hard to say goodbye to when you knew you would be home to see them again soon.

Sally finally came out with the cider. John drank his quickly. Sally looked tired to him and he figured he'd leave and let her get some sleep. Besides, there wasn't much more to say.

"I'm going to Mexico, Sally. I'll try to write to you, though I don't know about the mails," he said.

She said quietly, "I'll understand if I don't hear from you, John."

He put his empty glass down. "Well, goodbye then."

"Goodbye, John. Please take good care of yourself. . . ."

John took his time on the moonlit walk home. There remained, of course, his father to confront with his final decision. It was nine o'clock by the time John got home. He braced himself when he found both of his parents waiting on the porch for him.

John managed a tentative, "Hello, ma."

Abigail Bell, a stoutish, grey-haired, pleasant-faced woman, said, "Hello, John. Is Sally well?"

"Yes, she is, ma."

His father surprised him then. "I take it you're going," James Bell said.

"I want to see things for myself, pa."

James said sourly, "For yourself or for DeWitt's self?"

John said nothing.

"Don't be so hard on DeWitt, dear," Abigail said. "He's a sensitive boy and intelligent too, just like our John."

"I think so, ma," John said quickly.

James Bell grumbled, "The boy's no damned good. Well, never mind. . . . who's going to help me in the shop while you're away?" he asked John.

"Danny Jenkins can do that," John said promptly. "He told me he'd like a summer job with us. If he starts now, I'll be back before he goes back to college."

His father nodded. "I'll speak to Danny about it." Then James Bell frowned. "I don't know what word to send you off with, son." There was an awkward silence while his father thought and John waited. "The only advice . . ." James Bell shrugged, then looked squarely at his son. "No matter what anyone tells you to believe—general, president or anyone else—hold on to your own thoughts, your own feelings and, once you have them, your own convictions. And choose your actions. Never let yourself believe, even for an instant, that you have no choice in what you do. We—we have always tried to embrace those ideals in New England."

"I intend to do the best I can, pa."

"Tell DeWitt to make sure to stop by here before you leave," Abigail said. "I'll have a basket of food for you both."

"I'm sure he'll do that, ma."

Later, upstairs in his bed, John could not sleep. Eyes wide open, staring at the moon shining in the window, he pictured the Halls of Montezuma, which he saw as tall stone towers filled with silver and gold. He envisioned the spread of America westward, himself a part of the movement of wagons on the trail, with creaking wheels and friendly fires at night, en route to green new lands in California. He envisioned tanned Mexican girls with shapely figures bathing near-nude in the Rio Grande, and his eyes glowed.

He did not feel that he could wait until the next day to tell Dooey. He got up, dressed hastily, tiptoed down the stairs and out of the house, then ran to the high road on the far side of town where Dooey had his smithy.

The shop was dark but there was a lamp lit in the loft above it. He could see Dooey in bed reading a book. John picked up a handful of pebbles and flung them at the loft window. He saw Dooey come bouncing out of bed, laughed, and had flung more pebbles at the window before Dooey finally got it open and stared down at him.

"Hey, you son-of-a-bitch," John shouted. "Let's go fight Mexicans . . . !"

3

DOOEY AND JOHN went to a cafe on Broadway, in New York City, and there met a French count by the name of Gustave d'Orleans, who was raising a company for the New York First Volunteer Regiment.

This was the man Dooey had found through a newspaper advertisement on his scouting trip to the city. Dooey had explained to John that the Frenchman "had connections." Volunteers from northern states were being held back from action in favor of Texans, Missourians and others closer to the fighting. But the Frenchman had promised, Dooey said, that for a fee he would persuade the recruiting agency at Fort Hamilton to send all "his" volunteers to Mexico immediately.

John didn't like Count d'Orleans, a man of about forty-five who was entirely too smooth in speech and manner for him. Nor was John particularly comfortable in the cafe, which was overcrowded and noisy. As they sat waiting for the other recruits, John watched the Frenchman go to the bar for a glass of wine. "I don't believe he's a count at all," he said to Dooey. "And it's pretty clear he's not raising a legitimate company."

Dooey said, "It doesn't matter. If you want certain things, you have to put up with certain things."

John grew ever more uneasy. "How much did you pay him, Dooey? I want to know what my share is."

Before Dooey could answer, the Frenchman came back. He sat down and began to speak of "Taylor's gallant little army," which was a phrase in the newspapers and on everybody's lips now that the general and his three thousand U.S. Army Regulars had won two quick, successive battles on the north side of the Rio Grande. These battles, at Palo Alto and Resaca de la Palma, had been fought and won at about the same time President Polk had asked Congress for a declaration of war, though the president could not have known this due to the delay in communications from the field. The news had come out during the past few days, however, and now patriotic fervor was at its height.

"It is good news, eh?" The Frenchman beamed at them. "General Taylor's gallant little army has destroyed the Mexicans, *absolument*. They have fled. The general will be your next president, mark my words. And you boys—you will have only to swim in the Rio Grande and taste *la joie*. Ah, *la joie!*" He kissed his fingers.

"Where did the Mexicans run to?" John asked.

"But I do not know," the Frenchman said, as if surprised at the question. "They have left Matamoros and gone away. But surely they will sue for peace within the fortnight, do you not think so?"

"I don't know," John said. "Aren't you going to Mexico with us?"

"If only I could." The Frenchman sighed, shaking his head sadly. "But I must return to France to look after my family's estate."

John regarded him sourly. Dooey, who had been listening quietly, only grinned. To him, this was so much idle talk. He was eager to get started south—for reasons that had little to do with the fighting in Mexico. On the way to the cafe, he and John had passed the Bowery tenement where Dooey's doomed parents had died, nearly taking him with them. He had been filled with such black, raging hatred at the memory that, for a moment, he had felt dizzy. But then "the dream," the dream that would come true thanks to this fortuitous war with Mexico, had returned to soothe his troubled soul. In a way, President Polk and the U.S. Army would be paying his way home. . . .

"What time are the others in our company due here?" Dooey asked Count d'Orleans now.

"Any moment. Perhaps on the next trolley. And then we shall all go to Fort Hamilton." The Frenchman hesitated, then volunteered some additional information. "There will be a Dutchman, an Irishman like yourself, and—I hope you don't mind—a little Jew boy."

Dooey shrugged. "All the same to me."

John, who was beginning to despise the bogus count, thought about the other recruits' nationalities and put that together with what he'd heard about newly arrived immigrants volunteering quickly for the war, for the seven-dollars-a-month wages and free board they could get. Jobs were scarce for the foreign-born, particularly for Catholics. People didn't like them; there had been large-scale anti-Catholic riots in Philadelphia just a year or so before.

The others soon arroved. There was tall, blond Hendrik ten Hoor; shorter, burlier Michael Reardon, and 15-year-old Jacob Herschel, who had an open, innocent expression and wore a *yarmulka* on his head.

The names were exchanged and greetings, of a sort, went round. The red-faced Reardon had a snicker for the Dutchman. "Ten Hoor!" he said. "Ten *Hoor!* Do people ever call you just plain *whore*?"

The young Dutchman thought a moment. "Not intelligent people," he said with a sparkle in his blue eyes.

Reardon's red face got redder and John and Dooey suppressed grins, warming to ten Hoor immediately.

Dooey turned to young Herschel. "What do you want with this man's army, Jake?"

The boy spoke French and German but did not speak English too well, and he had to grope for words. "I am an orphan in this city. My mother lives in Bavaria. I wish to fight for America and hope to see a great deal of the world."

Reardon snickered nastily again. "Probably got his kikey eyes on the quartermaster corps so he can peddle our supplies to the greasers."

Dooey ignored him. "Do you think the Army will accept you at your age, Jake?" he asked.

The boy looked troubled. "I do not know," he said. "Count d'Orleans said he could arrange for me to be accepted."

Dooey nodded. "Well, that's all right then. You can count on the count . . . isn't that right, Count?"

He winked at the Frenchman, who looked away, as if ashamed.

As they got up to leave for the horse-drawn street car that would take them to Brooklyn and Fort Hamilton, Reardon let the others go ahead and waited for Dooey. "Damme, I thought you was Irish!" he growled. "Why're you stickin' up for them peckerheads?"

Dooey answered genially enough. "You've got me wrong, friend. I'm just plain American." Then the controlled anger in him rose to the surface. He turned on Reardon. "Especially if being Irish means being like you."

Reardon flushed deep red. "Why you—!" He shoved the wooden cafe table aside to give himself some room and swung a punch up from the floor towards Dooey's jaw. It was an awkward punch and Dooey saw it coming. He stepped in close, rage boiling inside him, and grabbed the shorter man's beefy wrist. Then he grabbed a handful of Reardon's shirt at the chest and jerked him in close. Dooey was breathing hard; there was murder in him. Eyeball-to-eyeball with Reardon, he spat, "Don't you touch me, you bastard! Don't you ever touch me!"

He shoved Reardon away. The Irishman stared at him. For a flickering instant he was frightened, but then he charged after Dooey, who had turned and walked out the door. He was too late; Dooey had joined up with the others. Reardon would be quickly overpowered, even by them.

They were all waiting, with the count, to board the street car when Reardon came up to Dooey and muttered: "I'll get you for that, just wait and see."

Dooey turned and looked at him. By then his rage had subsided and he was contemplating what he had almost done. It was true; he could have killed Reardon. He had been surprised by the strong urge to violence that had risen in him. In a way, he was pleased, even exhilarated, for Reardon was physically stronger than he was. But he was troubled too. Standing there, Dooey had a weird premonition. Smiling tightly at Reardon, he said:

"You may not be alone in trying."

True to the count's word, neither John, Dooey nor any of the others had any problem in getting what they wanted from the Army. While they waited in a large entrance hall at Fort Hamilton, the Frenchman went behind the counter and spoke to a sergeant. Then the count left, passing them with a wink. After a while, the sergeant came over to them, holding a notebook he had been studying.

"Here's what I can do," the sergeant said, looking down at his notebook. "I can put two of you in with the Indianas and the other three with the Kentuckys. Neither is up to quota yet."

"You can do that?" John said.

The sergeant regarded him coldly.

"I'm Dolan and this is my friend John Bell," Dooey said. "We'd like to stay together, so if it's all the same to the others, we'll take the Indiana Regiment."

There were no objections voiced, though Reardon glowered.

"Fine," the sergeant said, nodding. He referred once more to his notebook. "Now, we have a convoy of supply ships leaving here in a week's time. You can all board the *Redoubt*. When you get to Point Isabel, see Sergeant Harraway. Tell him Sergeant Dunnock sent you. He'll take care of you from there. Any questions?"

John blinked. "What do we do in the meantime?"

Dunnock acknowledged the question with another nod. "You'll bunk here. In the meantime, you'll take your physicals, sign up and pay for your uniforms."

"You mean, you have Indiana Regiment uniforms here?" John said, surprised.

"No, we don't."

"Then why should we pay for—?"

"Because I said so, that's why!" Sergeant Dunnock exploded. "The uniforms will be ten dollars apiece. You'll pay for them here, or you won't leave here at all! Any more questions . . . from any of the rest of you?" He avoided John's steady gaze.

Ten Hoor, the tall Dutchman, was standing at attention looking straight ahead. Young Jake Herschel seemed totally uncomprehending, and Reardon had nothing to offer but an impatient look. Dooey was amused but remained dead-pan.

John asked, "Will we get any training here?"

"Oh, for Christ's sake! Son, you'll get all the training and drilling you need on the Rio Grande. There's no fighting going on there now, and there may not be for months. Depends on the War Department." John kept looking at him. Exasperated, the sergeant turned and pointed to a rack of arms on the far wall behind his counter. "See those? Those are some old Brown Bess muskets. The Mexes are still using them, but we're not—you'll probably be issued new Springfields by your regiments. But you can get the heft and feel of those while you're here. Just help yourselves, only don't get in anybody's way."

Sergeant Dunnock spun on his heel and walked away, leaving John and the others looking at each other. Finally, Jake Herschel asked softly, choosing the words uncertainly, "What do we do now?" to which ten Hoor replied stolidly: "We bunk. Come."

The two trooped off to the barracks area, carrying their satchels, Reardon trudging along after them. Dooey, lingering behind with John for a bit, said softly, "You know, you can really give a fella a laugh sometimes. Maybe that's why I asked you to come along."

"I don't ask questions to be funny," John snapped. "I like to learn things." He'd picked up his satchel, ready to follow the others, but put the thing down again. "Now that you've brought it up, why *did* you ask me to come with you?"

Dooey grinned. "Can't stop asking questions." He thought a moment, then spoke the truth. "Because I needed someone along to admire me."

John frowned. "I do admire you, Dooey, you know that."

"Yes, but I don't know why."

John said solemnly, "Because I believe there's a power in you that's greater than what the rest of us have. I don't know if it's for good or evil, but I feel it's a power for change. I—look, Dooey, pa says that this country is doomed, that it's splitting up, North against the South, and that this war with Mexico is the beginning of the end."

"So?" Dooey said. "What's that got to do with me?"

"I'm trying to tell you! I don't believe that, I believe something else. I believe this country is like a growing child, changing all the time, for good and bad. And I believe you're going to play a big part in that change—maybe even help lead it!"

Dooey laughed nervously. "I don't know what you're talking about, Johnny. I'm just a nice boy from Connecticut, like you."

"No, you're not. You're from New York," John said

pointedly, "remember? And you're an angry man, Dooey, angrier than anyone I've ever known—don't you know that about yourself yet? That's what's going to make you do things. That's what's—"

But Dooey had had enough. "You're exaggerating, John. You're imagining things—and you're talking way over my head. Come on, let's join the others. . . ."

Before they sailed on the *Redoubt*, two incidents occurred which John found disturbing. Both involved Dooey. The first came during an indoctrination visit by a State Department official. The other involved a desk officer at the fort, Captain Robert E. Lee.

John didn't catch the State Department official's name. The man showed up on their third day at Fort Hamilton to outline the causes of the war to them. They all gathered in a large lecture hall to hear him. There were perhaps a hundred new recruits present, all dressed in the blue uniforms of the New York First Volunteer Regiment that had been issued to them. Most of these men were due to be "held in readiness" at such places as Fort Jessup, Louisiana. It seemed that only Sergeant Dunnock, of the Fort Hamilton staff, knew that five of them would be heading for the Mexican border.

The man from the State Department did his best. It was obvious that discomfiting reports from the Rio Grande had begun to reach Washington. There had been some early desertions by American regular troops, some of them even forming a turncoat "San Patricio" battalion to fight on the Mexican side. There had also been reports of reckless behavior, of rape, and pillaging of Mexican civilians, and of American deaths from dysentery and other diseases. The State Department man had come to reaffirm the volunteers' purpose in joining up.

This was something John did not need, for he had already determined to fight for his country. But he listened along with the others.

"As you all know," the State Department man began, "the Mexican government, under its present leadership, reacted violently when Texas was annexed last year. To prevent Mexican incursion into Texas lands, we stationed a small army, under General Zachary Taylor, at Corpus Christi, which is *here*—" He pointed it out on a large map, at the mouth of the Neuces River. "At the same time we tried to negotiate Texas's claim to a border south of that, on the Rio Grande—here. Not only were we unsuccessful in these negotiations, but it was subsequently demanded of us, by President Herrera, that we withdraw our forces to the Sabine River . . . here, on the border of Louisiana. Thus, Texas's right to exist was not acknowledged at all. It was an extremely hostile act. We of course could not yield to the Mexican demand without sacrificing our commitments to the new state of Texas and our honor and pride as a nation. We waited for the Herrera government to come to its senses. When it did not, we sent General Taylor to the Rio Grande—in February of this year—to show our determination. The Mexican Army attacked General Taylor and we had no recourse but to announce that a state of war existed." The speaker hesitated. "Am I going too fast for any of you?"

Sitting next to John, Reardon muttered, "We ought to cut that Herrera's balls off," and John's head jerked up. It was hot and stuffy in the hall and John had dozed off. He blinked and forced himself to pay attention.

The State Department man moved away from the map. "Some of you may be too young to remember the humiliations we Americans suffered at the hands of various dictatorial Mexican governments over the past fifteen years or so. It was a Mexican government that invited Americans to settle in what is now Texas in the first place. It was another Mexican government that expelled them, rudely, by force. Many of those expelled had damage claims against Mexico—legitimate claims which have never been paid. When those Americans who remained rose to fight for their independence—against an unstable nation that was making a mockery of their lives—it was still another Mexican government that sent General Antonio Lopes de Santa Anna and a Mexican horde to destroy them. Who here remembers the Alamo?"

Every hand in the hall shot up and there were growls and hoots of anger.

"Who remembers Goliad?"

There was more angry growling. A recruit half-rose from his seat to shout, "I do! I had an uncle murdered there by that bastard Santa Anna! He was a prisoner and drew a black bean from a jar and Santa Anna had him shot down in cold blood!"

More growling and heads turning to look at the man.

"Yes, you remember, all right," the State Department man went on quickly. "Well, we took care of Santa Anna at San Jacinto, didn't we?"

"You're goddam right we did!" Shouts and nods of approval.

"We captured him and we could have executed him on the spot for his crimes against *hundreds* of prisoners! But did we? No, because we had a *worse* punishment for him. We exiled him to Cuba where, for the rest of his life he can rue the day he ever took up arms against Americans! And we'll do the same to any other Mexican general who dares to pursue this totally unjust war against us!"

There was silence while the recruits took this part of the speech in. There was some grumbling, but nothing was said. The speaker took advantage of the silence.

"Now, I must tell you," he began slowly, "reports have reached us from Mexico concerning certain misguided young Americans who are *not* helping our cause. Some—only a few—are reportedly harming Mexican civilians. We are, after all, a civilized nation. Further, it is not to our advantage politically to stir up general resentment against us. Sooner or later, you may all find yourselves in Mexico, and I wish to offer you guidance along these lines. I—"

"Bullshit."

It was Dooey Dolan who said it, sitting three seats away from John.

The State Department man smiled. "Someone has a comment to make?"

"Why didn't we execute Santa Anna? He had it coming to him, didn't he?" Dooey said. He remained seated.

There was some mild, approving grunting from other recruits. John, knowing Dooey, hearing his tone, knew something more was coming.

"Well, but I already explained that." The State Department man peered into the blue-uniformed audience, looking for his questioner.

"Maybe you did, maybe you didn't. It's not what I really want to know, anyway." Dooey stood up then.

"I'd like to know why Polk has made a secret deal with this vicious, villainous, murdering Santa Anna to get him back into Mexico."

There was absolute silence. John stared over at Dooey, shocked.

The State Department man frowned. "I don't know what you're talking about, young man. Where did you ever hear such a rumor?"

"What difference does that make? But if you must know, I heard it in a tavern on the Bowery three weeks ago. I heard Polk has told the Navy to lift the blockade at Veracruz and let Santa Anna in. I heard he's given Santa Anna ten thousand dollars for his own pocket and enough money to raise a new Mexican Army besides. Is it true or isn't it?"

The State Department man's eyes narrowed. "I want to know who told you that."

"And I'm not telling you. If it isn't true, just tell me. Maybe I'll believe you."

The State Department man glared at him. "If you can believe that to be true, maybe you shouldn't have volunteered for the Army. Your patriotism is highly in question. You didn't have to volunteer, you know."

"Oh, I'm in the Army, all right, and you can't get me out of it. I'll fight six of them and seven of you. Mister, I just want to tell you something. You've filled this room with so much hot air it figures to balloon up to the sky any second now. I'm getting out of here before it does!"

And Dooey stormed from the room, flinging aside empty chairs as he went.

The other incident involving Dooey occurred two days after his disruption in the lecture-hall and was preceded by a bout of moodiness that tried John's patience. He had been astounded by what Dooey had said. The president of the United States making a secret deal with the infamous Santa Anna? How was that possible? And if it were true, what did it say about the American war effort? And, yes, who *had* Dooey heard it from?

John got a clear answer only to the last question. "It was a reporter for the New York *Sun*," Dooey told him wearily when they were alone. "He was feeling low and I bought him a drink. He said he had it from the paper's Washington bureau that Polk had had a meeting at the White House with an emissary of Santa Anna's back in February. The information was 'off the record' and the paper couldn't print it, he told me. We both got pretty drunk after that."

"I see," John said. "Well, maybe there's more to the story."

"What more?"

"I don't know." John thought a minute, then went on. "Santa Anna's a hero in Mexico, and the people in power there now don't seem to know what they're doing. They won't negotiate with us—won't even talk to us. Maybe President Polk has reason to believe that if he helps Santa Anna get back into power, we'll get concessions from him that will end the war."

Dooey grunted. "Would *you* trust Santa Anna?"

John hesitated. "I don't think that's the point, Dooey. You and I, we don't know enough to trust Santa Anna or not to trust him. What you did to the State Department man was like spitting in his face."

"He stank to high heaven. He was pulling everybody's strings as if they were puppets."

"Maybe so. But if you go on that way, Dooey, you're not going to have a friend left."

"Except you, right?"

John just looked at him.

Dooey stayed pretty much alone after that, brooding, until the morning after the next when John happened to turn a corner too fast and ran smack into him. Dooey backed off, putting up his hands in mock alarm and grinning.

"Where are you going?" he wanted to know. "Looks like you're mounting a charge and there's nary a greaser in sight."

John smiled. "I thought I'd go fool with those muskets."

"Oh. Would you like some company?"

"Sure thing."

John was pleased, partly because his friend seemed to have recovered his good spirits and partly because Dooey knew a lot more about guns than he did. Dooey was a hunter, whereas John had never really liked to kill anything and had passed up the sport after trying it once or twice.

They went to the front area where the wall-mounted gun racks were. Sergeant Dunnock was busy at his desk and the area was crowded with other Regular Army personnel, both officers and men, engaged in routine duties. Remembering Dunnock's admonition not to "bother anybody," John quietly took a Brown Bess down from the rack, hefted it, then examined it.

"What makes this gun old-fashioned?" he asked Dooey. "I mean, I know we were using them during the Revolution, but what's wrong with it exactly?"

"Well, look," Dooey said. "In the first place, it has no front sight, see? And it has a heavy kick. But its worst feature, maybe, is this exposed touchhole. If there's a breeze up when you light it, the flame's going to blow back toward your face. You're going to have a tendency to fire from the hip, in which case you're likely to shoot high and miss your target altogether."

"I see," John said slowly. "And the Springfields we'll be getting aren't like that?"

Dooey laughed. "Not at all. They work just fine, relatively."

John reflected. "We're lucky to have them, then. I mean, if we have Springfields and the Mexicans have these muskets—"

Dooey nodded. "We have better artillery too."

Something in Dooey's tone made John look up.

"And it could be," Dooey went on, "that we have the likes of Reardon's guts on our side, whereas the Mexican privates—the ones in the line—have no guts at all. So it should be easy for us, real easy."

"Dooey, I don't understand." John was perplexed, as much by the sarcasm in Dooey's voice as anything else.

"To win this war, you've got to have better arms or a stronger urge to kill and preferably both," Dooey went on irritably. "Ask anybody around here. Ask this captain, for instance."

"Dooey, don't—"

John was too late. A Regular Army captain, carrying papers, was coming their way and Dooey planted himself in his path. The officer wore the insignia of the U.S. Army Engineers on his blue uniform. He was a man of about forty, with a black mustache and a glint of humor in his eye. Dooey had make a lucky choice.

"Captain," he shot at him, "what the hell are we fighting this war for?"

The officer stopped and stared at Dooey. His eyes took in his questioner's volunteer uniform and his youth. "When you see an officer, salute and call him *sir*, soldier," he said quietly.

Dooey suddenly felt uncomfortable; the officer's demeanor, rather than his rank, commanded respect. Dooey saluted. "I repeat the question . . . sir," he said. "I'd like your opinion. Why are we fighting this war?"

The officer smiled. "My name is Robert E. Lee," he said politely. "May I ask yours?"

"DeWitt Dolan, sir. Private, New York First Volunteer Regiment."

Captain Lee's black mustache twitched. "Not one of Sergeant Dunnock's favorites, by any chance?"

Dooey said stonily, "Yes, sir. I'm leaving for Mexico in three days."

John, with a thump in his stomach, felt they were done for, but the officer showed no concern over their having bypassed official recruitment procedures.

"So, you want to know why you're going and you want me to tell you. Well, Dolan, I don't think this the proper place to discuss your question, nor do I think I could give you an answer that would satisfy you . . . or totally satisfy myself. However, I can tell you this: I envy you."

Dooey waited for Lee to explain himself.

"I am a soldier, you see. My orders keep me here at Fort Hamilton at present, but if I could have my way, I'd be on the border fighting with General Taylor right now."

Captain Lee looked at Dooey closely. "You show spirit, Dolan. I've enjoyed meeting you, and I wish you well." He nodded at Dooey and John, then continued on his way, only to stop after a few steps and turn. "There's one thing more I should tell you, Dolan. If we should happen to meet again, perhaps somewhere in Mexico in a more military situation, I hope you'll be with me. Because if you are not with me, you'll be against me, and I shouldn't like that. Do you understand my meaning?"

Dooey didn't say anything. Captain Lee walked on.

"I like that man," Dooey said.

"For God's sake, Dooey, what's the matter with you?" John said angrily. "We don't need the kind of trouble we could have gotten from him!"

Dooey made no comment.

That night, lying in his bunk, thinking about Dooey, John wondered if maybe he didn't just need a girl, someone to show him some warmth and love and tenderness.

Every man needed that, John reasoned, and went to sleep thinking about Sally, and about how lucky he was to have her close and dear to his heart.

4

THREE DAYS LATER John and Dooey sailed on the *Redoubt*, which was due to stop at New Orleans before proceeding on.

At about this time, on the Rio Grande, two young Regular Army lieutenants happened to be walking alongside the river while a black-eyed Mexican girl was swimming in it. One of these men was Sam Grant, a 23-year-old Ohioan who had mule-tending duties with the 4th Infantry and had already seen much action. The other was Braxton Bragg, a tall, lanky North Carolinian some six years older than Sam, who had distinguished himself in artillery action both at Palo Alto and Resaca de la Palma.

The two were walking towards Fort Texas, an Army-built earthenworks that had been shelled by the Mexicans a month before and was still under repair.

"There's Maria again," Bragg commented. "She sure does hate us, don't she?"

The girl wasn't exactly swimming; she was standing waist-deep in the water, her fists clenched before her, glaring at them. It was sunset. The other Mexican girls—those who encouraged *gringo* soldiers to swim with them now and, for a dollar, bed with them later—had gone back across the river to the white stuccoed houses of Matamoros, beautiful now with the low sun on them. Only Maria remained.

"Her folks should be here soon to fetch her," Sam remarked.

The two men stopped to watch.

"Kind of purty, isn't she?" Bragg said. "Looks pure-blood Injun to me. She's sure not one of those Spanish *gapuchines*, and she don't look half-breed *mestizo* neither. Almost black," he mused. "Could be one of those we got over to home if she wasn't so durned purty."

Sam didn't comment on the girl's looks. She was slim, had coal-black tresses and eyes, and was, to his mind, very fiery-looking. If looks could kill, he thought, and waited with interest for the peculiar evening ritual involving Maria that the Army had been observing for weeks now to begin.

Soon, two stolid-looking men appeared on the opposite riverbank, which was only about fifty yards away.

"There's Juan and Carlos," Bragg said. "I wonder which one is going to call her in tonight."

It was Carlos, the heavier of the two. He cupped his mouth and called: "Maria . . . Florita *se quiere venir por la comida ahora.*"

"*Une momento*, Carlos."

"Calling her to dinner, that's it," Bragg muttered.

The girl, after giving them one last glare, turned in her wet, clinging cotton skirt and slowly swam towards the opposite bank. "My, what a lovely ass," Bragg said softly.

Sam allowed himself a smile, though not at Bragg's remark. "I guess she's done her day's work," he said. "She stands there for eight hours, hating us, and then she goes home to dinner. One may presume there's an equitable labor-management arrangement somewhere along the line."

The two men trudged on toward Fort Texas, for there was much to do there and much else you couldn't do but had to worry about.

Bragg had a jibe for Sam as they walked along. "What's the matter, Sam, don't you admire lovely asses?"

"I do indeed," Sam said. "I admire beautiful women. I admire the girl in the river, and I admire the one I got back home."

"Oh, yeah, I forgot," Bragg jeered. "The lovely Julia Dent, who waits patiently while you wander. Don't see what you got against the name Ulysses, Sam—it fits you."

"I prefer Sam, I don't like Ulysses," the Ohioan said doggedly. "There are other things I don't like. I don't like what I've seen of this war so far. In fact, back there at Palo Alto, when Major Ringgold got killed and a man next to me got his jaw blown off, I was sorry I ever enlisted. I'm not even sure I like you, Bragg."

Bragg grinned. "Oh, but we get along fine, don't we, Sam?" he drawled. "We're Regular Army. It's them lunatic volunteers we have to worry about."

* * *

None of it mattered, Dooey Dolan was thinking; none of it. Not the idiot from the State Department, not the deal with Santa Anna, not the shipload of garbage like Reardon—none of it.

Even before the *Redoubt*, sailing down the Atlantic coast in a nest of six other Navy-manned ships, had reached balmy southern waters, Dooey was yielding to the dream, the fantasy that had swollen in him with time.

He stood on deck and studied the convoy's billowing white four-masted sails, seeing their surge as somehow equal to the surge he was experiencing in himself. He watched the coastline go by, the land to starboard changing gradually in configuration and color as they passed New Jersey, Chesapeake Bay, Virginia, North Carolina, headed for still greener, lusher climes. He was going south at last.

He dressed in blue, he ate, he lent a hand to the sailors with their lines; he chatted with John and little Jake Herschel, teaching the latter some more English. But mostly he couldn't be reached, not even by John.

"I'm going below to write some letters," John said, finding Dooey, on their fifth night out, leaning on the deck rail as usual. "Is there any message I can pass along from you?"

"Give my regards to your folks," Dooey said absently. "Tell your pa I'm fond of him, no matter what he thinks."

"And Sally?"

Dooey shrugged. "Give her my regards," he said.

Still John hesitated. "You sure do like the moonlight."

"Sometimes the moonlight's best."

"Yes, I guess it is," John agreed, not knowing what else to say. "I'll see you later, Dooey."

Dooey's moonlight was not John's moonlight; it didn't have the Halls of Montezuma in it. His dream had been born years earlier, when he was eight and his mother had taken him to south Carolina during a temporary separation—much welcomed by Dooey, who was glad to get away from his drunken father. It was the winter of the year his parents would set fire to their house, during an alcoholic binge, and murder each other.

Dooey had still had some hopes that winter. In South Carolina, he'd thought he'd have his mother's love for himself, but this had turned out not to be the case. Staying in the Charleston home of some friends —James Hunter and wife—Catherine DeWitt had railed bitterly at her absent husband, ignoring Dooey, so that he'd taken to sneaking out into the soft Carolina moonlit night, breathing in the wet palmetto leaves as if their tang alone could nourish him, and gazing at the sea. By day he gazed yearningly at the golden-tanned Carolina girls, who walked along with their easy strides and tender, welcoming eyes. The lithesome girls were his secret objects of desire; he was too frightened to talk to them, so fearful had his parents made him of life.

Dooey despised the memory of his parents, was glad they died when they did; they had been nothing to him that was not destructive. He'd done well enough without them, for he had always been quick and alert—maybe *had* to be, just to stay alive in their house. He could count up his accomplishments and sometimes did. He could shoe a horse, run a business, hunt, fight and beat his weight, hump girls, read books and learn from them—he could do all these things and do them well, could he? He could get by; he always would.

But John was right. Always, there was this terrible rage-filled emptiness inside him that it seemed only the dream could assuage. The dream that made him eager to get to the Rio Grande, to the scene of the war. For the South had long ago become Dooey Dolan's mother, replacing the one he never really had. Some day, somewhere inside its sensual warmth, his dream told him, he'd have *his* girl. She wouldn't be a thin-lipped Northern Protestant bitch like Catherine DeWitt, nor a fat Irish sow like the aunts who had clucked over his hated father. She would be glowingly "southern" and soft and foreign to his blood, defiant at first—for he always needed the spark of competition—but ultimately yielding. She would be young, as a child is young, and beautiful. They would go off with their shared love together, it didn't matter where.

All his years in Connecticut, Dooey had dreamed his dream, telling nobody about it—not even John—for fear of ridicule or worse. Sometimes even he was embarrassed by it, considered it "unmanly," even crazy. But he could not break free of it; he did not want to. The light in which Dooey regarded the war with Mexico came from the moon and the Southern stars. Barring the few dollars he'd paid to the count and Sergeant Dunnock, this was his free trip back to the land of lost content . . . and to the promise of its renewal.

Below deck, John wrote his letters:

Dear Pa:

I am now on the ship Redoubt, *and I hope I have the strength to live up to its name. Since my last letter, a lot of things have happened. For one thing, Dooey heard a rumor that President Polk has let Santa Anna back into Mexico. I think it's probably true. My guess is that it's to let Santa Anna raise an army, overthrow Herrera and then make peace with us. But if it doesn't work out that way, we may have our work cut out for us.*

Have you heard the reports that we have about a hundred deserters who have gone over to the Mexican side as the "San Patricio Battalion?" I asked around at Fort Hamilton about this. They are mostly Irish Catholics (which is why they call themselves the San Patricios) who have either been offered free land, or have been convinced by the Mexicans that we are waging an anti-Catholic war against them. We have an Irishman with us named Reardon who says if he catches up with these fellows, he will 'chop them to pieces.' And can you imagine Dooey, who after all is part Irish, deserting and fighting for Mexico like that? I guess that shows you just can't pin labels on people because of their nationality or religion or anything else, though I find this harder and harder to avoid, I must tell you. According to most folks I've met, we Americans are out-and-out saints and the Mexicans are out-and-out devils.

Well, pa, I don't want to go on and on. I hope you've gotten over your surprise that I'm to join an Indiana regiment. It surprised me too! I'm to report to a Lieutenant Lew Wallace, but as I know nothing about him aside from his name, I'll close now.

Love, John.

P.S. Dooey wants you to know he's fond of you, regardless of what you may think.

Dear Ma:

I've already written pa some news that he can pass along to you. I just want you to know that I love you and am always thinking of you. Ma, I met a volunteer on this ship named Dunning Foster, from Cincinnati, who joined us in New York. He has a young brother who writes songs and he played one of them for us on his banjo last night. It's called, "Oh, Susanna, Oh Don't You Cry For Me." It's real cute and perky, and sad at the same time. I know you could play it great on our parlor piano. It hasn't been published yet, Foster says, but I bet it will be sweeping the country before the year is out, so get your copy from Mr. Wilkins fast! (You can ask for it by title as I'm not sure I got the brother's name right—Steven, I think.)

Not that I won't be home long before year's end. From what I hear, there's no army in Mexico now to fight! I am going to go straight into Mexico City and bring you back a piece of gold from the Halls of Montezuma, mark my words. The food on this ship is all right and the sea breezes are cooling. As you can see, it doesn't take too much to make me happy, and I know I owe you and pa a good deal for that. Dooey's fine too. He sends his love, as I do mine.

Your son, John

When John wrote to Sally, the words didn't come as easily. He had to chew his pencil a bit and finally put down:

Dear Sally:

I know I shouldn't call you "the girl I left behind me," as it might embarrass you, but it's the way I feel.

John crumpled that page up and began again:

Dear Sally:

Do you know how the swing in your yard creaks? Well, I am on a ship that creaks the same way. A strong wind comes up, you hear the deck planks and beams creak and you think the ship's going to fall apart, but it never does.

We are off the coast of Virginia, which I never thought I'd see. Thomas Jefferson's state. I wish I could go ashore to Monticello to see all the things he designed and made with his own hands. Jefferson was a great man, a sane and sensible man during times of great trouble. (I remember it made you angrier than it did me to learn that he owned slaves—I don't know why.)

I will soon be in Mexico with an Indiana infantry regiment. Sally, you didn't look too well the last time I saw you, though I told my ma you did. You looked so upset that, when I thought about it later, I thought maybe some fellow was trifling with your affections. I thought you met somebody in Litchfield. It wouldn't bother me so much if I thought you were seeing somebody who was making you happy, but

John suddenly stopped writing and flung the pencil down. He found himself shaking with anger. He was angry with himself for the lie he was telling; he was jealous and he knew it. He remembered the way Sally had looked and behaved the night he'd said goodbye. It seemed to him now that she'd just treated him like an old dog she was mildly sorry to see wander off.

And he'd just wagged his tail and gone! He'd complimented her on her dress and gone! For Christ's sake! He was *sure* she was seeing someone else! He didn't give a damn whether whoever it was was making her happy or miserable, only that it wasn't him! Oh, for Christ's sake, for Christ's sake! He should have grabbed her, flung her down on the swing and done . . . something he'd never done, something he'd promised himself he'd never do until they were married.

Now it was too late. John writhed in anguish as Sally's face and body floated into his mind. She was naked on that damn swing, her legs spread, her eyes glazed with passion. He tried to work himself into that picture, but he couldn't. Somebody bigger and stronger, or smarter and cockier, or lustier and greedier than he was, was mounting her. And she was liking it!

For agonizing moments, John's sense of himself left him. He wasn't with Sally and he wasn't where he was either. He felt insubstantial, as if he were straddling an abyss, caught between two worlds and existing in neither one.

Then, almost as quickly as it had come upon him, John's rage left him. He saw himself as a fool for believing, even for an instant, that Sally would do anything such as he'd been imagining. He comforted himself with his conviction that his mother wouldn't and that Sally, who shared so many of his mother's values, wouldn't either. He held fast to the likenesses in character he saw in the two women until his mind eased.

But he was still faintly troubled and decided not to write to Sally at all until he had better control of himself. Because he could not rid himself of another black thought that had succeeded the first, which was that somebody in Litchfield might have forced himself on Sally, even raped her, leaving her too frightened and ashamed to speak of it. If that were the case, he would kill him, whoever he was.

But there was nothing he could do about it right now. He was on his way to Mexico.

5

IT TOOK the *Redoubt* seventeen days to reach New Orleans where, on a War of 1812 battlefield east of the city, the volunteers from New York waited for a week in mosquito-infested tents and mud up to their boot-tops for thousands of other volunteers to join them.

They came by Mississippi River steamboats south from Illinois, Indiana, Missouri, or they rode in from Alabama and Georgia, their horses' hooves still caked with red clay. Wherever they came from, they came grumbling and cursing, and plunked themselves down anywhere in the staging area tents.

"Jesus Christ, it's hotter'n hell here!"

"Y'all think it's hot in N'Orleans, boy? Yuh'll fry yur balls off in Mexico," predicted an Alabaman who'd never been there.

"Where do you s'pose they keep the women in this

town?" one man asked, speaking to no one in particular.

A burly southerner responded quickly. "Lest you got niggers in mind, son, you keep your paws off'n our southern women. There's gash aplenty in Mexico, they're sayin'. So you just keep your pants on—what's your name there, boy?"

"Name's Crossman, First Indiana."

"Well, howdy, Crossman. I'm Collins, great state of Georgia. We got two others from your outfit in this here tent. This one's Bell and that one's Dolan."

"Never seen 'em before in my life. Where you boys from? You sure as hell didn't come down with us from Indianapolis."

John came up from his cot in the rear of the tent and stuck out his hand. "I'm Bell. We're not from Indiana, exactly, but we'll be joining Wallace and the rest of your regiment in Matamoros."

"That's great, the more the merrier," Crossman said. "We'll be moving out most soon as we get there."

"What do you mean?"

"Didn't you hear? Ol' Zach's quit farting around. He's moving outfits out of Matamoros right now and taking 'em upriver towards Monterrey. We're going to wipe the greasers out there and take hold of all northern Mexico."

"That ain't the way it was tole to me," Collins objected. "I heard that Taylor's going straight down to Mexico City to end this thing right quick."

"Naw, why'n hell would he do a thing like that? Too damn risky, and if he failed, he'd no more get elected president in forty-eight than you or me."

John said hesitantly, "You think that's what General Taylor's aiming for, Crossman?"

"Hell, that's *all* he's aiming for! Were you born yesterday, kid? He's the Whigs' big hope. He's been sitting on his white horse loving everything they're saying about him. Shit, if Polk had his way, he'd keep Taylor penned up in Matamoros until he found some Democrat general to replace him. Only, he can't find no other goddamn general who knows beans about fighting 'cept Winfield Scott, and he's a goddamn Whig, too! What you got is a president and a general both their fingers stuck up their asses—'cept Taylor's pulled his out. I say, let's hear it for Taylor! It don't make no never mind to me where we're moving as long as we're moving!"

Cheers and shouts of agreement went up in the tent, which was crowded with volunteers. John began to cheer up himself at the prospect of seeing some action. Where was Monterrey? He didn't know, but it didn't matter. What mattered was sharing the eagerness for battle and sharing the gripes—of which there were plenty right there in New Orleans.

For one thing, there was a yellow fever epidemic that steaming hot summer, and the volunteers were confined to the camp with bad water, bad food and a Regular Army contingent that hated them as much as they hated the regulars. The Regular Army doctor who treated them for dysentery they took to calling Doctor Death.

It was only the beginning.

They were packed into the holds of schooners and shipped across the Gulf from New Orleans, cursing and vomiting when a storm came up, rocking the convoy so that the horses tethered belowdecks kicked at the plankings in maddened fear.

On July 8th, from the deck of one such schooner,

John, with Dooey alongside him, got his first glimpse of the land in dispute.

It was Port Isabel, Texas, at the mouth of the Rio Grande. In the distance, John could see Fort Polk, Taylor's supply depot. He couldn't see much else. The land was scrubby, flat and brown. John stared at it, his hopes somewhat deflated. There was little that was green and growing on it; it sent no odors seaward, no fresh breeze to blow away the sour smell of vomit on board. As the schooner came into harbor, the water got browner and more sluggish. The stillness of the land seemed to be accentuated by a lone wagon, packed with Mexicans, rolling up a dusty road to meet them.

"You thinking what I'm thinking?" John asked.

"I don't know." Dooey answered. "What are you thinking?"

"I wish I was home."

"Cheer up. Looks like you'll be able to get your clothes washed, anyway."

As they came ashore, a platoon of soldiers came riding up from Fort Polk to greet them, but the Mexicans were already there, piling out of the wagon, edging each other out for selling space.

"*Mi esposa, señor. Una buena lavandera.* Wash uniforms. Fifty cents, one month."

"Sorry, we won't be here that long," Dooey said, pushing past.

"*Señor, por favor. Mi carta. Tequila, muchachas Mexicanas y Americanas, todas en case de Pedro en Puenta Isabel.*"

"Thanks, Pedro, I'll remember that."

"*Señor, por favor . . . señor, por favor . . .*"

One was more pleading than the next, the darting, greedy eyes seeking out the most vulnerable.

A blue-uniformed sergeant rode up and jerked to a stop, his rearing horse kicking up dust. "Don't eat or drink anything they sell you," he shouted. "All you new men hear that?"

About three hundred volunteers had debarked from the ships. The sergeant had them form up roughly into companysize groups before addressing them right there on the beach.

"Now, I'd get you men out of the heat except that's all we got here," he said. "I'm Harroway, U.S. Fifth Infantry, and that there's Fort Polk, where we got our supplies and our hospital. We got us some good American doctors there—I don't want you to worry about that. Now, I'll need a hundred of you to go right on down to Matamoros. The rest of you will stay here until there's a call for you. Since I can't do it no other way, I'm asking for a show of hands. Who wants to go to Matamoros today? Them that's got horses can ride them. Them that don't can ride the wagons and help with the oxen and mules."

"What do they need a hundred *fer*?" a black volunteer from Illinois said. "Is they fightin' down there again?"

"No, they're not fighting. They need a hundred to replace the hundred that came back here yesterday."

"What did they come back *fer*?"

The sergeant glowered at the negro. "Because they're sick. Because they ate the food and drank the water I'm telling you not to. Now listen—all of you men. We had five killed and forty-five wounded at Palo Alto and Resaca de la Palma. That's in action, from bullets or cannon, and that's all. But we have lost near to fifty percent of this army at one time or another to dysentery, mosquito fever, the clap and every goddamn thing else. Some men are dying in that there hospital right now just because they didn't listen. Nobody can save them now. I'm telling you this as a warning and because you asked me. Now, who wants to go on to Matamoros now and who wants to go back home where you came from? Because if that's what you want, General Taylor will be only too happy to send you."

There was no question but that John and Dooey would choose to go on, John because Fort Polk seemed dead as a doornail and Dooey because what he'd seen of Point Isabel so far offered no fulfillment of his dream of romance. The place was just plain ugly. Things had to be better upriver in the Rio Grande valley.

Among the other men there was grumbling. To think they'd come this far and General Taylor didn't want them! They'd show him. They'd show the whole goddam Regular Army what stuff they were made of. If the Regulars couldn't get on with the war, the volunteers would.

The upshot was that nearly all three hundred raised their hands, opting to go on, and Sergeant Harroway had to pick a hundred at random. Before he did, he gave them time to get out of the wool uniforms they'd been issued in the States, for it was well over one hundred degrees in Point Isabel. There was grumbling about that too.

John stepped out of line and spoke to Harroway.

"Sir, Sergeant Dunnock in New York said you'd take care of us."

"He did, did he?" Harroway appraised the young man in front of him, strapped with a tin canteen and sweating like all blazes. "Who's *us*?"

John pointed to Dooey, then ten Hoor, Reardon and

Jake Herschel, who'd all indicated that they'd wanted to go on. Harroway nodded wearily.

"All right. You five can stay here and help in the hospital."

"That's not what I meant," John said quickly. "We want to head out today."

The sergeant merely grunted. "With *that*?" He jerked his head toward John's canteen.

"What's wrong with it? They gave them to us in New Orleans."

"You like your water boiling?" Harroway got wearier. "Son, when you get out in the desert later, find yourself a gourd and throw that tin can away. You got a knife to cut a gourd?"

"I've got my jacknife."

"Good. Good for you."

John hesitated then asked, "Anything else I ought to know, Sergeant?"

Harroway thought that one over and shook his head. "Either you'll pick things up as you go along or you won't. If you don't pick things up, you'll probably die." Then Harroway relented. "Look, son, you're now in Texas, or northern Mexico, whatever the hell it is. All plants here have thorns, everything that crawls has a poisonous sting and every son of a bitch carries a weapon. Remember that."

"Mexican bandits, you mean?"

"*Every* son of a bitch," Harroway repeated. "Regardless of nationality, creed or color." He looked at the ground and spat.

John wet his lips. "Will I find Lieutenant Wallace in Matamoros?"

"With the Indianans? Sure thing. They're still there. A good bunch."

The sergeant watched as John turned and went back into line. He felt sorry for these men. Sergeant Harroway was one of those Regulars who thought of this war as being completely unorganized. They didn't need all these green recruits dumped on them through the administration's excessive zeal. Half of them deserted sooner or later anyway. They sure as hell didn't need them to show up with shit for clothing and equipment. He blamed that on the War Department too. Things were so confused by politics that the Army hadn't even been able to move. Now Taylor—Ol' Rough and Ready—*was* moving, but slowly, sometimes as little as a company at a time, as if he felt that if he moved slowly enough towards Monterrey, maybe Polk wouldn't see him doing it and complain to the press that he wasn't courageous enough to go straight to Mexico City.

As if Zach could take Mexico City without enough trained men and supplies to cross the Sierra Madres in between. There were seven thousand men in the U.S. Army, which was the government limit, and only half of them were here! And they were talking about closing down West Point!

Christ, what a war, Harroway thought. It was like shitting bricks. Taylor was inching out and, meanwhile, Harroway was getting all these sick and dying bodies back in Point Isabel by the wagon load. *If* they made it across the desert and past the two-legged vultures who wanted their boots.

In the confusion of finding wagon space the next morning, John got separated from Dooey and found himself with Reardon. Four wagons laden with foodstuffs and guns in wooden crates had been readied for the journey.

Some of the southerners had horses to ride, but most of the volunteers didn't, so there was a rush to find seats on the wagons. No one wanted to face a twenty-odd mile trek on foot—or an uncomfortable ride on the back of one of the mules that also went along. The pugnacious Reardon bulled his way through to a wagon and John followed in his path. A mounted guard of six sneering Regulars watched them. There was room for all, it turned out, if you didn't mind sitting cramped, feet up on the gun crates.

John, who hadn't had much sleep, blinked into the early morning sun, already at blistering intensity, and waited for someone to shout, "Giddup, that!" When they moved, it might at least create a breeze. He was down to his shirt, and he noted that all the other wool uniforms were gone, stowed in the men's bags. Some of the men were bare-chested, and most had rolled their pants up to the knees. Some wore straw sombreros they'd bought from the Mexicans the night before. Most everyone had sewed or tacked on his regimental insignia somewhere. Aside from that, they looked about as ragged and disorganized as the scornful Regulars made them feel.

Thinking of what Harroway had told him about "the sons of bitches" in the desert, John turned to Reardon. "Do you suppose there's any ammunition in these gun crates?"

"Don't know, don't care," Reardon growled. "I got mine." He opened his shirt and let John see the belt of bullets he had strapped around his stomach.

"Where did you get those?" John asked.

"Stole 'em."

John nodded. He felt he was learning things already, and that what he was learning wouldn't hurt him. He wished he'd thought to pick up the Colt pistol he'd seen lying on a table at Fort Polk, but he hadn't. Instead he'd spent a lot of time being sick about all the death and suffering he'd seen and smelled there. And at the time he had trusted the Regulars to look after him. He knew now that he would have to look out for himself.

The ordeal started about a half-mile out of Fort Polk, when they lost sight of the sea and civilization altogether. The only plants that grew in the sandy ground were the tangled brown chaparral and the cactus, which drooped as if it was a struggle even for this hardy vegetation to survive here.

It was everywhere the same, and a man could torture himself numb with vain hopes that he might be able to distinguish one feature from another on this torrid landscape. It was all sea-level flat, but there was no sign of water. The oxen dragged the wagons at a slow pace. Eyes glazed, the men grew very quiet.

John found himself thinking: "What do we want this land for? Is it all like this? What do we want it for?" and was overcome by depression. He was very thirsty, but when he opened his canteen the water in it was—as Sergeant Harroway had predicted—near to boiling. The tin mouthpiece burned his lips when he tried to drink from it. John let himself go numb, taking the desert into his heart as the wagons jolted along.

The straining oxen made about six miles in two hours. Some of the mounted volunteers wanted to race ahead, but the Regulars ordered them not to—the one order they gave, based, they said, on this route still being prey to Mexican guerrilla forces who camped on the other side of the Rio Grande.

John wondered if this were really so. As the tedium

of the desert bore into him, making him more and more irritable, he began to wonder if the Regulars weren't just being sadistic and got mad.

"Those bastards," he muttered. "Look at that one grabbing that recruit's reins. Why doesn't he just let him be?"

Reardon heard him and growled, "Because they're bastards." John felt a little better hearing his view shared.

They traveled for another hour and then, just for fun it seemed, two of the Regulars unlimbered their rifles and began to shoot the heads off snakes. There were snakes everywhere. You would see smaller ones slithering away through the chaparral as the wagons came up to them and huge ones sitting coiled in the sand, maybe thirty yards away, motionless except for flickering tongues as the wagons passed. It was at these the two Regulars shot, knowing they were poisonous. They made it a contest between them. Their shots would crackle through the dead air, and then one or the other would shout as his bullet blew a snake away. John felt a flicker of interest and admiration for the Regulars' sharpshooting. But there was something in him that would not let them have their fun without negative comment.

"Look at them using up ammunition," he grumbled. "What if we run into those Mexican guerrillas they keep talking about?"

Once more he got Reardon's glowering support and some responsive action from him as well.

"Me, I'm getting ready," he said. He raised the lid of the gun crate at his feet, took out a shiny new Springfield and loaded it from his ammo belt. Others in the wagon who saw him do it came out of their lethargy, grinning, chattering:

"You show 'em boy . . . You know how to shoot that thing? . . . Just shove down that lever . . . You see a greaser, line him up a tick below the front sight and just go pop . . . Hey, boy, hand me one of those rifles and lend me some of them shells you got. I'll pay you back, on my honor. . . ."

It was about an hour later that they reached the pond. It was a small, clear pond with no scrub around it. By then, the volunteers—John included—had parched, swollen lips and a sullen conviction, not without foundation in fact, that the Regulars couldn't care less about their suffering. When they saw a pond a quarter-mile ahead, the noon sun glinting on it, cheers went up. John could almost taste that water. Some of the men were ready to jump out of the wagon and run ahead, then saw that they didn't have to, that the Regulars were bringing the wagons to a halt beside the pond as they came up. There was a huge cactus some ten yards from the pond. The Regulars dismounted and went over to sit in its shade. A couple of them pushed back their hats and one man opened a whiskey bottle.

When John and the men in his wagon reached the pond, they found a dozen other volunteers standing around it, not drinking but staring with dark hatred at the Regulars. John's group didn't know why. Reardon, for one, didn't care why. He pushed through to the pond's edge, kneeled and cupped water from it. It was very clear water, clear as any you might drink back home.

"I wouldn't drink that if I were you," one of the whiskey-drinking Regulars cautioned with a grin.

Reardon looked up. "What's wrong with it?"

"Pure salt. That's why you don't see nothing living

in it—no fish, no bugs, no nothing. The salt killed 'em all."

Reardon slowly got to his feet.

Someone else from John's wagon said, "What the hell's the matter with you, man? Why the hell did you stop here if we can't drink the water?"

The Regular shrugged. "A man's got to rest."

Reardon bellowed, "Gimme some of that whiskey!"

"Come get it, mick."

Reardon started to do just that. He lowered his head and charged across at the Regular, who quickly put his bottle down and picked his rifle up, pointing it at Reardon's midsection and bringing him up short.

"It's called learning the hard way," the Regular said. "You'll pick it up as you go along."

John, coming up to Reardon, made an instinctive gesture to grab his arm and get him away from further trouble. Reardon shook him off and stood there, breathing hard, immobilized by his rage. John turned away and moved slowly back towards the wagons. He felt sick to his stomach at the meanness of the thing the Regulars had just done to them. Oh, they'd get to Matamoros without the water, making do with the hot trickles left in their canteens, but why did the Regulars have to torture them?

By the time John got back to his wagon, he had decided that he himself would rise above such meanness and make things better for all. All it took was diplomacy—and some good old New England horse sense. He had a plan. As he thought about it, he happened to glance up and see Dooey, two wagons away, watching him. John flushed and looked away. It was as if Dooey, who hadn't gone near the pond in the first place, could read his mind and was telling him to leave it alone, that he couldn't make things any better. Damn Dooey! Dooey never thought you could make anything better. You could. You had to! If someone didn't, Reardon might shoot that Regular in the back once they got started again, and then there would be hell to pay.

What John did was wait until a sulking Reardon returned to the wagon. Then he climbed out and approached the soldier with the whiskey bottle. The bottle was still about three-quarters full.

"Corporal, can I buy that from you?" John asked him.

"Buy it? Well, that's more like it." The soldier, who was about to remount, stepped down from his horse and gave the young volunteer an amused grin. "What'll you give me for it? It don't look like you have much."

"Don't know." John thought. "How about three dollars?"

"Well, now."

"That's two weeks' pay."

"I know that. You gonna drink this all yourself?"

"Yep," John said.

The Regular laughed. "Well, whether you do or don't, it don't matter. Just try to hold the ruckus down in that wagon. We got a ways to go yet."

"Sure thing." John took three dollars from his pocket and gave them to the soldier, shielding the transaction from the volunteers behind him with his body. Being basically frugal, he had plenty left over from the advance he'd gotten at Fort Hamilton and was convinced this was money well spent.

He took the bottle back and gave it to Reardon.

"What's this?" Reardon asked suspiciously.

"That soldier told me to bring it to you," John said.

"He said he felt bad about what he did and wanted you and the rest of us to have the whiskey."

"He did? He said that?"

"He sure did. Said he felt rotten. He figured it was the heat that got to him."

Reardon frowned. "Yeah, well, it sure is hot." He hefted the bottle and peered at its contents. "Don't know about this," he muttered.

"I don't either," John said quickly. "You got to think about this. I mean, why would he give it to me? Why not to you? You're the one mostly he tried to make a fool of. Could be rotgut in there—or worse."

"Naw, that ain't it. Didn't you see him drink it himself?" Reardon waved John off impatiently, then sat still and pondered. The sun was beating down hot enough to liquefy brains; everybody felt groggy, including John.

"See, Bell," Reardon said slowly, "meanin' no offense, you're just a thin little kid. Me? Well, he was scared to face me, that's all." He started to grin broadly. "Hell, I wouldn't hurt him. We're all here to fight greasers, not each other, ain't we? A man can make a mistake. Shit, anybody's likely to blow off steam in this heat." Reardon lifted his head and shouted. "Hey, Corporal!"

The Regular, mounted and getting ready to move out with the rest of the guard, turned in his saddle. Reardon held the bottle high and gave him a deep nod, a gesture of thanks. The soldier, who'd been paid well for the bottle, nodded back briefly, then returned to his task.

"See that?" Reardon roared gleefully. "See that?"

As the wagons started rolling and drew away from the pond, John settled back, relieved and a bit proud of himself. He felt he'd helped avert a fight that could have had lasting effects, even if somebody hadn't gotten himself killed right there. Now they were all happy—at least, those in his wagon were—as the bottle got passed around.

At first John didn't drink, just tried to stay attuned to the talk around him. A lot of it was interesting, as the men began to open up about themselves, their homes, their dreams of conquest in Mexico. And some of it was revealing.

He could remember later that someone started the rounds of self-revelation with, "Gawdamn, can you imagine tryin' to make a livin' growin' cotton in this country? I seen maybe two, three li'l patches of dirty ol' bolls back yonder by a li'l ol' stream we passed." John was surprised; he'd seen none, but then, he hadn't been looking for it. "I wouldn't put a niggah down here," the man went on. "Paw and me, we got five niggahs back home in Kaintuck. The cotton ain't no good there neither. We're going to take them niggahs to Californy oncet it's ourn. We're going to grow oranges, paw and me, an' they c'n just stuff theirselves on wawtermelons."

Someone else said, "The niggers we got in Illinois ain't worth shit. We got ourselves a congressman now, name of Lincoln, he don't think they're worth shit either. Least that's what they say and that's why I voted for him. We don't get rid of the niggers, send them back to Africa or something, I'm going to take my pay and go out to the Rockies once this war is over. Trap beaver or something. There's good money in that."

"Barber, you don't know balls about beaver. An' you wouldn't know a good niggah if you saw one. You're prejudiced, is what you are."

"Barber, what's that black buck doin' over in that wagon?" somebody else wanted to know. "Ain't he one of yourn? Mean-looking son of a bitch, likely to skewer you with that sword he's got."

Both John and Barber looked over. The black was the one who'd asked at Point Isabel if fighting had resumed at Matamoros. He had a shaved head, carried his own bayonet and did look mean.

"Name's Hentle," Barber said. "James Hentle. He's a student of the military, you might say. Says he's going to cut himself up a heap of Mexicans, learn what there is to learn, then go join up with one of those negro cavalry troops they got fighting Indians out west—with rank."

"Shit, more power to him, long as he don't come after me."

The wagons crawled along.

"O lolly, lolly o, I think I'll sing me a song." The man who said that belched and began, "*Green grows the laurel . . . all sparkling with dew . . . I'm lonely, my darlin' . . . since a-parting from you. . . .* Hey Bell! You! Kid! You think that's why the greasers are calling us *gringos*?"

"What do you mean?" John asked, puzzled.

"Well, it's got 'green grows' in it. The boys are singing it down by the river, they say, and the Mexicans are hearing it. I thought maybe that's why they're calling us *gringos*."

"I don't know," John said.

"Bell, you don't know *nothin'*. You don't *say* nothin' an' you don't *know* nothin'. You just sit there. You know what the trouble with you is? The trouble with you is you're ossified."

"I am?" John said, startled but beginning to grin.

"Thas right, you're ossified. Now, whyn't you have yourself a drink from this here bottle and get yourself un-ossified like the rest of us?"

"Go ahead, Bell," Reardon urged. "You got it for us. It's as much yours as anybody else's. Go ahead and wet your whistle. Do you good."

"Well, fine, all right," John said. "I'm not much of a drinking man, but you all seem to be enjoying yourselves so much I think I will have a bit."

John took a swig from the bottle and it was good. It burned his throat going down, but it instantly warmed his insides in a way much different from the way the sun was baking his outsides. He took another swallow, then a last large gulp, just to catch up with the others. Then he handed the bottle back to Reardon and smacked his lips.

"Not bad," he said. "Not bad at all."

Very quickly the whiskey went to John's chest, if not to his head. It gave him the power of song. He began: " '*The buckwheat cake was in my mouth, the weather it was dry, the sun so hot I froze to death, Susanna don't you cry.*' "

"What's that?"

"A song. Foster's song," John said importantly. "What happened to Foster anyway? Haven't seen him since the *Redoubt*.

"Search me. Where's he from?"

"Ohio . . . Pennsylvania . . . not sure. Everybody here's from everywhere there." John thought he had that concept down pat.

"To hell with Foster—how's that song go?"

John filled his lungs. The whiskey *was* going to his head now, but it felt good there too. He sang:

" '*O Susanna, O don't you cry for me, I'm gwine to Alabama wid a banjo on my knee.*' "

A fellow in the wagon from Alabama perked his ears up, liking what he heard. But a fellow from Arkansas thought it might as well be his state the song was calling him to, and another man thought Susanna could well be his girl Nancy, left way back home in Michigan. They all picked up on it and were soon roaring into the desert:

"*'O Susanna, O don't you cry for me, I'm gwine to Alabama wid a banjo on my knee.'*"

The mounted Regulars looked back and grinned. The volunteers in the other wagons looked over and grinned. That is, most of them did. When John glanced over happily at Dooey, wanting to yell, "How'm I doing, pal?" he saw the same expression on Dooey's face that he'd seen at the pond, as if John were making a total ass of himself.

He grew moody. When the singing stopped and there was a short silence, John said, much drunker now, "You know, everybody's going away. They're going to be strangers to me."

"Who's everybody?" someone asked.

John shrugged disconsolately. "Sally, for one. She may already be gone. And Dooey—" John had the strangest of insights. "You know, I think Dooey really is going away."

"Who's Dooey?"

"Dolan," Reardon growled. "He's a bastard. He ain't going nowhere that we ain't going, and I hope the greasers shoot the shit out of him the day after we get there."

John said slowly, "No, Dooey isn't a bastard. He's—"

"Kid, you were doing fine up to now. Come out of it or we'll dump you overboard into the cactus."

"Sing us another song, kid."

But John couldn't think of any more songs at that

point, so the others started a round of ribald chants that had to do, in some vague way, with cursing out various kinds of authority—from factory bosses to plantation overseers to Army generals. There were also some crude lines about the physical ability of Indian girls. John couldn't follow all the words, being too drunk to, but he was alert to the tone, a kind of roughshod belligerence, and joined in, roaring and shouting with the rest as the wagons crawled antlike through the desert.

John was bursting with bellicose feelings and was enjoying them. When, as the wagons neared the Rio Grande, John saw something strange lying in the grass near a stand of timber, he roared out his disapproval.

"What are those funny little black balls?" he shouted.

"What little black balls?" someone as bleary-eyed drunk as he was asked.

"*Those* little black balls, you blind bastard!" John said, pointing.

The other man focused with difficulty and finally muttered, "Christ, they're cannon balls—three-inch cannon balls."

"Well, what are they doing there?" John demanded.

"How the hell should I know?"

"Well, I'll find out," John said. He hiccuped. "You men keep your mouths shut because you're all too damn unossified to learn anything. Corporal? You there!"

A mounted Regular, not the one who had sold John the whiskey, had reined in to look at the cannon balls as the wagon drew up.

"Corporal, would you please tell us how those cannon balls got to be lying in that grass?" John hiccuped again.

The Regular looked at him, hesitated, then decided to provide these raw and raucous recruits with some sobering information. This was Palo Alto and the corporal was proud of what the Army had done here.

"We fought the greasers here about four weeks ago," he said. "Some of their artillery was off, and you could just step aside and let their balls roll to a stop in the grass. That's what those are."

John blinked woozily. "Heck, whyn't you just pick those balls up and fire 'em back?"

The Regular looked at him narrowly. "I guess because we were too busy. The greasers did well enough otherwise. They had us outnumbered two to one. Major Ringgold got his legs blown near off and bled to death later. If Lieutenant Bragg hadn't commandeered the major's flying artillery when he fell, you cackling sons of bitches would be coming into more cannon-ball fire than you're ever likely to have to face now."

"Oh," John said uncertainly. But the others in his wagon voiced objections to the soldier's slur.

"Who the hell is Ringgold? Who's Bragg? We'll show the greasers what men are made of, you bastard, and we'll show you!"

The Regular looked at them. "You men are drunk," he said coldly. "That's against regulations. Hand over that bottle—*pronto*."

There was a rebellious outcry, but John—who happened to be holding the bottle at the time—gave it up. The Regular rode to the head of the line with it, spitting on the ground in disgust as he went.

In the ominous silence that followed, John, in his

drunken state, grew more and more confused. He had tried to smooth things over between the Regulars and the volunteers, but everything had turned out wrong, and he felt that he'd played a part in making them wrong. He was uneasy and a little frightened as the others in the wagon sat sullenly or kicked at the gun crates in frustration. They were still several hours from their destination. Reardon had handed around bullets and the Springfields were right there for them. It did not seem possible to John that the volunteers would start shooting Regulars with those rifles, but he'd been proven wrong about so many things—like bringing Reardon the whiskey in the first place—that he would not bet against that happening. All John could do was sit there and pray silently for the volunteers to restrain themselves and for the sick sensations that had suddenly seized him to pass away.

The wagons crawled on another five hours or so when suddenly, on the cloudless blue horizon ahead, a horseman appeared. His small, distant figure shimmered in the waves of desert heat.

"Who's that coming?" Reardon barked.

Nobody answered him. The men, John included, stared at the approaching horseman until, as he galloped nearer, they could see he wore a sombrero and carried a musket. He was loading his gun from a shoulder strap as he rode.

"Greaser," Reardon muttered.

A Regular came riding back swiftly. "You men hunker down in those wagons. We'll take care of this." The Regular then rode back up toward the front again, unlimbering his rifle as he went.

Reardon growled, "I'll be damned if I let them have all the fun. Gonna get me a greaser. Who's with me?"

"I am, goddam it!" Barber, the Illinoisan, shouted.

Six others in the wagon concurred noisily. They grabbed Springfields out of the crates and quickly loaded them.

John, watching the Regulars, could see that they were aiming low at the horseman, who had come on very fast—recklessly so, considering the contingent of armed men waiting for him. When the horseman had approached to within a hundred yards, the Regulars were still aiming at his horse's flanks, probably planning to bring the man down without killing him.

John tried to push aside the barrel of Reardon's rifle, which was aimed squarely at the horseman's head. Reardon shoved him aside roughly. "Hands off, Bell. Watch this," he said.

It was impossible to tell which of the volunteers killed the horseman, because all six rifles exploded almost at once. The man, fifty yards off at the point of impact, rose in his stirrups and jerked convulsively. A bullet had blown his sombrero off and his sun-blackened face was a mass of red. His musket bounced off the hard-packed sand a moment before he pitched from the saddle and fell face down next to it. He had died without uttering a sound.

There wasn't a word spoken by anybody for several moments, save for Reardon's muttered, "Goddam it, we did it." Then a Regular came riding back. He eyed the six smoking Springfields and the men who had fired them.

"Proud of yourselves, ain't you?" he said. "Think you're gonna get medals for this?"

"Didn't say that," Reardon said. "We just did our duty as we saw it and don't want no thanks for it."

"Come on out, all of you, and take a look at the man you killed. I'm not ordering you," the Regular added. "I'm inviting you."

Reardon shrugged. He climbed out of the wagon, followed by the others, John among them. They all trooped out to the body, sprawled in the sand. When the Regular turned the dead man over on his back, they saw he was an American.

"He was a Fifth Infantry deserter by the name of Luke Johnson. 'Trapper Luke' is what he called himself," the Regular said, shaking his head.

Reardon frowned. "Then we did right, killing him, if he was a deserter."

"Trapper Luke was crazy as a loon and just as harmless. Look here." The Regular pointed to Trapper Luke's bandoleer, which was empty of bullets. "He went through the motions. What we did whenever we met up with him out here was play with him. Sooner or later, he would've gotten hungry or sick and we'd have taken him in. Now we won't have to do that, poor bugger."

Reardon growled, "How were we supposed to know?"

The Regular looked at him, spat and walked away.

For once, John remained silent. He had had his welcome to the war with Mexico, and it had not been a pleasant one.

6

THE MOVE toward Monterrey by the Taylor-led American forces did not include John Bell until August 3rd, which was three weeks to the day after he joined the First Indianans at Fort Texas, on the north bank of the Rio Grande across from Matamoros. The move never did include Dooey Dolan. The parting of these friends resulted from a sequence of events neither could have predicted.

On arriving at Fort Texas, the two friends, along with the bona fide Indianan, Crossman, reported to Lieutenant Lew Wallace. John and Dooey were astonished at this officer's youth. Wallace, who had raised a company of volunteers in Indianapolis and led them to the Rio Grande about a month before, was a broad-shouldered young man of nineteen. But John soon decided he was about as mature a leader as anyone could wish for, with a fine, sensitive intelligence to boot.

"Crossman! Good to see you," Wallace said, shaking his friend's hand warmly. "What held you up so long?"

"Well, Lew, I got stuck in New Orleans for a while, but I finally made it. These fellas are Dolan and Bell. They've come from the East and want to fight with us, if it's all right with you."

Wallace looked at John and Dooey politely, but at the same time sizing them up. He must have liked what he saw well enough. "Guess that's all right, since the regiment's still way below quota," he said genially. "I don't suppose you fellows have had any more military training than the rest of us, but can you shoot?"

"I'll need some practice," John said, "but Dooey is a fine hunter."

"That so?" Wallace, who'd been quick to observe Dooey's withdrawn expression, was curious. "What do you hunt?"

Dooey shrugged. "Grouse, doves, what we have in Connecticut. Sometimes deer."

Wallace smiled. "That's more than I've shot in Indiana."

"Lew writes stories," Crossman said.

"I just tinker, mostly," Wallace said modestly.

"What do you write about?" John asked.

Wallace thought. "People," he said finally. "I like a good adventure story, as most folks do, but mostly I think about people, what makes them behave the way they do. I think about hope and faith sometimes, what it means to have it and where you are when you don't." Wallace was silent for a moment, then he added, "I'm just beginning. The way I look at it, it can take a lifetime of pain to sort out what's worth caring about from what isn't."

"I guess that's right," John said, surprised at hearing such feelings after his experience with the soldiers in the desert.

Wallace's manner became brisk and businesslike. "I ought to fill you fellows in on what's been happening around here so you can find your way around better. In the first place, Fort Texas is now Fort Brown. A Major Jacob Brown was killed here trying to defend the fort while most of the Army was at Palo Alto, and General Taylor is having the War Department rename the fort in his honor."

"Is that so Taylor will look good in the papers back home?" Dooey asked bluntly.

"That's part of it," Wallace answered easily. "You may get a kick out of learning, Dolan, that old Zach has an adjutant translating all the cuss words he'd like to shout at Washington in his dispatches. Man named William Bliss. Zach calls him 'Perfect Bliss.' Zach tells Polk to go to hell, for instance, and Bliss writes, 'Dear Sir: We should like to honor your latest request that we pursue and attack Mexican forces forthwith, but are unable to comply due to the inclemency of the weather, the sickness of the men, and the lack of sufficient supplies, many of which we are still waiting to receive from the War Department.' Amusing in its way, don't you agree?"

"Don't know," Dooey said shortly. "We just got here."

Wallace nodded. "That's so. I guess I'm talking too much. Tell you what, why don't you fellows get your billets and then go out and have yourselves a good time? We'll be drilling in the mornings until the regiment is ordered out. Meanwhile, you'll find we have theaters here, grog shops, women, ball games—whatever your pleasure is. Just don't drink—"

"The water. We know," John said. "Thank you, Lieutenant."

"Lew."

"Lew," John said.

When John and Dooey went off, Wallace was left with Crossman for a moment.

"A lot of them are so damned tense when they get down here," Wallace observed. "That's what worries me. If only Taylor could move out of here faster and they had some Mexican artillery to face."

Crossman said, "That Bell's all right, just maybe a little too earnest, you know what I mean? But he'll settle down and do good by the regiment, don't you worry about that, Lew. Dolan, now, to my way of thinking, he's a bad one. It's like there's nothing or nobody in the world good enough for him. That's the kind that makes trouble. They either drag ass or just aren't there at all when you need them. I wouldn't want Dolan fighting in the line next to me, Lew. You ought to get rid of him. Pull some strings and dump him on the Mississippi Rifles or something."

Lew Wallace smiled. "There are various reasons why I can't do that, Bill. For one thing, Jefferson Davis—he's the captain of the Mississippi Rifles—he rarely sees things my way. He's a West Pointer, you see, and I'm not. But that's not the point, is it?"

The strapping young lieutenant began to muse out loud: "It's not this man Dolan we should be concerned about, Bill, you know that. What you say about him is true for thousands of other men down here. They're dissatisfied with the places they came from and are here because they have no place else to go. Is this to be our destiny, Bill—to be wanderers without purpose? Is it just the free ice cream they all want and damn why they're here and damn the man next to them? Or is there a challenge we all have to face—to find the true Christian faith again so that we can all share and live by it? Dolan hasn't found it. You can tell by looking at him how empty he must feel. But maybe he will find it down here. You never know."

"Lew," Crossman said gently.

Young Wallace came back to the present.

Crossman put a hand on his shoulder. "Lew, everybody back home knows you're going to sort all this out some day and write a fine book about it. But for now, do me a favor, will you? Get Dolan out of the regiment so's I can breathe a little easier."

If anybody had told Dooey Dolan that he lacked Christian faith, he would have conceded the point and walked away. If anybody had thought to inform John Bell that down here on the Rio Grande you could call officers by their first names and that many among both the officers and the troops found fun and excitement in the same things he did, he would have felt a lot better about being there.

The two friends went to a saloon run by a Mexican sutler, sat at a table and had a brief argument over a beer. The saloon, not more than a hundred yards from the fort, was crowded with soldiers in uniforms of all sorts and colors. There were also some unshaven Texans in weather-beaten buckskins, and one portly old man in a waistcoat and slouch hat whom John could swear he recognized from newspaper drawings as General Zach Taylor himself. If it *was* Old Zach, he was having a pretty good row with the Texans over something. John itched to join them at the bar and get in the swing of things, but he had something to get off his chest with Dooey first.

"Back there in the desert when you saw me getting into trouble you could have warned me, instead of just sitting there with a blank look on your face."

Dooey sipped his beer. "You were working very hard, John. I don't like to interrupt people when they're working so hard."

"C'mon, Dooey," John said. "You could see I was getting mixed up in something that wasn't any of my damned business!"

Dooey nodded. "That's right. And you wanted me to get involved too?"

John stared at him blankly, then shook his head. "Dooey, nobody can get anywhere with you. I'll see you later."

He got up and walked across the sawdust-covered floor, which was being wetted down and mopped up by the Mexican saloonkeeper. Nimbly dodging past the puddles of sawdust, John reached the bar just as the man in the slouch hat finished giving the Texans a mighty tongue-lashing.

By God, it *was* General Taylor!

John worked his way into the circle of onlookers. Ol' Zach was really rough and ready. He was red in the face from shouting. Sixty years old or not, he looked like he was about to grab the tall, grizzled Texan he'd been yelling at by the throat and throttle him. But that fellow was giving the general what for right back.

"Zach, we'll do damn near everything you want us to. We'll ride up ahead and scout for you, or we'll join you in battle like we been doing. But don't tell us to keep our paws off Santa Anna. We got a score to settle with that prissy bastard. We catch up with him, we're gonna shoot off his socks, then work our way up *real* slow to his necktie."

"Goddam it, Sam Walker," General Taylor roared. "It ain't *me* tellin' you to stay clear of Santa Anna—it's the goddam president. I'll stick a Colt up your ass and pull the trigger myself if I find you disobeyin' orders I'm doin' my damnedest to obey—even though I don't like it any better'n you!"

A neatly attired, grey-whiskered officer next to the general coughed to get Sam Walker's attention.

"General Taylor means he will be forced to resort to strong measures if you—well, if you attempt to circumvent official U.S. Government policy with regard to the man who will soon be reappointed President of Mexico, General Antonio Lopez de Santa Anna."

Ol' Zach wasn't through yet. "Goddam you, Bliss, I don't need you now! When I need you, I'll tell you. I meant what I damn well said, Sam. My hands are tied. You think I want to take this shitpot town of Monterrey? You think I got Worth and Twiggs and Pillow and all them West Point fellers here just to do that? But I can't *do* nothin' else—can't you get that straight? I go down to Mexico City after Santa Anna like you want me to, Polk's sure as hell gonna find some way to recall me. And I don't want to be recalled. I been fightin' Injuns too damn long to want to go back and get older and older just doin' it some more."

Sam Walker said, grudgingly, "Mebbe so, Zach, mebbe so."

John listened, all ears and wide-eyed, fascinated by General Taylor's speech and manner, so different from the knight on a white charger the Whigs were making him out to be back home.

He watched sympathetically as Old Zach fell into a kind of hopeless head-shaking. "O mi god, Sam, o mi god, Bliss, what a stinking war! Got no good reason for bein' here in the first place, we don't. Do you know I've sweated off twelve pounds just in the July heat alone? Twelve pounds! Can't keep my britches up no more. Got to get myself a new belt, that's what. Goin' to get a new belt an' then I'm goin' to take Monterrey."

Old Zach lifted his head and peered at the room behind John. Then, returning his gaze to the foreground, his eyes settled on John. A sour expression crossed his face and he put out his hand.

John was startled for a moment, then thrilled to the core of his being. General Taylor wanted to shake hands with *him?* A new recruit? He could hardly believe it! He stuck his hand out to grasp the general's.

"General Taylor, I'm John Bell. I'm pleased to—"

"Son, meanin' no offense," Zachary Taylor stopped him tiredly. "You might do well to take a step back and to the side. Otherwise, Alfredo there, he's gonna sweep sawdust all over them new shoes."

John reddened and fumbled awkwardly for words that didn't come. He took a quick glance around at Alfredo and his broom and complied with the General's suggestion. When he looked back, Ol' Zach, Walker and Bliss had already started moving off, in renewed conversation with each other, down the length of the bar and out the door, leaving John hot with embarrassment.

Dooey, watching from his table as John did his hop, skip and jump for General Taylor, just shook his head grimly, put down his empty glass and strolled out into the late afternoon sunlight. He had a longing for solitude—continued solitude. Wrapped snugly in his dream almost since boarding the *Redoubt*, he had felt aloof from the other volunteers, even John, and everything going on around him.

It was a conceit Dooey Dolan had that his dream somehow made him better than everybody else, made him rise even above those parts of himself that he didn't like. As he walked outside now onto the lush green grass on the bank of the Rio Grande, he felt that dream surging within him, putting an eager spring into his steps that he hadn't felt since he was eight years old.

He ambled along in the 100° heat, feeling a curious mixture of peace and joyful anticipation. The leaves of the palm trees hung motionless in the hot afternoon air, but now and then there came a light breeze that rustled the grass pleasantly. A small grey cloud drifting across the sky cast its shadow on the low hillocks that rolled away from the banks of the Rio Grande. It was all Dooey Dolan needed, these slight transformations of light and sound and color. He was home. He was home right here in the valley of the Rio Grande, a place he had never visited but which was enough like his South Carolina of long ago so that it could stir in him anew the longings of the child he had once been.

He walked to the edge of the river and looked down into its stillness, aglint now with more blue than muddy brown with the lowering sun shining on it. To Dooey, the Rio Grande he was looking at was a river out of time—it could be any slow-moving southern river, really—and it instilled in him that same rare mixture of peace and excitement. Yes, you could be a child again . . . you could. Dooey knelt to test the temperature of the river, considering a swim. The water was plenty warm enough. He was about to withdraw his hand when he heard a sharp cry of pain and anger from the otherwise silent town of Matamoros across the way. This was followed by a woman's shout. As Dooey squatted there, staring toward Matamoros, a huge brown turtle rose in the river and nipped at his dangling fingers.

Dooey howled and yanked his hand out of the water. "Damn it!" But when he saw what had bitten him—one of several large turtles floating around at his feet—he started to laugh.

"Enough of this, buddy," he told himself. "What you need is a playmate."

Dooey got up and looked around for someone to talk to. About fifty yards downriver from him, standing on a point where the river curved, were two soldiers and a mule. The soldiers, with their backs to him, seemed to be gazing at something down the river and out of Dooey's sight. But what mostly piqued his curiosity was the mule, which the shorter of the two soldiers held behind him by a rope. The mule wore a thin Army blanket on which Dooey could just make out the white-stencilled letters U.S. GRANT. Dooey frowned, pondering the meaning. Had the short soldier been given his very own personal mule by the United States government? Dooey doubted it, but he was curious enough to go over and ask.

As he came up to them, the two men turned.

Dooey grinned. "Mind if I ask what the U.S. GRANT on the mule stands for?"

The taller man said dryly, "Stands for one hell of a lot of muleshit, for one thing."

The shorter man didn't blink an eye. "It's my mule.

That's me. I'm Grant," he said. "Ulysses Simpson Grant."

"Oh?"

The man named Grant smiled. "It's a hard nut to crack, I know. I'm generally called Sam around here. This is Bragg—Braxton Bragg."

Dooey nodded. "I'm Dolan . . . nice to meet you both." He hesitated, then said to Sam Grant, "You won't believe this, but I thought maybe your mule might have been a grant you received from the U.S. government."

Braxton Bragg frowned. "Sort of like a homestead grant?" Suddenly he was laughing and slapping the slight, slender Grant on the back, so that the latter winced. "Sam, did you ever hear that one before? Damn, that's a good one!"

"I can't say that I have," Sam Grant said, smiling. "Unfortunately, Dolan, I have not been singled out for any such honor."

Bragg was still shaking his head. "Damn, I like that one!"

Dooey laughed. "Guess I made a mistake. Are you fellows Regulars or volunteers?"

"We're Regulars," Grant said pleasantly. "I take it you've just arrived?"

"I'm with the Indiana regiment," Dooey said.

Bragg showed some interest. "That's not a bad outfit at all, from what I've seen of it. What brings you out in the heat, Dolan?"

Dooey shrugged. "Just walking."

Bragg grinned impishly. "Us, we're on a special mission."

"Oh? What's that?"

Grant said, "You never want to take Bragg seriously,

Dolan. Fact is, things are slow here right now, as you may already have noticed, and we make it a habit to stop at this spot most every evening to watch a certain Mexican girl in the river. You're welcome to join us."

Bragg had already moved off and was gazing again at the river.

"Sam, you can set your gawddamn watch," Bragg called out without turning. "I do believe they're coming for her."

Grant grinned at Dooey. "Come on, Dolan. We have here an interesting phenomenon. Besides, Maria's an attractive lady of some dark appeal."

Dooey walked up to the lip of the bank with Grant and looked out at the girl. Then he found himself staring at her.

The girl, who was clearly Indian, was not merely attractive but, in his opinion, spectacularly beautiful. He could see immediately what Grant meant by her "dark appeal," which could apply to both her coloring and attitude, as she stood waist-deep in the river not twenty yards away, glaring at them. She had coal-black eyes and a mane of long black hair that now clung wetly to her high cheek-boned face. To Dooey she looked like a waif, a starved and angry and beautiful waif.

Dooey found himself grinning, to which the girl responded by focusing her hate-filled glare on him, her upper lip curled in a sneer of contempt. Dooey grinned all the more.

"Who is she?" he asked.

"Her name is Maria," Grant said, observing Dooey wryly. "That is all we know. And all, apparently, that you *need* to know."

"Except that she has a lovely ass you haven't seen yet," Bragg muttered.

"Is she a whore?" Dooey asked, interested.

Grant said, "No. You see, Dolan, about all we know of Maria is that she was seen with General Arista before we drove him and his army out of Matamoros. Arista left and she remained, under the custody or protection of a group of Indians who are either her family or acting as such. Maria's hostile attitude toward us has made it impossible for any American to get close enough to her to learn more. It's a matter of many having been attracted but not chosen."

"She could be this Arista's private whore, or maybe even a spy," Dooey suggested.

"Now, that's possible," Grant agreed. "However, if she is a spy she's committed no culpable act of espionage yet. She comes and goes in the river, one of hundreds of Mexican nationals who, by policy, the Army lets be."

Bragg muttered something about the volunteers not letting the Mexican civilians be, but Dooey's mind was still on Maria. "This family of hers . . ." he began tentatively.

"Wait. You'll see," Grant said.

As Dooey watched, a Mexican appeared on the far bank, cupped his hands and yelled to the girl in the river. She continued to glare at them—most particularly at Dooey, who found himself stirred by the venom in her narrowed eyes. He felt challenged by her hatred—and ready to rise to the challenge. As he stood there grinning, she tossed her head at him, spat contemptuously in his direction, and turned and swam gracefully toward the opposite shore.

"Oh what an ass," murmured Bragg. "You see it, Dolan?"

"I sure do," Dooey said.

"Well, we can go now and get some work done. That's it," Grant said.

"That's it?" Dooey was perplexed. "But all that Mexican fellow did was come and call her for dinner—I know that much Spanish. You mean to say you fellows come here most every night, just to watch a girl being called home for dinner?"

Bragg turned and glowered at him. "He does it every night at *exactly the same time*. You're on the Mexican border, Dolan. What do you expect. A regular three-act New York musical show with Joseph Jefferson in it?"

"No, but—"

"Because if it's a real big show you want we can give you cute little Sam here playing Desdemona in Shakespeare's *Othello*. Sam did a fine job with that when we were putting on camp shows up at Corpus Christi last winter. And we can—"

"Come along, Bragg," Grant said commandingly.

His hand resting on his mule's rump, ready to try and slap it into motion, Grant turned to Dooey.

"Did that little scene in the river make you wonder? Did you wonder for instance, why an Indian girl should hate us so much? Why she should be so loyal to a Mexican government that cares so little about its Indian citizens?"

Dooey stared at him.

"When we were fighting at Palo Alto," Grant continued, "we had occasion to throw grape—tons of it—into the Mexican infantry ranks. There were hundreds, perhaps a thousand of them, mostly all Indian conscripts and apparently under command to hold fast to their positions. So they just stood and took the grape. They didn't fire at us—there's little they could have accomplished with their muskets anyway, not against our artillery. Bragg had an artillery battery there. He can tell you how it was."

"We knocked the shit out of them," Bragg said.

Grant nodded. "That's right. And they just stood there for a while, screaming and dying. Later, their survivors and the rest of the Mexican Army gave us a merry old time. But that those poor Indians should have obeyed a command to stand there and die, that bothered me, Dolan. Tell me; I like to get people's opinions. Would it have bothered you?"

"It's bothering me right now," Dooey said.

The girl in the river appeared in Dooey's dreams that night. Dooey saw her as an orphan like himself—straddling the border, not knowing whether to turn north or south; living in defiance and contempt, unable to reach out in friendship.

Dooey felt he knew her already.

The next day, during the lunch break he drifted away from his regiment and went back to the river again. The girl was standing in the river, alone, with no one near her. She was in the same spot he'd seen her in the evening before, and glared at him as he watched her.

Dooey cocked his head at her. Maria . . . For some reason the name seemed special to him. He liked it. He wanted to hear her say it.

He leaned forward a little on the bank and called to her, "*Que es su nombre*?" No answer, only a deeper glare. Dooey scratched his head. "No . . . wait. I have that wrong. *Como se llama*?"

Again no answer. Dooey, irritated, yelled out to her. "All right, we'll call you Injun girl. Injun girl, are you anybody at all? Injun girl, why do you work so hard at being unfriendly."

There was a change in her expression. She frowned, and Dooey was sure that she had understood him. He leaned forward and called out softly, "Maria." She said not a word but her frown deepened.

Dooey sat down on the riverbank. The girl watched him as he took his shoes off and stepped into the river to wade out towards her. She didn't move, only watched his approach with unblinking eyes.

When he was standing only three feet from her, he stopped and smiled at her. Then he dove underwater and came up a foot closer.

"Water's nice and warm," Dooey said. "We could swim. We could race." He hesitated. "Of course, I have my uniform on, but you have yours on too, so we'd be even."

Underwater, he had seen that she indeed wore a skirt—one of those Mexican "emblem" skirts, with tiny green-and-white flags around the hem.

Up close, Dooey could see that Maria was pure Indian. He was captivated by her dark, hawk-like features and the fiery glint in her eyes. It occurred to Dooey that, had she been living on this land three hundred years ago when the first Spaniards arrived, she would have fought them to the death. He felt his heart pounding with excitement. And then she spoke.

"Go away!" she spat at him. "General Arista will come back and cut you to pieces!"

Instantly, Dooey was on firm ground. He nodded soberly. "I'm sure that's true. But could I possibly hear you say your name before I die?"

She bit her lip. She had understood every word he'd said. How dare this *gringo* mock her? How dare he intrude on her deep devotion to the Mexican cause?

"My name is Maria Alora Martinez de Jesus Caldez Heran."

Dooey said, astonished, "I've never heard of such a name!"

She glowered at him. "What is your name, *gringo*?"

"Dooey," he said absently.

She scoffed, aping him. "I've never heard of such a name."

Dooey smiled at her. "It's short for DeWitt."

"De-Witt. De-Witt." She bit the name in two. "Dooey," she decided.

She lost interest in him then. She thought he was a foolish boy. He did not know what she knew; otherwise he would not have come wading out to her like a small child. Another time she might have found him attractive, with his dark good looks. But they had nothing to talk about.

She let her gaze drift past his head. Her eyes narrowed. Dooey, turning, saw hundreds of volunteers regrouping outside their tents with their Springfields, ready for the afternoon drill.

He turned back to Maria. "We're practicing to kill people," he said quietly. "What are you practicing for?" She did not look at him. "Are you a spy? Are you going to find General Arista and tell him what you've seen here? Are you going to poison our water? Would you like to dance?"

She flushed. "You killed two of the sweetest boys I ever knew," she said suddenly. Her eyes blazed at him. "You killed Ramon and Goya at Palo Alto. They never hurt anybody—they were just sixteen. And you killed them!"

Dooey stared at her for a moment. Finally he said,

"Well, what is this then, a wake? Do you come here to mourn them?"

She began to nod her head violently. "Yes, yes, yes! They were my friends. They were beautiful boys—beautiful! And you killed them! You killed them!"

Dooey felt a rush of pity. He stepped forward and put his arms around her. Maria let him, sobbing violently against his shoulder. They stood that way for what seemed a long time.

Finally, Dooey stepped back and put his hands on her shoulders. "Look, you'd better go back. Coming here isn't going to help you, and I have to go now."

She looked at him, her eyes still moist with tears.

He said hesitantly, "I didn't kill Ramon and Goya, you know that. I wasn't even at Palo Alto."

She looked at him steadily. "Yes, I know that. You are a good boy, Dooey. You would not kill anybody."

"Maybe that's right." For some reason, anger flashed in him. "Maybe I wouldn't kill anybody at all."

"Well, then. Go back to your camp and play."

Dooey stood there, exasperated. "Listen, do you mind telling me where you learned to speak English so well? And could you—"

But Maria turned and Dooey watched her wade slowly back toward the silent houses of Metamoros. Suddenly, he had a desire to follow her, to take her in his arms and protect her.

But he told himself to forget her—this wild creature who lived in a world completely different from his own.

7

THE INDIANA VOLUNTEERS remained in camp for the rest of July, as orders to move up the Rio Grande were posted, retracted, reposted and retracted again. Most of the Indianans, with other regiments, were marched into the chaparral north of the river, where they had target practice with their Springfields —shooting mostly at snakes—and got more and more acquainted with the nearly intolerable heat. Day after day they trained for a battle that never seemed to come.

It was difficult, sometimes impossible, to sustain the men's morale. Despite the warnings they had received, men got sick—from bad water, bad food, bad whiskey, bad *something*, for their illnesses were often beyond diagnosis. Many got so sick that they couldn't function and had to be returned to Point Isabel and the States.

John and Dooey held on well together for a while. After some initial fumbling, John had found a niche for himself in the Army. For one thing, he had come to admire and respect General Taylor, and was going to do his best by the old buzzard—come hell or high water. Also, John had found a host of new friends.

Dooey, on the other hand, had been keeping more and more to himself. Haunted by a vision of Maria's face, he went to the river daily in the hope of seeing her, but she had not returned since the day they had met.

"Dooey," John broke into his friend's reverie. "I found out who's waiting for us at Monterrey. There's a General Terrejon there with an army of twenty thousand men."

Dooey looked up from his cot. "Not Santa Anna?"

"No, he's supposed to be reorganizing the government in Mexico City."

"Twenty thousand Mexicans," Dooey mused. "How many men do we have . . . four, five thousand?"

John nodded. "But we'll knock the shit out of them."

Dooey looked at him sharply. "You haven't been talking to Braxton Bragg by any chance, have you?"

"Sure. And to Sam Grant. By the way, he asked about you. . . ."

When Maria did not reappear at the river after several days, Dooey went over to Matamoros to look for her.

He joined the crowd of volunteers going over in the boats one night to let off some steam. He hit several saloons with them, but when he did not see Maria in any of them and no other girl took his fancy, he wandered up the street alone, looking for her.

In an alley between white stucco houses he found

a Mexican vagrant, an Indian, lying against a wall with a bottle in his hand but not too drunk to speak. Groping for the right Spanish words, Dooey asked him if he knew an Indian girl named Maria and where she might be.

The man's eyes lit up and he became crafty. Dooey gave him some money, at which point the Indian stood up, wavering, and pointed to an open field on which Dooey could see a small shack, smoke curling from its chimney. Dooey started that way.

"There are better ones, *mas gorda, mas alegra, mas bonita*. I will take you to them," the man called after him. "*Bobo Americano*," he muttered when Dooey did not turn.

As Dooey neared the shack, Maria came out of it, carrying a dishful of scraps for dumping into a nearby garbage pit. She stopped and waited when she saw him.

"Hello. How are you?" Dooey said, feeling silly. "I thought I'd drop by to ask."

She seemed to be suppressing a grin. "Come in," she said.

Whatever she was feeling, she was aglow with it. Dooey, warmed by her greeting, followed her inside. Around a low cook fire on the shack's dirt floor were three other Indians, one of whom Dooey recognized as the one who had called to Maria from the riverbank. There was another stolid-faced young man there, who might have been the first's younger brother, and an old white-haired woman. They were eating beans and looked up impassively from their plates as Dooey entered.

"This is Dooey," Maria said, taking his arm in hers and beaming at them. "He is the one who was kind to me in the river."

"Ah," the old woman said, smiling at Dooey.

"This is Carlos and Juan and Florita," Maria said.

Dooey nodded at them. Looking around, he was struck first by the poverty of the shack, then by its neatness, finally by a small gold-framed portrait that was sitting on a low table. The figure, looking like a Mexican dignitary, wore a black velvet coat with wide red lapels; the thin-lipped face struck Dooey as smug.

"Who's that?" he asked.

"That is General Santa Anna," Maria said proudly.

He looked at the girl. She was pathetic, a pretty girl in a torn dress looking with worshipful eyes on a smug, evil-looking man. What was going on here? Dooey was angry—and jealous. It didn't make sense to him that Maria could adore such a contemptible face.

He grumbled something and turned away.

"What is wrong with Santa Anna?" Maria said, following him.

"Nothing. He's not on our side," Dooey said.

"Your side! You have no side!" Maria spat at him. "What are you doing here, *gringo*? Go back where you came from! Why do you come here to insult me? What have I done to you?"

"Not a damn thing," Dooey said. "You bother me, that's all."

"Why? What have I done?"

"You're too goddamn pretty to be wasting your time on a mutt like that."

"Pretty! Is that all you can say?"

"Yes, goddamn it! Who the hell are you, anyway?"

The old woman at the fire stirred herself. "Sit down with us, *gringo*. Eat."

"I'm not hungry!" Dooey shot at her.

"Yes, yes you are. Maria, bring him something."

Maria glared at Dooey a moment longer, then strode angrily to a cupboard at the far end of the shack.

"Come, *gringo*, sit."

The one called Carlos made room for him, pointing to the ground, and Dooey sat. He felt confused, but more alive than he had been for many a moon, as if he were confronted by some danger.

"We are Huasteca Indians," the old woman said.

"I know you're Indians!"

"Ah, but you don't know everything."

"What else is there to know?"

"That you like our Maria," the old woman said, more softly, so that the girl wouldn't hear her.

"I'm not sure about that."

"Yes, yes, you do," the old woman said, nodding. "Calm yourself, *gringo*. We are Huasteca Indians and Matamoros is not our home. Our village is in the Sierra Madres, many miles south."

Dooey waited.

"We would like you to go home with us."

Dooey stared at her.

"We would like you to bring your gun with you and your promise that you will join the San Patricio Battalion, for that is the way to win Maria—the only way."

"Loco," Dooey muttered. "You're all loco."

"Nevertheless, this is what you will do," the old woman said. She sounded as if she knew.

Maria came back to the fire. Dooey looked at her. She was just a girl, only a girl . . . and yet Dooey was somehow afraid of her.

Maria said, "Here. Here is a plate of beans for you."

"Thank you," Dooey said. But he did not touch the beans.

"We would like you to come away with us," Maria said.

Dooey stared at her, then looked away in confusion. "I'd prefer not to. Tell me what you are doing in Matamoros."

"I told you."

"No, you didn't."

"I am a spy."

"I didn't believe you before. I don't now."

"I am nobody."

"Everybody on this earth is somebody."

"Do you believe that?"

"Yes. Sometimes it's hard to remember, but it's true."

"My name is Maria. I do not know my last name—my father's name, that is. He was Indian, as was my mother. My mother died when I was born, and my father left me on the doorstep of the Hernan family, in Mexico City. He left me there in a paper bag. Señor Hernan took pity on me and took me in. He and his wife had no children. I stayed with them until I was six, then Señor Hernan was called into the army to fight the Texans. He was killed. Señora Hernan died—of grief, it was said—and I went to the Calderon family, who were neighbors. I was pretty at six, do you know what I mean?"

"You're pretty now," Dooey said.

"Señor Calderon thought I was pretty at six," Maria said bitterly. "Nevertheless, I learned to speak English in his house, for he was a government translator. He raped me often and then I began to like it, for he could be a king when he was not drinking. He explained certain things to me. How your President Polk, for instance, was trying to steal our country from us, humiliating us, always humiliating us."

Dooey shook his head. "What do you want me to do about all of this?"

Carlos, munching a taco, mumbled, "Listen to her, *amigo*."

"No. I've listened and I am not moved. I've had a tough life of my own."

"Ah."

"I had a mother and father who were no better than yours, probably far worse. More to the point, I don't give a damn about this war."

"Then leave it!" Maria shot at him.

"*You* leave it! It's not your war any more than it's mine!"

There was silence. Finally, Carlos grunted, then pointed to a leftover taco on Juan's plate which Juan handed to him. Carlos licked his fingers and ate some more.

Maria and Dooey glared at each other, at an impasse. Into the silence came a sound from outside. Some volunteers, roaring drunk, were heading their way. Carlos got up. He and Dooey reached the door of the shack together.

There were six or seven of them coming across the open field. They were Texans. One of them had a Colt pistol out and was pointing it up at the sky. He fired it once. The others roared with laughter and kept coming.

Carlos looked at the oncoming group, then at Dooey. "*Amigo*, we are not armed. We cannot defend ourselves."

Dooey nodded. "Maria, Florita, go out the back and hide there. Keep low against the wall. Carlos, Juan, you stay with me."

There were broken slats in the rear wall of the shack. The two women, instantly alert to the drunken roars and knowing what they could mean, crawled out and hid as directed. There was no place to run except across the open field on which the moon shone brightly.

The Texans came on. Dooey couldn't be sure what they wanted. Maybe just a good time they would give up on when they saw no women there. As they neared the shack, Dooey stepped out the door to meet them.

The Texans stopped and one of them said, "Gawdamn, it's one of us. What you doin' here, boy? Got yourself some hot greaser pussy?"

Dooey thought quickly. "If I did, it would be mine. But I ain't."

"Well, what *do* you have in there? I c'n see somebody moving around."

"A couple of male greasers. I've been talking to them, that's all."

"Shee-it! Talkin' to greasers out here in the middle of the night? Don't that beat all? Let's just see what you got in there, boy!"

They crowded by Dooey, one after the other, into the shack. Dooey had started to bar their way, then thought better of it.

They saw Carlos and Juan and all but ignored them, for their eyes had fastened not on what Dooey was most apprehensive they would see—the many plates around the fire—but the picture of Santa Anna on the table.

The Texan with the Colt promptly shot at the picture, and Santa Anna got a hole in the middle of his forehead.

"Now that's taken care of, whar's the ladies?" The Texan tucked the Colt back in his belt.

"What ladies? I told you there weren't any here," Dooey said. "That was a good shot," he added.

"The ones you been chompin' with, you danged fool," another of the Texans said. He was pointing to the extra plates.

It wasn't going to work, Dooey realized. They were drunk, intent on what they wanted, and he didn't have the wits to put them off. He felt even then that he was going to take a bad beating. But all at once he hated these men, and the words came busting out of him.

His eyes narrowed. "Get out of here, you sons of bitches."

"Well, now . . ."

As the Texans started to move toward Dooey, Carlos said, "*Señores, por favor,* leave him be," but Dooey seized an iron bar leaning against the wall near the door and lashed out—at thin air, as it turned out, for the Texan who had shot Santa Anna jumped back quickly.

Dooey stood there breathing hard.

"Put down that bar, boy," the Texan said steadily.

But Dooey wasn't about to; he was ready to split the man's skull with it.

"Now this *is* serious," the Texan commented.

"Come on, Tom, let's get out of here," one of the others said. "He's crazier than you are. Let's head back to town."

"I don't want to fight you. I didn't ask for this," Dooey said.

"You're asking for *something* when you got a piece of iron aimed at my head!"

Dooey flung the bar away and put up his fists. The Texan smiled. Dooey didn't wait to be attacked but stepped forward quickly and unleashed a blow at the man's jaw. Up until that moment, he truly hadn't wanted to fight. But once the Texan sidestepped his punch and awkwardly belted him in the shoulder, Dooey didn't think anything at all except that he could take this man, that there was more power in him than he'd believed.

The blow to his shoulder was hard enough to numb the muscles in that arm, but Dooey bored right in, aiming for the man's stomach, chest, arms, anything he could hit. He was pummeling at flesh with tunnel vision, not a thought in his head.

A tremendous smash caught him flush on the jaw and Dooey went down flat on his back. He lay there looking at a big spiral of stars. He felt no pain, only utter astonishment. It was an amazing thing. One moment he had been standing there with a kind of murderous power in him; the next, he was lying on the floor with nothing in him at all, it seemed.

"Come on, Tom, that's enough. You done real good."

The Texan who had hit him stood over Dooey. "You want a hand up, boy? There ain't no hard feelings on my part."

Dooey didn't want a hand up. After a moment, Tom shrugged, turned and left with the others. Dooey heard them whooping and hollering as they headed back to Matamoros.

He rolled to his knees and got up painfully, rubbing his jaw. Some sense had returned to him and he saw Carlos eyeing him.

"Well, I stopped them," Dooey said ruefully. "I guess they got all they needed here. You can call Maria and Florita back in now."

The women came back. Maria came over to Dooey, took a look at his cut jaw, then got some water to wash it with. Dooey sat down heavily on a straw mat by the fire and looked up at her. "And you want me to fight with the San Patricios?"

She dabbed at the cut, cleaning it. "I thought you were a fighter."

"I guess that was back in Connecticut. There wasn't much competition."

"Anyway, you would not have to use your fists if you joined our army. You could bring your gun."

Dooey shook his head. He could not believe that Maria was serious. Over her shoulder, as she tended to his bruises, he saw Carlos and Juan grinning at him. The old woman, Florita, was beaming.

"Zorro," she said.

"What's that?"

"The fox, the clever fox. You are Zorro."

"I'm not so clever."

"You are. You just do not know it yet. It is nothing to be ashamed of. It is something to take pleasure in."

"I don't know what you mean."

As if these people had somehow brought out feelings that he usually denied, even to himself, all Dooey knew at that moment was that he hungered for relations, for a family. And strange though it was, he found himself wondering if he might find one with these Indians, who were as poor as he felt himself to be.

"Tell me about your village," he said.

It was Florita who answered him. "It is a green place in the mountains north of San Luis Potosi. It is cool there—not hot as it is here—and peaceful. It is not on the route of the war."

"It will be," Maria said.

Dooey pricked up his ears. "How do you know that?"

"Even now we are forming an army in Mexico City, a large one, under General Santa Anna, that will come north and put an end to your General Taylor and his plans to conquer us."

"You know what we'll do to your General Santa Anna? That." Dooey pointed to the bullet-holed picture.

Maria frowned. "Sit still."

Dooey thought while she finished washing his cut and put a cloth on it to stop the bleeding. "So the army will be coming up through your village, I take it."

"Yes. Our only road north leads through it. The army will have the San Patricio Battalion with it. Its commander is John Riley, who left your infantry and joined us in April, even before the war started. You can meet Lieutenant Riley and enlist in the battalion there."

Dooey's pulse quickened. He thought about taking this information back to Fort Texas. He could really be a hero if he did that. "How do you know this?" he asked.

Maria colored. "I know Lieutenant Riley. I was here in Matamoros when he swam the river and came to us. And I—I hear from him occasionally."

"You mean, you slept with him? Is that what you do? Sleep with deserters?"

"What if I do?" she challenged him. "It is not your business."

"No, no, it's all right," Dooey said, soothing her. "I just want to get things straight. You mean, that ritual you were going through in the river—for Goya, Ramon, whatever their names are—was only an act? You were really out there to lure deserters, a whole flock of Rileys?"

Maria looked confused. "I did miss them—they were my friends. But I also—I also. . . ."

Dooey surveyed her. "You're a very interesting person, do you know that? Well, now you've lured Dolan, so what are you going to do with him? It seems to me I've already rescued you from a fate worse than death. Do I have to desert too, just to go to bed with you?"

"No."

Dooey was surprised.

"But we cannot do it here," he said.

"I don't see why not."

Maria looked significantly at the others in the shack. But Carlos and Juan were already on their feet, helping Florita to hers. They left the shack silently, as if much-practiced in the procedure.

Dooey watched them go. Then he turned back to Maria.

She stood before him and slowly unbuttoned the blouse she was wearing, a U.S. Army shirt that was open at the collar. Her legs were spread flauntingly, and he now noticed she was wearing army pants too. Leaning forward a little, ostensibly to get the shirt's bottom button, her hair brushed his cheeks. Dooey saw the seductive purpose of it and was filled with admiration.

She had her eyes fastened on his as, with one hand, she tugged the shirt out of her trousers, still leaving the top buttons closed.

Dooey sat where he was, on the straw mat, watching.

"How much more of this do I have to do?" she complained. But she was enjoying herself, Dooey could see, and he grinned at her. "More," he said.

Watching him intently now, she slowly undid the top buttons. The inside swellings of her breasts appeared.

"You're skinny," Dooey said.

"I am not!" She grabbed the shirt and flung it open to his gaze.

Dooey swallowed. She had gorgeous breasts, round, firm, uptilted.

"I take it back. You're not skinny," he said.

He got to his feet, no longer able to just sit there and look at her. There was a feeling in the pit of his stomach that had a touch of dread in it, but it was no match for his longing. He moved to her, put an arm around her shoulders and pulled her close, cupping a breast with his other hand and caressing it tenderly. Maria shivered, and her legs were trembling. For an instant, Dooey wondered if maybe she hadn't done this for a while and if that was why she was as eager as he was.

The thought amused him, but only for an instant, for the touch of her skin and the sight of her lips reaching eagerly toward his drowned all speculation in a sea of ecstasy. He closed his eyes and kissed her. Then Maria's arms were around him tightly and they went down on the straw mat.

Dooey took great care. A welling tenderness toward this girl restrained his lust so that he felt as if he were dancing with her, guiding her across some great private ballroom with courtliness and grace. For a brief moment she had a startled look in her eyes, as if she had never been treated in such a way before. Then she entered into the dance, became a willing partner to it, and unleashed the storm of her own passion in this unfamiliar mix of feelings he had induced in her.

After a great soaring lurch, she came down from some blissful heaven in an excruciating agony of pleasure. She lay silently under him, dazed, almost stunned. He was lying on top of her, her legs still straddling his hips. Their clothes were scattered all over the floor. After awhile, they got disentangled. Maria stood and began to dress.

"Are you going to stay here tonight?" she asked.

"I don't know," he said. "There's no room for me."

"Yes there is." Maria nodded toward a straw pallet in one corner of the shack. "We can sleep there. The others won't mind."

"I'm due back at the fort," he said.

She didn't answer this.

From the floor, he watched her pull on her trousers. She had long, slim legs, he noted, disproportionate to her height. They were smooth, like the rest of her. She wore no underpants. When she bent to get into a pants leg, he looked at the smooth curve of her buttocks, and passion stirred in him.

"Maria," he said. "I've always liked that name."

"Oh? You have known a Maria before?"

"No, but—" Dooey shrugged.

He wanted to argue some more. "What I don't understand about you is your loyalty to the Mexican flag. It's crazy. It makes no sense. Nothing you've said has made any sense."

"You don't have to worry about that anymore, Dooey."

He looked at her, surprised. From where she stood, buttoning her trousers, she smiled at him. Then she came over, knelt before him and wrapped her arms around his bent knees, pressing her bare breasts against them.

"Perhaps I *was* crazy, but I am not crazy now," she said. There was a soft look in her dark eyes and a twinkling of happiness too. "I will not be crazy again, I promise you."

She took his hand and rubbed it against her cheek and jaw. A hint of tears now came in her eyes.

"Stay with me, Dooey . . . ?" she said.

8

WHEN PRIVATE DOOEY DOLAN did not return to Fort Texas that night, about the only person who noticed or was concerned was John Bell. John woke up the next morning and there was nobody in the adjacent cot.

Some other cots in the large tent were empty as well, so there wasn't anything unusual about that. During the enforced waiting period, men were spending the night in Matamoros with little being said about it. But those were the hell raisers, of which Dooey was not one; they'd invariably be back by noon, some still half drunk, ready to resume drilling.

Dooey didn't return by noon. There was nothing John could do about it except hope, for Dooey's sake, that he'd get back before the day ended. Because there was a definite stirring in the air that day, more than a hint that the Indiana Regiment, along with others, would be moving out very shortly.

The first indication of this came at noon, when Lew Wallace mustered the regiment for roll call—a distinct break in the usual lax procedure. Lew didn't let the gathered volunteers wonder long either.

"Well, you've got what you wanted, most of you," he said, smiling. "General Taylor has given orders for the Kentucky, Mississippi and Indiana regiments to be ready to ship out tomorrow morning. That is, the others will be shipping out. There aren't enough steamboats for all of us, so we'll be heading overland to Camargo, where we'll make camp."

A mixture of cheers and groans, mostly groans, came from the men.

"Lew, is this one more time when we pack up the mules and then unpack 'em when Taylor calls it off?"

"No, I think Zach means business this time. Next—?"

"Well, why just Camargo for us?" someone else wanted to know. "Hell, Camargo ain't more'n halfway to Monterrey. He's got us walkin' our asses off across the desert just to get us someplace where there's no more goin' on than there is here. Lew, I coulda stayed home an' shot birds an' had more fun than I'm havin' here!"

Wallace nodded. "Maybe so, Jim. Point is, our Texas scouts have reported seeing a large Mexican guerrilla band in the desert. Our job, if we run into them, is to keep them away from the river so's the boats can get through."

"Well, that's somethin', anyway," Jim growled.

"We'll stage at Camargo and go on to Monterrey when all the Regulars come up," Wallace continued. "Monterrey is a well-fortified city and General Taylor has no plan of attack yet—probably won't have until he sees the place and gets the feel of it himself. So yes, Jim, unless we run into those guerrillas for your turkey shoot, you're just going to have to wait in Camargo a little longer. Any more questions?"

John, in a rear rank, spoke up. "Lew, what if we're not all here and ready to go tomorrow?"

Wallace grinned. "In my opinion, none of us are all here. What do you mean? Who's missing?"

Crossman looked around. "You don't have to call roll, Lew," he said flatly. "Dolan's missing."

John said, "I mean, could he catch up with us if someone told him where we'd gone? Or could I go look for him?"

"The bastard must have deserted," Crossman said.

"His rifle's here. His pack's here," John argued. "He can't be far."

"He could be carrying a Mexican gun and riding a Mexican horse toward Monterrey right now," Crossman countered angrily. "Meanin' no offense, but the bastard's Irish, ain't he?"

John shook his head. "You don't know Dooey."

Lew Wallace, after a moment's thought, said, "Bell, go ahead and look for him, so we can get this cleared up one way or another. If you find him, fine. Bring him back in time to leave tomorrow. If you don't, I'll have to report his absence and we'll leave without him." He took a step backwards. "That's it. You men have all the information I can give you about tomorrow. Until then, dismissed!"

So John went looking for Dooey, though he didn't feel much like it. John had changed: he was anxious to get on with it, eager for the war ahead. He was fed up with inaction and the introspective brooding it brought on. He was fed up with Dooey's moping around. Mostly, he was fed up with himself.

But he felt that he had this one last obligation, not so much to Dooey as to the feelings of loyalty so deeply ingrained in him. Dooey was going to get himself into a lot of trouble if he didn't return to the regiment in time for the departure next morning.

He rowed across the river to Matamoros and found himself to be one of the few Americans there, it being midday. A couple of Regulars he found in the saloon, coming groggily awake with the aid of a morning-after tequila, didn't recollect seeing any Indiana volunteer answering Dooey's description the previous night. John's few halting words of Spanish brought him cold stares or helpless smiles of ignorance from the Mexicans he approached, but no useful information as to Dooey's whereabouts.

The town was small enough so he could walk through all its streets in an hour, peering into doorways, hoping he would find Dooey drunk and sleeping it off somewhere, but not really believing that he would. Dooey didn't, as a rule, drink to get drunk; he would have been easier to find, John thought, getting madder and madder, if he did.

He was about to give up on his increasingly onerous task when he ran across a tall Texan, sprawled on his back on a street corner, snoring with his mouth open, a cigarillo stuck to his lower lip and the brim of his sombrero down over his eyes. John reached down and shook the man's shoulder, to which the Texan responded by instantly reaching for the Colt at his belt. Only then did he open his eyes.

John grinned. "Excuse me," he said.

"What fer? What you goin' to do?"

"I just want to ask you a question."

The Texan groaned, hauled himself into a sitting position and blinked into the sun. "Time to get up anyway. What time is it? Fire away, boy."

"It's about noon. I'd like to know if you happened to see a tall, black-haired fellow in an Indiana uniform around here last night."

"Irish-looking fellow?"

"That's it."

The Texan, who'd been trying to frown away his hangover, now smiled. "I think I beat the living shit out of him."

"Where'd you do that?" John asked with interest.

"Over yonder." The Texan pointed west. There was a rose-colored stucco building ten feet from his pointing finger. "Not that, that's a cathouse," he said. "Past it is an open field and a greaser shack. Why you lookin' for him anyway?"

John told him.

"Hot damn! You mean we're moving out?"

"I don't know about you, but we three volunteer regiments are. Tomorrow morning."

"Well, if you are, then Taylor is, and if Taylor is, then I am." The Texan got to his feet, swaying. "Where's my horse?"

"I don't know. Where you left it, I guess. Thanks." John started off at a trot and the Texan called after him. "If you find that boy, tell him Tom Watts says hello an' that he done give me a purty good fight—even if he is crazy in the head."

John reached the field, saw the shack and loped across the field to it. It looked dead-quiet to him. There were a couple of scraggly chickens outside, but nobody was up and about tending to them, or to any other chores.

He ran up and knocked loudly on the door. No response from within.

"Anybody home?" John called out.

When there was no answer, he stood in indecision for a moment, then shrugged and tried the door, which was stuck but gave way under one shove of his shoulder.

"Well, I'll be damned," he said. "Who'd have thought you had it in you?"

What met his eyes was Dooey in bed with the Mexican girl. Dooey was on his back and the girl was leaning over him protectively, her upper arm shielding her naked breasts and most of Dooey as well. There were three other people in the shack, sitting up on sleeping mats on the floor, but John ignored them.

"Oh, it's you," Dooey said. "Hello, John."

John ignored the girl too, noting only that she was a dark-haired, seductive wench.

"For Christ's sake, Dooey! Hop to it and get back to camp with me. We've got orders. Six A.M. tomorrow. Sharp."

"Where to?" Dooey asked with a flicker of interest.

"Camargo first. Come on, Dooey, you've had your fun. Shake a leg. I'll wait outside and we can go back together."

"I'm not going, John."

"You're not—what?"

"I'm not going."

John stared at him.

"He said he's not going," the girl in the bed with Dooey said defensively.

"I can handle this, Maria," Dooey said.

"Handle what? Dooey, do you mind telling me what's going on here? Who are these people?"

He meant Carlos, Juan and Florita, who were sitting on the floor regarding him impassively.

Dooey shook his head. "It's no good, John. I quit. I've resigned from this war. These people are friends of mine. They don't want to fight either. We're all just going away together."

The girl, Maria, fumbled for and found a shirt under the sheet that was half-covering her and Dooey. John watched her put the shirt on, still under the sheet. Dooey swung off the mat and went over to the remains of a fire to get some cold coffee. He tasted it, screwed up his face and said, "It's awful, but it's the best we've got. Would you like some, John? Sit down and we can talk."

John ignored the offer. "Dooey, I'm leaving. It seems to me there's nothing to talk about. If you intend to go native and live with these Indians, that's your business. I don't want to know why and I don't want to know where you're going. I just want to remind you that it's desertion, and if you go through with it and the Army catches up with you, you'll be shot."

Dooey shrugged. "I guess that's part of the game. Maybe the Army won't catch up with me. I can be pretty elusive."

The old woman, Florita, gave John a toothless grin. "He is Zorro," she explained.

John tried one last time. "Dooey, I just spoke to a Texan, name of Tom Watts, who said he licked you in a fight last night. From the looks of you, I'd say he certainly did. He also said you were crazy."

"I guess he spoke true on both counts. Goodbye, John."

The quiet in Dooey's voice convinced John. He

turned to go. As he did, he caught the bright, eager look in the girl's eyes as she watched them both from the sleeping mat behind Dooey.

John hesitated. "I just hope we don't have to face each other across some barricade," he said.

Dooey shook his head. "No chance of that. I told you: I'm quitting before I start. I'm not going to be shooting at anybody."

Still, John lingered. He wanted to say something about the girl, who did not seem at all placid to him, whose proud, defiant gaze did not suggest that she could live in peaceful harmony with anyone, anywhere. Anymore, John felt deep in his heart, than Dooey could.

But he left, saying nothing else.

When John got back to Fort Texas, the American camp was bustling with preparations for the departure the next day. John decided that, considering the noisy preoccupations of Lew Wallace and the rest of the regiment, he could afford to hold back information about Dooey unless Wallace asked him for it. He might even lie, if questioned, might say that he'd searched for but hadn't found Dooey. John couldn't help noticing, though, that he didn't feel particularly dismayed about Dooey's unexpected behavior. Through some radical change in his own outlook, John felt separated enough from his erstwhile friend to think of him almost with indifference; with curiosity, perhaps, but without that nagging sense of worry he'd always had about him. In short, he no longer saw Dooey as a kind of wayward "older brother" to whom he owed allegiance; he had himself to think about.

With that new outlook, it came to him that nobody in camp gave a damn about Dooey's continued absence. Not even Lew Wallace, who was off getting the mules and supply wagons together and having last minute conferences with members of General Taylor's staff. In fact, the only one who mentioned Dooey's name to John was Jake Herschel, who would be traveling by steamboat with the Kentucky Regiment and came over to say goodbye.

Little Jake was all excited. John hadn't seen him in a while and was quick to note the change in him. He came into the Indiana area while the men were loading their packs and dismantling their tents. Jake was all eager to help out his two friends from New York with a small portion of the food supplies he'd bought from Mexican farmers for the Kentuckies. Somebody over at the Kentuckies had noted the pleasure Jake had taken in a few personal transactions he'd made with the Mexicans and assigned him to quartermaster duties. He was pleased with his job.

"Join the army and see the world, eh?" he said, beaming at John. "Here's what I have for you." He gave John a bag of tacos, enough to eat on the four-day march the Indianan's had been told to expect.

"Take them. They're good," he urged. "They're kosher."

"Kosher?" John said, perplexed.

"Made with unleavened flour and blessed by a *shagitz,*" Jake explained.

John looked at him doubtfully. "Jake, do you mean to say you found a Mexican Jew in these parts?"

"Why not? We're everywhere," Jake said disarmingly. "Where's Dooey?"

"I don't know," John said.

"Would you give him some of the tacos when you see him, please? I have to get back to my stores now. I'm a redneck Kentuckian and I'm raring to go!"

Everybody else was "raring to go," too. Nobody went to Matamoros that night and the sleep of most was restless. The feeling of wanting to break loose and being on the verge of doing it seemed to permeate the camp.

They got up the next morning, fell in in front of Fort Texas, packs loaded, ready to march. As he had before, Lew Wallace tried to get some discipline into the ranks. He did his best. "General Taylor wants me to tell you men that we're *not* on a turkey shoot, that you're not to molest civilians, that you're to save your fire for Monterrey, barring any—"

"General Taylor don't give a shit about us!" someone shouted.

"Stop gabbing and let's get on with it, Lew!"

"If the ol' man don't give us something to shoot at soon, I just as lief shoot *him*!"

There were cackles of approval and Wallace said heavily, "All right. Let's go."

9

THEY WENT. They marched away from Fort Texas in some semblance of order, crossed the river in longboats and proceeded to the western outskirts of Matamoros, where they picked up the one road that led through the desert chaparral to Camargo. This was at dawn on the last day of July, and already the humid heat, the sand flies, spiders and mosquitoes were adding to the men's irritability. They shambled along, drifting into groups of three, four or five, in a line that stretched backward a quarter-mile or so from where Wallace walked, nominally leading them. Which caused no particular problem at the beginning.

It took on the form of a day's outing, this rifle-toting journey to Camargo. At the outset, John walked pretty much alone, or at least with his own silent thoughts. As they passed the shack where he'd last seen Dooey, he saw that it seemed totally deserted now; not even the chickens were in evidence. Wondering whether Dooey was really going to find a better life for himself, John began drifting back in the line, looking for some companionship to the rear where the ox-drawn supply wagons and the larger clusters of men were.

Life at the rear was abominable, but no more so than it would be at the war front, John figured. You had to make the best of it. The regiment had been given no clear idea of what it was up to, except that it was moving from one pesthole to another.

"Did you ever see such heat?" Crossman said. He was squinting out at the monotonous desert terrain.

"No," John replied after a moment's thought.

Crossman looked at him. "You're not much of a talker."

"You're not much better."

"Do you think we'll run into those guerrillas Lew talked about?"

"How the hell should I know?" John asked.

"Didn't ask what you knew, asked what you thought."

"Don't know," he said at last. "One thing I think is that we shouldn't be all stretched out like this. If we do run into them, they could ride down the line and pick us off."

"Maybe," Crossman agreed.

"Do you think I should go up and tell Lew about it?"

"Don't see what good that would do. Look at everybody. Look at us. With this heat, all you can do is drag-ass along. Besides, I can shoot a man riding down on me just as well here as anywhere else."

"Guess that's true," John agreed.

"Another thing. How're you gonna catch up with

Lew in this heat?" Crossman pointed out. "Gonna ride a mule up to him?"

"I could do that," John said.

There were mules in the wagon train behind them. The more John thought about it, the more it struck him as a good idea to at least bring his concern to Wallace's attention, though Lew probably had it in mind already. He was commanding them, wasn't he? Still . . .

John had walked far enough in heavy boots. He thought it might be a relief to ride a mule for a while.

"See you later, Crossman," he said.

He went back and borrowed a mule from one of the drovers, who told him that if he wanted to ride the thing for a while, it was all right with him, but warned that the animal was going to be balky and hard on his ass—worse than walking.

This did not turn out to be exactly the case. John got on the mule, kicked its sides, and it started off at a fast trot—back toward Matamoros, followed by the hoots of just about everybody in the wagon train. John was glad he was providing some amusement. Still, he had to get the mule turned around. By the time he did that, the last of the train was a good half-mile ahead of him, and moving on and paying him no heed. Then the mule just up and quit.

He was in a fix now, John thought. He sat on the absolutely still animal and hollered ahead for help—which produced no result other than bringing a tarantula scurrying out from under a nearby bush.

Despite being alone now in the desert, John saw his predicament as comical more than anything else. A mule was just one more bit of Army paraphernalia he'd had little experience with. He swung off its back and started tugging at its head. When that didn't work he tried pushing it from behind. It stood like a rock.

John swore, scratched his head. Then he got an idea. He unslung his rifle from his back and loaded it. First, on the off chance that a simple threat might do the trick, he pointed the rifle squarely between the mule's eyes and said, "Move, you son of a bitch." The mule remained impervious.

With a sigh, John climbed back on its back, dug his knees into its sides and flung an arm around its neck to get a firm seating. Then with his free hand he fired the rifle into the sky.

This brought about unforeseen results. The mule did not bolt forward as John had hoped, but twitched encouragingly. Moments passed. About to fire another shot and try his luck once more, John sensed rather than heard the mule swishing its tail and turned around to look.

What he saw over the mule's rump brought him instantly alert. In the distance was a cloud of dust being raised by some fifteen to twenty horsemen. They were coming toward him from the direction of Matamoros and were spread out across the desert flats, not bothering with the road at all. A glance at their white clothing and their sombreros told John that they were Mexicans. That same glance, taking in their waving muskets, told him he'd better get away from there—fast.

He leaped from the mule and headed for a copse of trees bordering the river. It was obvious that he could be seen running by the guerrillas, but that didn't worry him. The trees might not do him much good for long, but this way, out in the open, he hadn't a prayer.

His neck-prickling fear served to give him added speed. He reached the trees and kept right on going, splashing into the Rio Grande, half-wading, half-swimming, until he reached the far bank and clambered out. There were trees on the Texas side too, and John made for a thick one, reaching it and getting behind it just as the Mexicans reined in their horses at the point where he had entered the trees on the other side.

John loaded his rifle, which he had managed to hold out of the water, and waited. There was no point in running any further because that would just take him into miles of Texas desert.

He could hear the Mexicans across the river muttering to each other. For a moment, he had hopes they would consider him not worth pursuing—which was the truth, after all, he being just one man and the rest of the regiment, with its supplies, being far up ahead. But logic didn't enter into the case. Two of the Mexicans walked through the trees, leading their horses, and peered across the river.

John gripped his rifle and held his breath.

"Hey, *gringo!* We doan wanna hurt you. We only want to ask you something."

John waited. The man who had called out turned to his partner and said something in Spanish to him. The other shrugged and started to argue, as if the first man had failed to consider something vital.

"Hey, *gringo.* We only wanna ask you how you have the mule? That is the mule of my mother. It was stolen from her."

Oh, Christ, John thought, gritting his teeth. They'd have to do better than that.

"It is true, *gringo.* That is my mother's mule. Did you see the long scar on its ass? That is how I know."

John held steady.

"Miguel, I tole you *gringos* have no heart," the caller

complained. "This one, he doan care somebody take my mother's mule. Let us jus' take back the mule and go."

Miguel got clapped on the shoulder, and then both men turned and led their horses back. John waited for their next move.

It came as a surprise to him. Through the trees on the far side, he saw horses mounted in a flurry of arms and legs, then the Mexicans simply galloped away. He could see them heading directly across the desert toward the motionless mule. On reaching it, the man who had called out to John lassoed the animal and tugged it by the neck toward Matamoros until the mule broke into a run. Then, mule in tow, the Mexicans rode eastward, vanishing over the horizon.

John blinked. Could it be possible that they had been telling the truth? That all they wanted was that lousy mule? Send twenty men after a mule? He didn't believe it for a second. Sure, the Army had probably taken some Mexicans' mules. They weren't getting them fast enough from the States, so they had to make off with a few now and then. But using up all that manpower to retrieve one didn't make sense to him. Still, what other explanation could there be?

John waited ten minutes more, just in case the Mexicans changed their minds and returned. Another thought had occurred to him: he couldn't wait much longer, because he'd have to run like hell as it was to catch up with the regiment.

Taking a deep breath and holding his rifle with his finger bent around the trigger, John stepped out from behind the tree and began a slow walk towards the river. He'd reached the bank when a voice called out from behind a rock half-hidden by branches twenty feet up from where John had crossed the river.

"Hey, *amigo*. Got you."

John spun toward the sound of the voice, jerked up his rifle and fired. The pistol Miguel was pointing flew from his hand as John's bullet caught him in the shoulder, driving him to his knees. A look of consternation on his face, the Mexican got up, clutching his shoulder, and started to run.

John barked, "Stay where you are!" Miguel froze.

"Good trick, Miguel, but it didn't work. Now talk. Why did the rest ride east? To get more men while you stayed to shut me up?"

"*Si, señor.* Miguel's teeth were chattering. "We ride ahead for Garcia, our leader. We were looking for your regiment, but did not know where it was until we found you."

John thought swiftly. "Where's your camp?"

"Five miles from here. *Señor*, don't shoot! It will do you no good to kill me. The others will have reached Garcia by now. Many men will be riding after your regiment. It is too late to stop them. We could talk. I could tell you many things. I—"

But John had stopped listening. He was peering up and down the far bank. He cut the Mexican short. "Where's your horse?"

"*Señor*, I have no horse. The others, they took all the horses. They—"

A sudden whinny from beyond the trees and some thirty yards downriver froze Miguel in his lie. John turned his head sharply that way, then, his fact taut, and looked back at the Mexican. Miguel's eyes instantly widened in fright.

"*Señor*, don't shoot, don't shoot, I beg of you, don't [illegible]t—"

[illegible]here—fast," John said. He jerked his rifle [illegible]e him. The Mexican responded with alacrity. He jumped into the river and waded swiftly toward John, his arms outstretched in pleading.

John wasn't going to shoot him unless he had to, and he hoped he wouldn't have to because he was afraid that a shot might scare off the horse he now had a desperate need for. He wanted to rejoin the regiment both for his own safety and to warn Lew Wallace. When he had Miguel clambering up the bank in front of him, he stepped aside, motioned him against a tree trunk, then got into the river and began to wade backwards, keeping his rifle pointed at the Mexican's chest.

"When you see me halfway across, you run," John said. "I'll give you that much chance. Three counts after you start running, I start shooting."

"*Si, señor, si,*" Miguel said hastily. He moved his eyes left, then right, as if uncertain about which direction to run in.

John moved steadily backward, keeping his eyes on the Mexican. The water got chest-deep. He didn't know if he was halfway across yet or not, only that if he took another step he might go under, the rifle with him.

"Now," he called out softly.

Miguel ran. He took two steps to his left, which was east, then bolted north, crashing through the woods, reaching open ground and racing in the general direction of the Louisiana border.

John turned and plowed swiftly to the opposite bank. Then he was up and running for the placidly waiting horse, mounting it and riding at a gallop due west after the regiment.

Fifteen minutes later, riding hard all the way, he had the rear wagons in sight. The me[illegible] along ahead of the wagons were, if[illegible] dispersed than when he'd last seen them, tiny dots on a landscape that covered at least a half-mile north and south. As John rode up, the drover who'd lent him the mule turned to stare at him and his new steed. John rode right past him; he didn't stop until he'd reached Wallace a mile further on.

"Lew!" he cried, jumping to the ground. "That guerrilla band's coming after us. They should be here any minute now. Somebody named Garcia with about three hundred men!"

Wallace was with a Regular Army lieutenant, who'd apparently debarked from a steamboat to march with the Indianans for a while. Both listened while John reported all he knew, which was little more than that the guerrillas would be coming from the south of them.

When he was finished and Wallace was about to speak, the lieutenant, whose name was George McClelland, said, "Wait, Lew. While you round up your men, I'll see if I can get some infantry help. Private, lend me that horse."

John turned the horse over willingly. Lieutenant McClelland mounted and rode ahead, veering north towards the river, which was not in sight at this point. All that *was* in sight was the flat desert, thinly populated by walking targets, and the empty blue bowl of the sky.

"There's part of the Fifth Infantry in boats not too far upriver from here," Wallace explained. "If McClelland can get back with them, we'll be in good shape. Otherwise . . . Damn, we don't even have a horse now to go after those men."

"How about firing our rifles to get their attention?" John suggested.

Wallace nodded. "We can try that. Better get all the

guns we have here fired at once. Otherwise they'll think we're just shooting at snakes. You! Thompson! Get up here fast with the first ten men you can get hold of!"

Forty yards to the rear, close enough to hear the shout, the Indianan did what he was bid—plus more. A full dozen men came running up to find out what the commotion was that had penetrated their heat-induced lethargy. Wallace gave them the briefest of explanations, then told them, "All of you fire at the sky on my command. One . . . two . . . *now*!"

Twelve shots rang out simultaneously, echoing off rock foothills too far distant in the south to be seen. Men shambling along in the vast circumference of the desert picked their heads up. Some of them seemed loath to increase their dragging pace even then. But one did, then another and another until all began to converge.

"Like calling in the pigs!" Wallace said. He cupped his hands. "Hooo—hooo-hooo!"

The gathering regiment, all 212 men, came up to within shouting distance in five minutes or so. Wallace said dryly, "Thanks for joining us. We expect an attack of mounted guerrillas shortly—probably outnumbering us and probably out of those foothills yonder. Their leader is Pedro Garcia. What you may not know about him is that he was given an artillery piece captured from us at Resaca de la Palma. He's likely to have it with him. A force of Regulars has been sent for. Our job is to hold Garcia off until they get here. I suggest we do it this way. . . ."

On Wallace's orders, the Indianans quickly formed a large semicircle and got down on their bellies in the underbrush. A distance of ten feet separated one man from the next. They waited that way, leaning on their elbows, holding rifles cocked and ready and watching the southern horizon. John, using a fair-sized cactus outgrowth for cover, found himself between Crossman on the left and Wallace on his right.

"What happened to you back there?" Crossman wanted to know. John told him, briefly. Crossman nodded admiringly. "Scared the greaser off, did you?" he said.

"I was pretty damn scared myself," John said. "I still am."

Crossman answered him with a grunt. If he was afraid, he was holding that fear inside him. John, taking a deep breath, made up his mind to do the same.

It was hard. There didn't seem to be any relief from the queasiness that bubbled up inside him. He tried to remember what he had just done and so buoy himself up, but it didn't work; he still felt queasy in the face of this new challenge—the one coming up, the one blowing away anything substantial a man might have done like a giant wind.

Soon enough, the first of the Mexican riders came into view, a figure fly-size in John's front gunsight.

The regiment waited, still as death. Only Wallace turned to look at the supply wagons he had drawn up between the regiment and the river. He'd laid out a concave semicircle of hidden men in the hope that the guerrillas would come charging through its center to get to the wagons. If the Mexicans did take the bait, they'd be squeezed by a pincer of riflemen behind them.

The trap might work if the men at the ends of the arc—a quarter-mile out into the desert—let the Mexicans enter it, then opened fire at their rear. What Wallace was concerned about, with reason, was individual heroics: a man out there taking it upon himself to shoot down the lead rider for his first taste of glory, or out of panic, one or the other.

The Mexicans came on. There were hundreds of them, John now saw, and they were spread wide across the desert—wider than the jaws of the trap set for them. He feared for an instant that they would overrun the Indianans' outermost positions, alerting themselves to the danger they were in. Then they appeared to have spied the wagons, for they funneled together and came riding hard toward them.

But it was far too early to judge if Lew's plan had worked. All John saw were musket-bearing horsemen riding down on him, in their van the fat scout who'd tried to ferret him out of his hiding place earlier and alongside him a saber-waving, sturdy fellow in a green-and-white uniform jacket—the only guerrilla so dressed—who had to be Garcia. Behind them, in the throng, was a flying artillery battery pulled by a four-horse team and ridden by two men in position to jump off quickly, load and fire the battery's four-foot-long guns. The battery, on large carriage wheels, kept pace with the horsemen; it could blow the men to pieces with one ball.

John wasn't about to become part of a mass target; he wasn't about to move from his spot. He wet his lips, his heart pounding madly but his finger steady on the trigger. They came to within two hundred yards of his position, still out of range but closing rapidly. Quick looks out of the corners of his eyes showed John that Crossman and Wallace were waiting intently, just as he was. There was nothing else sensible for any of them to do.

Suddenly, for no apparent reason, the leader Garcia pulled his horse up sharply. As the animal reared, Garcia raised his saber for his troops to stop. They all did. The desert gradually became very quiet again. The last sound John heard for a while was the creak of the flying artillery battery's wheel hubs as, on a barked order from Garcia, its riders jumped off the carriage and prepared to unlimber the gun.

John saw Wallace give a swift look behind him, where the supply wagons were massed.

"Damn," Lew muttered. He'd been wrong in his estimate of Garcia's intentions. The guerrillas did not intend to capture the supplies, which would have been time-consuming, but to destroy them so that they could not be used at Monterrey.

Also, it became apparent that Garcia had discerned the trap prepared for him early on. The horsemen around him began to fan out from the artillery piece, even now being loaded, to face the wide encirclement of Indianans bellied down in the brush. Garcia may or may not have caught sight of the defenders on his way in; the point was, he'd sensed they were there!

The continuance of his ploy being useless, his hopes that the Regulars would arrive in time obviously in vain, Lew Wallace leaped to his feet, shouting, "Come on, let's get the bastards!"

Only John, Crossman and some ten men to either side of Wallace heard him, but the sight of them following Lew's headlong rush straight at the artillery piece was enough to trigger a wholesale attack from more distant quarters. Some two hundred Indianans rose almost as one man out of the chaparral and charged the guerrillas from all sides, firing their rifles as they ran.

Volunteers stumbled, fell, saw the last of their picnic war right there on the desert as the mounted guerrillas recovered from their surprise and returned bullet for bullet. But the Mexicans were no match for the speed of the charge, nor for the many weaving directions from which it came, nor for its savagery. The Indianans ripped bullets into horses, and when the horses fell, dragging their riders down with them, other horses kicked at them, stumbled around in the melee and unseated their own riders with sudden rearings.

John, running toward the artillery piece, saw Garcia's horse become crushed between adjacent horses and go down. Garcia freed himself, only to stand futilely shouting orders at horsemen who could no longer hear or see him. Then John was charging into the muzzle of the carriage-mounted gun, with Crossman and Lew Wallace now shoulder to shoulder beside him.

The gun was their primary target. There hadn't been time for Lew to shout for help in capturing it, nor, possibly, was there another man in the charge who would have considered its capture vital in the heat of the hand-to-hand fighting they were now engaged in.

The gun's muzzle gaped at the bridge of John's nose. He vaguely noted the guerrilla holding a blazing taper about to ignite the powder. Three feet from the gun John made a mighty leap that carried him over its barrel into the chest of the Mexican about to light it. The man went down on his back. Unthinking, John scrambled to his feet, drove his bayonet deep into the Mexican's chest, then pulled it out.

He spun around just in time to see the fat scout, Vargas, riding down on him, his saber drawn and a wicked leer on his face. There was no way Vargas could have recognized John, but John recognized Vargas. When the Mexican was ten feet from him, John gritted out the words: "For your mother."

He raised his bloodied rifle and fired it point-blank. Vargas, his saber uplifted and the beginning of a frown of recognition on his face, toppled from his horse, dead.

John, turning quickly again to the gun, saw that Wallace and Crossman had already swung it around and were training it on guerrillas galloping south to get out of its range. Some of the volunteers, their unleashed fury far from exhausted, were chasing after them, which kept Wallace from firing.

John, looking elsewhere, spied Garcia desperately trying to climb a new mount. The guerrilla leader was only about twenty yards away, still afoot. John thought to charge him with the bayonet of his now empty rifle. Then he saw the pistol in Garcia's hand, pointed at him. He stood for the briefest moment before the pistol cracked and heard from behind him the cry of a mounted Mexican hit by the bullet intended for John. Garcia swore. Leaping astride the horse, he raced off, followed by the remnants of his band.

Flat on his stomach, John watched them until they had all but vanished into the desert. He was tired and he felt empty; he reckoned he had been through a lot that day and he didn't want to move. But he pushed himself up and went over to where Wallace, Crossman and a few others were tending to the wounded.

"Good going, Bell," Wallace said briefly. "Now, if you can pitch in and help here, it would be much appreciated."

"Sure thing, Lew."

An hour later, when the wounded had been placed in the wagons and the rest of the regiment was ready to march again, Lieutenant McClelland arrived at the head of a detachment of mounted Regulars.

"What kept you fellows?" Wallace remarked mildly.

McClelland's mouth twitched. "We got lost and had to follow the vultures in."

The rest of his comment was equally brief. Casting his eye over the many dead guerrillas lying unburied on the desert, his gaze fell on the captured battery.

"That our piece, Lew? Thanks for getting it back. We'll manage it from here." But his mouth wore a tight smile of admiration he could find no suitable words for.

10

THE REGIMENT stayed in Camargo for two weeks, long enough for some seven thousand men to gather there for the planned assault on Monterrey, fifty miles further on. There wasn't much to do in Camargo, and the heat there—enclosed by the town's blocks of uniformly pink stuccoed houses—John found to be even more stifling than it had been on the desert.

After the heat and the boredom and the boredom and the heat, General Taylor's appearance in Camargo, in mid-August, produced wilder yells of exaltation than the event merited, because Old Zach wasn't going anywhere just yet. It seemed he had once more been undercut by President Polk.

John got word of this from Crossman, who came bellowing into their billet one night. His anger and disgust sent the Mexican woman who owned the house scurrying away.

"Do you know what I just heard?" Crossman said. "I just heard Polk's going to pull Zach out and put Winfield Scott in his place."

John was writing letters home. He looked up and said, "So what? I don't give a damn."

"Neither do I," Crossman said. "Only, not *now,* for God's sake. Do you know how long it'll take Scott to pick a new staff and get here from Washington? We'll be in this hellhole forever."

Camargo was a hellhole, the worst of the Mexican towns in the vicinity for heat, dust, scorpions, armies of ants, and the pestilential chills and fevers these things brought with them to lay men low. Camargo was like a giant hand of destruction. It had swept hundreds of Regulars and volunteers into sick beds and raised among the others irritable, snap judgments like John's and rumors like Crossman's.

But it wasn't going to happen—at least, not yet. Taylor was going to stay on, despite the president's discomfort over the favorable publicity Old Zach had received while doing little, in Polk's view, to end the war quickly.

John was as disgusted with the delay as Crossman was. He had been venting his displeasure in a letter to Sally when Crossman had come barging in. First he'd told her about the action he'd seen in the desert, sparing her only a detail or two of how he'd killed two Mexicans after being chased and hounded by the bastards. Then he'd complained about the insufficient gratitude he'd received from Wallace for what *he'd* done and from McClelland for what he and the regiment had done.

We outwitted the Chaparral Fox, he wrote. *They*

should have brevetted Lew a general as soon as we got to this pesthole. But did they? No, not even a visit from anyone on Taylor's staff. It's as if we don't exist. Sally, I tell you, I'm stuck in some Mexican woman's pink house that runs rivers of her kids' pee on its walls. It stinks to high heaven here. Do you know what Dooey did? You won't believe this but, damn it, he ran off with some Mexican girl, and I'm not sure now that he didn't have the right idea. If it weren't for you, I might do the same.

He'd been writing furiously, blotting the page more than once as he swept his hand from it to bat at the ants crawling on his other wrist. Then, at that point in his letter, he took another swipe at the ants and succeeded in knocking the oil lamp off the table, which sent him into a murderous rage and brought his Mexican landlady running.

"*Que pasa, señor?*" she cried. "Why you do this?"

"Your house stinks!" John stormed at her. "Look at this place! You've got so much junk in it it's driving me crazy!"

The woman backed away. John picked up the lamp and slammed it back down on the desk. Then he looked for more clutter to straighten up. There wasn't any; everything else in the room, he realized, was tidy enough. So he just glared at the woman.

"*Señor,*" she said doubtfully and backed up some more.

"Well, it's the ants," John said defiantly. "Or it's Taylor, or it's Sally, or it's . . . something."

The woman smiled at him nervously. "*Mi casa no le gusta?*"

"It has nothing to do with you," John went on irritably.

The woman scurried out of the room.

That left John alone again. He felt miserable, in so foul a mood that he couldn't see straight. He decided to take a walk, anything to get out of the place of his present discomfort, though he had already walked the six streets of Camargo dozens of times and had found the town a pall of pink gloom.

Sure enough, it was the same town; it hadn't changed. He passed some men from other regiments who, in the one hundred five degree heat, had the half-glazed look of zombies. He himself was not so much conscious of the heat, only of the furor inside him. He might have looked for Crossman or Wallace or some of the other Indianans in Camargo's three dark saloons, but he didn't want to.

After a while, walking aimlessly, he began to simmer down. He thought, at first flickeringly, of his Mexican landlady, if he could call her that. He didn't know her name, but he hadn't treated her well. He had a vision of her face. She was a woman of about forty, dark-skinned and broad-nosed, with white even teeth. She had wide hips and a slim waist. She wore the same gold earrings every day and, to his way of thinking, the same print dress. But there had seemed to be something warm and genial about her—until he scared the living daylights out of her. He was surprised to find himself getting a semi-erection when he visualized this woman. The least he could do, he decided, was to go back and apologize to her.

He went back to the house and knocked on the front door. It had been noisy inside, and when the woman opened the door, he saw that three of her six children were tugging at her waist. "*Si, señor?*" She seemed to be—and was—surprised that he had knocked.

"I want to apologize," John said gruffly. Then, seeing her wide-eyed, puzzled expression fixed on his face while she slapped gently at the hands of her tugging children, he suddenly knew what for.

"I guess it did have something to do with you," he blurted out. "It's not as if you're nobody—I didn't mean that."

The woman frowned. She had taken little note of what the blond *gringo* boy had said during his battle with the ants. Actually, she felt kindly towards this young *gringo* . . . and she was lonely.

Her face cleared up and she smiled. "I am Consuela."

"I'm John. Juan."

"*Si*, I know. I read *ingles*. It is on your shirts."

"Well, I'll come back in then," John said awkwardly.

"*Si*."

He went past her to a couch and did not see her, behind him, shooing her children through the open door. But he saw that they were not there when he was seated. She turned to him, smiling. She looked comfortable to him as she moved to pin up her hair, and somehow he felt comfortable.

"Do you have any *vino*?" he said.

"*Si*, I will get it."

She came back with a bottle and two glasses, put them on the table, then sat on a chair facing him.

John poured them each a glass, then sipped his wine. He wanted to get to the point, but embarrassment held him back. He groped for something else to say, but was defeated by the enormity of this challenge.

She was surveying him, her head cocked in amusement. "You do not have to say anything if you do not wish to, *señor*," she said. "The ants—you have them now in your pants, eh?"

John swallowed nervously. "Well, yes. But we can't go to bed just like that."

"*Si*. We can. I am lonely, you are lonely. . . ." She shrugged.

John said, "You're lonely?"

"*Si*. I have no man. I have desires, as you do."

"I think you are very pretty," John said swiftly. "*Muy bonita*."

She laughed. "*Señor*, those are your ants speaking. Come. You do not need *vino*, nor do I. You are a good boy. I will give you what you need."

She got up and ambled toward a bedroom she shared with two of her younger children. John, sitting where he was for a moment, followed the swaying of her hips. He was enticed, but still this was going a bit too fast for him.

"There's no door on that room."

Consuela turned, sighing, and leaned against the wall. "*Señor*, I do not need a door to make love on. I have a bed. Come."

John got up. He felt light-headed. There was a boldness in him that he had never experienced. He wanted to crush this woman in his arms. He went over to where she stood in the doorway, pulled her roughly toward him and, surprised and joyful at all these feelings flowing through him, gave her a kiss that seemed to melt him into her mouth.

She pulled away, gasping. "*Señor*, we had better hurry."

She went into the room, sat on the edge of a lumpy, rumpled bed and began almost frantically to undress, pulling her dress off the top of her shoulders first. He stood in the doorway and she looked up at him, her expression pleading for him to hurry. Her wide face had softened. Night light through the narrow window shadowed her large breasts on which the nipples rose pink and firm.

John's lust rose as his eyes fastened on her breasts, but he did not move until he saw the yearning in her eyes begin to verge on impatience. Then he went quickly to her, put a knee on the bed and with a hand clasping her breast, began to force her down gently on the bed.

She moaned at his touch and put a hand quickly on the bulge in his pants. There seemed to be the same frenzy in her as there was in him, that had them both trembling until those first touches. Then the trembling ceased, and they were all over each other. She tore at the buttons on his pants to get his penis out and kissed it furiously, then licked it and put it in her mouth while he was still trying to get the rest of her dress off.

"Hold it! Hold it!" John swore, for he thought he might come immediately if she kept doing that and wanted her to stop. But she thought he meant for her to hold his penis more tightly and complied avidly.

Savagely, John got out of her grasp. There was no room for humor in the intensity of his passion. It became a wrestling match. They rolled around on the lumpy bed, one on top of the other, wincing when their backs hit unseen small wooden objects that were mixed up in the tangle of sheets.

John began throwing these things on the floor, not knowing or caring what they were. He was busy biting at Consuela's neck, stomach, thighs, and she was doing the same to him. Finally, in one of these rolls that ended with him on top, he reached down, motioned her thighs up and entered her. She was so wet that he slipped right in. Her body was larger than his, and it was like entering the darkest and most comfortable of caves.

She gave a moan and clutched him with her vaginal muscles. John waited a moment, his full weight on her ample bosom, then began to move. "*Si, si. Mas. Mas,*" she murmured ecstatically. So he began to move more, and faster. She started to grin, happily, and wrapped her legs around his waist. As he went in and out of her, John, lost in his own trance, looked down into her moist eyes, saw her smiling face, the glistening white teeth. He was oblivious to all else.

Thus it came as a rude surprise when a small voice called from the doorway: "*Mama, mama, quiero mis bloques?*"

John was startled, but only for a moment. He was too far gone in what he was doing. So was Consuela. Her head flung upwards now, she was answering his thrusts with her own.

"*Mama, mama, mama, mama!*"

"*Señor, pronto, ahora, pronto, pronto!*"

John answered the desperate call. He thrust one last time. Consuela gave a lurch, made a small, sharp sound, and then it was over. John lay still on top of her.

"*Es bueno, es bueno,*" Consuela murmured. She kissed his cheek. "*Pero ahora . . . por favor, señor.*"

She lifted her head and from under him called out, "*Sus bloques estan sur el suelo, chicita.*"

The little girl in the doorway ran into the room, studiously avoiding John and Consuela in the bed as she collected her blocks from the floor and ran out with them.

John grinned down at Consuela. Shrugging, she said, "I am sorry, *señor*, for the interruption."

"It's all right," John soothed her. "It was fine. It was wonderful."

They became friends during the one week John remained in Camargo. Perhaps more than friends. It became obvious, as the days ran out, that Consuela did not want to leave. John didn't want to leave either; the sex remained at a high level of excitement and, out of bed, he was comfortable in her presence. One day she warned him of a danger he'd be confronting if he left.

"Juan," she said, "there is a citadel in Monterrey which your army will not be able to pass. I have seen it myself. Many Americans will be killed there. You do not have to be one of them. Stay with me. I will hide you until the others leave."

"Where will you hide me, under the sheets with the blocks?" John said, smiling. "No, I can't do that, Consuela. Tell me about this citadel. Why won't we be able to pass it?"

"General Ampudia has placed many cannon there. You cannot avoid them, for the citadel is on a hill overlooking the one road that leads into the city." Consuela hesitated, then, as if to underscore the danger to him, said, "Your Texas scouts have seen the citadel too. They call it the 'Black Fort.' They can tell you how formidable it is if you don't believe me. Juan, stay. Let the war pass us by."

She coaxed him more along these lines, telling him of other Mexican defenses set up in and about the city of Monterrey, defenses she considered impregnable, but she succeeded only in giving John a fairly clear mental picture of what to expect. She coaxed him with sex, too, but to no avail.

One day Consuela struck him a low blow. In their talks, she'd prompted him to tell her about his life in Connecticut and he'd told her about Sally, among other things. Now, when John seemed determined to leave her, Consuela said stormily, "You are a fool, Juan. You do not love that girl. If you did, you would have sent her the letter you were writing her. You would have trusted her with your feelings!"

"You're wrong, Consuela," John maintained stoutly. "I was angry when I wrote that letter. I didn't want to upset her."

Consuela sneered. "Pah! You are angry with *her* because you think she has betrayed you with another man. And what if she has? Forget her, Juan. I am alive before you, and you have already struck her dead in your mind. It is not this girl you care about, but the unknown man who has taken her from you. How envious you are of someone who has taken from you something you do not want. How you wish to kill *him* now!"

She looked at him sadly. "How young you are, Juan."

John stood frozen for a moment. Then he muttered, "There's more to it than that, Consuela."

"*Si*, there is always more," Consuela said bitterly. "There is this war you have fled to. How your eyes lit up when you told me of how you shot to death this man Vargas, who had tried to trick you. But the one who *really* tricked you, the one who is too much of a man for you, he is not in Mexico, he is still in *your* country, is he not? Why do you not go back and find *him*? He can be no less stupid than Vargas. He can be no less stupid than you!"

Consuela kept railing at him. John felt there was some truth in her belittlement, and it made him sick to hear it, but he could also see that her ultimate aim was to get him to desert the Army and stay with her. He didn't interrupt her verbal assault, but when she finished at last he put his hands on her shoulders and said, "Thank you, Consuela."

That was all he said, but she seemed to understand then that she couldn't hold him, no matter what she said or did. She wanted to tell him what fears she would be left with once he had gone, tell him how other soldiers, less caring than he, would be billeted in her house and would rape her, as had happened before. But she had her pride and would not use these fears to barter for his continued protection.

"Will you think about what I have said?" she said. "For your sake, not mine?"

John nodded. "I'm already thinking about it, Consuela."

It was something John couldn't help thinking about from time to time, even as the regiment moved on toward Monterrey and more immediate matters demanded his attention. He noted that every time he let himself dwell on the possibility that he was simply running away from something back home, his fears of the Black Fort citadel—now only a day's march away—became strangely magnified.

It was a peculiar thing of the mind. The Black Fort depressed him, gave him a sense of doom long before he saw it. There were times when he trudged along in dread that he wouldn't be able to face this battle, that he would run from it in cowardly fashion. It was inconceivable that the Black Fort could be blacker than his mood. He found no more courage in himself than when he'd fled, wounded, from Sally's rejection of him in favor of someone else. He had Consuela to thank for this new, darker light in which he saw himself as a coward, the bristling guns of the Black Fort the sure exacters of the doom such cowardice deserved.

At times he wished Dooey were along to talk things over with. Dooey might even kid him out of his mood. As it was, Crossman got him out of it with a sharp rebuke.

"Goddamn it, Bell, move your ass before I run you down!"

They had come down south from Camargo and were marching in close file toward the town of Cerralvo, in the Sierra Madre foothills, where there was enough drinking water, so scouts had informed Taylor, to replenish his entire army of six thousand. But this was desert country still, and the men had many reasons for being savagely irritable, or alarmed, or both.

John picked up his pace and tried to stay alert, which he couldn't do, really, anymore than the other trudging Indianans could. Only sharp nags of discomfort, such as the one he'd caused Crossman, stirred any reaction in them. The march was a repetition of what they'd experienced en route from Matamoros to Camargo, but without the saving grace of enemy guerrillas to confront in hard battle.

Not that they didn't see any Mexicans. Always, a mile or so ahead of them on the straight, flat, broiling road, a thousand dragoons under General Torrejon—the same man, the regiment was informed, who had precipitated the war by capturing Seth Thornton's cavalry force back in April—rode along slowly, almost as if they were the U.S. Army's advance guard. Except that the Mexicans would turn in their saddles now and then, as if to make sure that the Americans were still following them.

Those dragoons, keeping close watch on their progress, exasperated the marchers. They were always too far ahead to engage in battle, and they led those with all-too-fertile imaginations to believe that some trap had been prepared for them at Monterrey and that they were being conveyed directly into it.

At one point, following the road, they came to the outskirts of a town. The road bypassed it to the west, following the bank of a river. Marching along, they could see the bell tower of the town's white church and could picture the *zocalo*, the town square, at the corner of which the church stood. All Mexican towns were alike. This one would have a fountain in the *zocalo*, maybe a park with green trees in it, and there would be arcaded buildings all around the square—cafes, shops, dance halls.

The marchers didn't go into the town; they were trying to make Cerralvo by nightfall. But civilians came out and stood at the roadside, watching them go by. They were boisterous, happy. John wondered why. The reason became clear soon enough when the man marching next to him called out to a girl, "Hey, *señorita*, any dances in Cerralvo tonight?"

The girl laughed. "In Cerralvo, no. In Monterrey, *si. Mucho fandango* in Monterrey!" She made a throat-slitting gesture.

11

THE ARMY MOVED on to Cerralvo and got some relief, finally, after its wearying march. It had taken them seven days to come fifty miles. But here were groves, trees, pastures and the Sierre Madre mountains in view, and the change in environment helped to lift flattened spirits.

John, still doubting his spiritual fortitude, readied himself for a battle that, it turned out, was still ten days off. They'd reached Cerralvo on Sepember 9th. John's enlistment was up, had been for over a month, but so were the enlistments of many others. They had stayed on, those who hadn't fallen too ill to carry a gun, and so would he. In Cerralvo there was a great deal of high-spirited activity that seemed to carry John along with it. General Taylor himself was there. John had seen him once on the march, riding up and down the lines on his horse, Ol' Whitey, looking as peeved and despondent as the men he was leading, if for reasons that had more to do with his distrust of President Polk than the arduousness of the march. Old Zach's personal problems, as mirrored in his face, still had the effect of weakening the ordinary soldier's confidence in his leadership.

But once Taylor came off the desert into Cerralvo's more invigorating climate he, too, underwent a change in attitude. He was seen in close, animated conversation with Generals William Worth and Persifor Smith, who had brought up brigades of the Second Division, and General David Twiggs, commanding the First Division.

The Indiana Volunteers were in Worth's command, along with other volunteer units and about a thousand Regulars. Lew Wallace, with his access to Taylor's staff, was able to tell the Indianans what to expect in the way of fortifications at Monterrey, if not what strategies were being planned to surmount them. Because, it turned out, no definite plan had been forthcoming from the generals' meeting.

"We'll be coming in from the north on the same road we've been on," Wallace reported. "There'll be the fortified citadel dead ahead of us and two bastions to the right. They guard the entrance to the city. In the city itself, word is that the rooftops have been manned by large numbers of men recently brought up from Mexico City. Then, if we do get through, we'll be running into two fortified hills guarding the road on to Saltillo, which is where General Taylor would like to go next."

John knew all about the citadel, but not about the other defenses. Someone said dryly, "We sure gave them a lot of time to prepare for us."

Wallace agreed. "That's right. We're outnumbered now two to one. Any further questions?"

"What's Taylor got in mind?" a man asked. "Anything? Or are we just supposed to charge that there citadel and them other places with bayonets?"

Wallace said, hesitantly, "General Taylor does favor the bayonet, as you know. However, he'll decide when we get there."

"You mean he ain't got a thought in his head about it?"

"I mean he's a gut fighter," Wallace said evenly. "I figure we're all gut fighters. You men proved that once already and I figure you'll do it again when you have to."

"Yeah, well, I suppose so . . . Heck, they're just a bunch of greasers. Just point us in the right direction an' we'll get 'em for you, Lew. . . ."

When the others subsided, John found himself asking a curious question. "Lew, do you have any word about whether or not there'll be a deserter battalion fighting against us?"

"No. Why do you ask?"

John shrugged. "Just wondered."

Wallace frowned. "If the Mexicans have some of our deserters with them, there couldn't be more than a handful. They shouldn't add much to our problem." He hesitated. "I don't like shooting at Americans any more than you do, Bell, no matter what misguided notions got them to cross over. But we may have to. It's part of our job."

"I guess that's right," John said. He couldn't agree more now that this war was a job—a rotten, thankless job. Still, he wasn't going to shoot at Dooey Dolan if he could help it. He had no real reason to believe that

Dooey would be on the Mexican side in Monterrey, only the hunch he'd had when he'd seen the girl Dooey had made up his mind to run off with. Whatever happened, he wasn't going to shoot Dooey. Deep down, Dooey was still like a brother to him, and he wasn't going to shoot his brother.

"—had his head boiled in oil. Ampudia's cruel, he's vicious, so the best advice I can give you, Joe, is *don't* get took."

There was some laughter and John shook the fog out of his head. Later he found out that somebody had wanted to know how the Mexicans here might treat prisoners. Wallace had replied with some information about Monterrey's commanding general, Ampudia, a man who more than once in Mexico's army internal revolutions had made particularly gruesome examples of the prisoners he'd taken.

This information was sobering. But what disturbed John more than anything else at this point was that he had heard neither the question nor the answer. Even though his heart was no longer in this war, he still had to survive the forthcoming battle, didn't he? And how was he going to do that if he let his mind wander all over the place? He envisioned taking a bullet through the eyes at Monterrey and never knowing the difference.

A week later, a chance incident tested John's true mettle, or some of it. On September 15th, the Army got its marching orders and left Cerralvo under its various commands. Worth's brigade, with the Indianans in it, moved out first on a cool dawn. It was a silent, determined Army now . . . or maybe a frightened one. There wasn't much talk on the road—nobody complained, nobody grumbled. Men kept their eyes fixed on the ring of mountain peaks surrounding Monterrey, which could be seen across the flatlands from fifty miles off.

The march lasted four days with stops for sleep at night. There were times when John would stay up and just stare at those mountains. One of the peaks he could see had two smaller peaks at its top, forming a cleft shaped like an upside-down half-moon. It was a natural feature that, in the moonlight, had a hypnotic effect on him during this time of his personal anguish. He used the welcome calm it gave him to give himself a message of hope. Come what may, John Bell, he told himself, just do your best. Even if called on to charge the city with a bayonet—the one possible order of Taylor's that scared them all—he would do his best.

Fortunately, Old Zach began to give up on ordering a bayonet charge as soon as he and the Army came in sight of Monterrey's citadel, on September 19th. It was impregnable. Even to John it looked impregnable—not simply a fort that men would die trying to capture, but one that couldn't be taken if the entire six thousand-man Army were sent against it.

At the point where the Indianans stopped and made camp in a walnut grove, there to await further orders, the citadel lay in clear view across an open pasture. Cattle grazed in the pasture. Beyond, dwarfing them, rose the huge, half-built cathedral. John could see why the structure had been dubbed the Black Fort. It wasn't just the cathedral that was made of black stone; a high black wall surrounded it, and a blackish moat surrounded the wall. Eight cannon, no less black, jutted from the cathedral's half-finished towers.

Moreover, about a quarter-mile to the right of the Black Fort, John could now see the two other defenses Wallace had alerted them to: a smaller fort on a hillside and a nest of four big artillery pieces close by. Any army that tried to run that quarter-mile-wide gauntlet into the city would be smashed to smithereens.

But Old Zach was stubborn and it took a while before word came from Wallace that the general had changed his mind about ordering a frontal attack. Wallace brought the news of an altered plan to take the city late that afternoon, after the regiment had, for six hours, been staring into what appeared to them to be the jaws of hell.

"Seems we neglected to bring the heavy artillery we'd need to soften the citadel up," Lew said. "Here's what we're going to do instead."

The men, having geared themselves up for a suicidal charge, breathed easier. But now they had to adjust to the new plan, which made for new tensions. Taylor's idea now, according to Wallace, was for General Worth to circle his division around to the rear of the city and try to take the two hills there that the Mexicans had guarding the road onto Saltillo. The Indianans would go with him. If the hills could be captured, they could then attack Monterrey from the rear while the remaining divisions went in from the northeast, around the smaller fort now facing them. Coming in from both sides, the Army would pinch the Mexican forces in the city's center.

There was silence while the regiment chewed that over. Then, "When do we move, Lew?" Crossman said.

"Tomorrow afternoon, about two o'clock."

So this was it, John thought. The battle he didn't want to fight wasn't going to go away; it was only going to become more prolonged, more complicated. He didn't know, he could only speculate now on the risks entailed in the new plan and he didn't want to be in that position, for new speculations engendered new worries.

Other Indianans seemed to share his view; there was much aimless cursing as the long day let them think too much. From when they were now, they could only see the two hills they were to attack as long bony bluish-gray ridges pointed at the sky on the far side of Monterrey's white houses. They were "over yonder," not here.

During that afternoon and evening, John got to hear what the hills were called—*Federacion* and *Independencia*—and learned something about their fortifications. The first had two gun emplacements at its top and the second was even more heavily guarded—by a fort called the "Bishop's Palace," halfway up it, as well as a gun emplacement at its top.

This information came from the Texas scouts, as filtered through all the volunteer regiments. The Texas scouts were some distance from the Indianans, in a part of the grove they shared with Taylor's staff. What little they knew came over the grapevine. Unfortunately, the scouts couldn't let the volunteers know how General Worth intended to take these hills; the rumor came over strong that he himself didn't know. About the only comforting news the Indianans received was that they probably wouldn't have too much trouble finding their way around the city to the hills, since the division would be guided by a Mexican prisoner under threat of immediate hanging if he betrayed them.

During the night it rained. The next day dawned gray, with angry black clouds hanging still for a long while and blotting out the sun. The weather seemed to suit the volunteers' mood which, by and large, had become one of sullen determination to put one foot after the other and get on with a slogging job. John, on line at the fire with his tin coffee cup, shared this mood and was somehow strengthened by it. All he had going for him was a dog-like tenacity of purpose, a pervasive gloom with the will to survive persisting under it. Did the others have more? He looked at some grim, tight faces, heard some bad jokes being nervously told and thought not. Better this way, John thought, than to hear the sounds of unwarranted optimism. When something like despair was appropriate you had a better chance, going off to battle, with men who did not pretend to feel otherwise. Or was it simply a case of misery loving company?

In any case, the pall that had spread over the camp lifted at about noon when the Indianans, in the process of getting their gear together, were diverted by an amazing, spontaneous charge at the citadel undertaken by the same Texas scouts who had passed along the bits of fact and rumor the day before.

It was a foolhardy thing the Texans did. Maybe they had been too long frustrated by the delay in action and now felt cheated by the change in orders. In any event, they charged the Black Fort on their own. Ten of them, whooping and waving their hats, suddenly came galloping out of their camp and made straight across the pasture toward the citadel's outer wall.

It was an astonishing sight. The Indianans stopped what they were doing to watch. They could see nothing to be gained from the Texans' venture, yet there they were, riding hard and fast into the range of eight large cannon pointed straight at them. As the Mexicans saw them coming, one of the big guns, then another, went off with tremendous blasts. The balls kicked up pasture grass not far from the Texans and started a cattle stampede. The cattle went with the Texans. Ten men and a hundred steers now charged the citadel. All splashed across the moat and headed for the high stone wall.

At this point the steers milled along the sides of the wall in moving confusion. The Texans, ignoring them, proceeded to scamper their horses up and down the length of the wall, firing their revolvers into the air and shouting taunts at an enemy now unseen by them, since the wall towering high over their heads totally blocked any sight of the citadel. The Texans seemed to be demanding that the Mexicans inside come out and fight!

"Those crazy bastards!" one of the Indianans muttered.

The onlookers stood and gaped as the Texans kept up their daring stunt. The sudden charge of ten riders had come as a total surprise to the citadel's defenders; they'd had no musketeers stationed on the wall's high loopholes to defend against it. For several minutes there was no response from within. Then the Mexicans must have gotten curious about the high level of noise being sustained outside—the shouts of men and the mooing of steers. Maybe they thought a plan of larger scope was underway.

They sent a man to climb a ladder into a loophole, look down and investigate. When the man's head appeared, a Texan promptly shot at it. He missed. The man quickly scurried back down the ladder, to be replaced by another investigator at another loophole in the wall. Another shot sent him too into hasty retreat. That was the extent of the Mexicans' scouting missions.

Some time passed in which the Texans continued to have their sport, waiting for more customers to appear on the wall, and the citadel remained silent. Then, before the Indianans' rapt gaze, a startling thing happened. The Mexicans, taking about the strangest measure available to rid themselves of the disturbance outside, slowly elevated all eight cannon on the parapets higher and higher toward the sky. John stared incredulously. He could see what the Mexicans were up to. They were going to loop sixteen-pound balls up into the air, just over the wall, and have them come down on the Texans' heads, squashing them like flies.

"Well, I'll be damned!"

By this time, Wallace had rejoined the regiment after a late briefing he had received at divisional headquarters. He had seen the band of Texas horsemen cutting up at the wall just as everybody else in the waiting Army had. It had been decided at headquarters to let the rollickers finish on their own what they, after all, had begun on their own. Wallace had orders from General Worth to get the regiment moving. He started to pass this along to the men, but Crossman stopped him.

"Wait, Lew, I got to see this."

"See what?"

Crossman nodded toward the elevated cannon.

"I'll be damned," said Wallace, noting this latest feature of the fray for the first time.

They all stood around and watched; the Texans' predicament had become fascinating.

"Crossman, do you think those fellows know what's about to come down on them?" John said.

Crossman shook his head. "Don't see how they could."

"Somebody ought to get to them and warn them."

"It ain't going to be me," Crossman said flatly. "How about you doing that?"

John said nothing, realizing that a race out into the pasture to warn the Texans would be as foolhardy a stunt as their own. Besides, it was too late. As the Indianans watched, all eight cannon boomed almost simultaneously—and deafeningly. The Texans, momentarily stunned, reined in their horses and watched eight cannon balls fly over their heads and come down about a hundred yards beyond them in the pasture.

"That was a little too close," Crossman observed.

"It didn't come anywhere near them," John protested.

"A little too close to *us*, you damn fool."

"Oh." John had been too taken up by the Texans' plight to note their own. The cannon balls hadn't landed *that* close to them, he saw—they'd hit pretty far out in the field—but he could see what Crossman was driving at.

"It's an interesting thought," Crossman said. "See, they were probably afraid of hitting their own wall, so they overshot. Now, if they got any judgment at all, they'll draw the range closer in the next round and—Oh, my God! Lew! Will you look at that! They're aiming them guns *lower* instead of higher!"

Sure enough, the snouts of the cannon descended, for some reason known only to the Mexicans. This time when they were fired, the balls came down and skipped along some fifty yards beyond the first batch. The Texans looking on jeered, and Crossman groaned, "Aw, hell, Lew, I'm with you—let's get the hell out of here before we get killed. Those dumb greasers don't know what they're doing."

"Wait a minute," John said. "We can't just go and leave those fellows out there."

"Hell, they'll get out of it," Crossman said. "The greasers can't aim straight. Next time, if they don't hit us, they'll be shooting balls up their own assholes. You watch."

Crossman was wrong about that. The cannons' range was more properly adjusted, and three of the balls in the next volley splashed into the moat not fifteen yards from the horsemen. The Texans got very quiet. One of them peered up at the wall, as if planning to climb it and put an end to the menace single-handedly.

Crossman snorted. "Some chance he's got. They've had it now. It's all over but the shouting."

"I'll bet they get out of it," John said.

"How?"

John didn't have the faintest idea how. All he knew was that he suddenly found himself rooting for the Texans, hoping they'd come up with *some* plan to save themselves and willing to bet they would.

"Never mind how. Crossman, you don't have any guts. You going to bet me or aren't you? I'll lay you three dollars to one that none of those Texans gets killed and—and that they'll do something terrible to the Mexicans."

Crossman looked at him. "Like what?"

"Something terrible, that's all. Terrible means—"

"I *know* what terrible means," Crossman said coldly. "Lew here'll be the judge of what's terrible. Okay, Lew?" Wallace nodded and Crossman said, "All right, Bell, you're on."

John watched intently. The Texans didn't move for a while, only stared into the moat, as if measuring the last cannonade's proximity to them. Then it was clear that they had come to some decision because their heads jerked up.

While the unseen cannon above them was slowly elevated again, three of them dismounted, splashed into the moat and retrieved three of the sixteen-pound balls that had sunk to the shallow moat bed. They tugged them back to the wall. One of the Texans stood on his horse's back. The cannon balls were passed up to him. One by one, he threw them over the wall, back, in effect, into the Mexicans' laps.

"I don't believe it," Crossman said softly.

The cannon stopped moving. All sound in the fort ceased. John couldn't figure out what the Texans were up to anymore than Crossman could.

"The thing is, we don't know what's going on in there," Crossman said slowly.

"I'll see if I can find out," John said. It had suddenly occurred to him that he might be able to do that. There was a tall tree nearby and he climbed it to its uppermost branches, from which precarious perch he could see over the distant wall into the citadel's inner courtyard. He couldn't see the returned cannonballs—they were too close to the inside of the wall—but he did see, after a while, three Mexican soldiers come trotting out of the citadel to pick them up. They ran back through the cathedral's open doors and disappeared. A few moments later he saw, through the cathedral's stained-glass windows, the shadows of the Mexicans lugging the balls up the steps of one of the towers.

"I think they're going to reuse the shot the Texans gave them," John called down. "I guess they don't have all that much ammunition in there. Hand me up my rifle, will you?"

He clambered halfway down the tree and took the

rifle from Crossman, then climbed up to the top again and fired to attract the Texans' attention. Even though he didn't know what they had in mind, he could see what they couldn't, and he could help them out by letting them know what that was.

When some of them looked his way, John put the gun down in a crook of the tree and began to show them, using imitative gestures, just what he had seen, eventually pointing to the tower over their heads. Squinting back at him they seemed not only to get the idea, but to take encouragement from it. One of them took off his hat and waved it at John.

"What's going on?" Crossman called up.

John didn't answer at first, he was busy studying what was now happening in the courtyard. Three Mexican privates came rushing out the cathedral door, then skidded to a stop. There seemed to be an argument going on among them as to which two would go and get the balls furthest off from them. This brought an angry general in a plumed hat out of the door after them. He ordered each private in turn to go in a certain direction. When they didn't budge, he began shoving them so they stumbled a few steps before stopping again.

"They're not going to pick those balls up," John said, reporting this action to the growing crowd of Indianans waiting below. "The man's a *general* and they're not going to do what he says!"

"That's about all the greasers got, privates and generals. Don't you know that yet?" Crossman said. "He's probably their cousin. What else is going on?"

But John was too intent on watching. By now he had a pretty fair idea of what the Texans in their wisdom, in their knowledge of Mexican ways, had been counting on. They'd been trying to delay the cannonade, and they'd succeeded. John now saw that the set-to in the courtyard had drawn the involved attention of the cannoneers. All had left their posts. They'd moved to the edge of the parapets and were gazing down with unhurried interest at the reluctant privates and the angry general.

Suddenly the scene seemed to freeze before John's eyes. The balky privates became like stone; the general too stood motionless. For the briefest of instants, John felt dizzy. He felt unreal, conscious of himself as no less a frozen object than the Mexicans were. Then he seemed to dissolve within himself, lose track of where he was again.

He became aware that the Texans were waving their hats at him, asking for a signal. Instinctively, John responded with waves and motions indicating that they could now get away. Whooping, the Texans spurred their horses into the moat and headed back to camp. They were three-quarters of the way across the pasture before the cannoneers got back to their guns and they were far out of range before the cannon could be re-aimed.

John came down from the tree. Whereas he had scampered up it, he came down slowly. The flurry of activity of which he had been a part was over. Somehow John took no pleasure in the contribution he had made to the Texans' escape; he'd even forgotten the bet he'd made.

He was struck by the absurdity of the entire affair: he couldn't believe that the Texans would make so senseless a charge, or that he could have gotten caught up in things to the extent that he had. All was unreal. He felt, not as if he had climbed the tree of his own volition, but as if he had been pulled up it by invisible strings. It was a miserable feeling.

Crossman didn't at first notice John's stunned expression. He was pleased the Texans had made it back to their camp. He remembered the bet, but was willing to overlook it. He greeted John warmly.

"Damn clever of you, Bell. Them scouts didn't exactly do something terrible to the greasers—we don't need Lew here to tell us that—but, what the hell, you don't have to pay me nothing."

John said hollowly, "But I lost. Don't you see that? I lost."

Crossman studied him a moment, then shrugged. "It's all right, Bell. It's all right. Look, I'll give you a hand with your gear if you like."

John shook his head. "Thanks. I can manage."

Crossman nodded. He went off to get his pack and John started after him. General Worth had sent a courier to get the regiment moving. The rain clouds had passed and the sun was high. The general wanted to get around to the back of the city by nightfall. The other Indianans were already moving off. John knew he had to go with them.

"Bell." It was Lew Wallace calling after him. John turned. Wallace was looking at him curiously, as if seeing him for the first time. John waited for him to catch up.

Whatever Wallace had observed in John's behavior, it prompted him to say, "Bell, you don't have to come along with us. There'll be no disgrace for you in my eyes if you don't—if you've changed your mind. After all, your enlistment's up."

Again, John shook his head. "Thanks, Lew, but I haven't changed my mind. I'm going on."

"The thing is," Wallace persisted, "you wouldn't be the first to drop out. We've had hundreds drop out since the war started. People get sick—from the heat, from the water, from the monotony of the desert marches. Over a hundred got sick just on this last march alone, the medics tell me. They're going back to Camargo. You can go with them."

"I'm not sick, Lew. I can walk and I can carry a gun."

Wallace studied him. John's face was ashen and his teeth were clenched. Wallace said slowly, "All right then. But would you mind telling me what happened to you up in that tree? Something did, all of a sudden."

John said, "I don't know, Lew, I just don't. If I knew I would tell you. All I know is—" He paused and Wallace waited. John went on, more slowly, "All I know is that one minute I was looking at what the Mexicans were doing in the courtyard and I was all excited. Then, suddenly, they weren't doing *anything*. They seemed frozen, a kind of suspended animation. And then I felt as if *I* were in suspended animation. Nothing seemed real to me. It was as if I were hovering somewhere between life and death." John stopped. He felt he had said enough—maybe too much. "It's crazy, Lew, I know, but I can't explain it any other way."

"Maybe you are in suspended animation," Wallace said quietly. "But if you are, it's you who are holding yourself there. And what makes you think that you're back living in time? Just because you made it down from that tree?"

John said slowly, "You do know what I'm talking about, Lew, don't you?"

Wallace shook his head. "No. But I know a little about you. You're a good soldier, Bell. But don't you have a friend you think has gone away, who isn't, let's say, such a good soldier but is inclined to be a little rebellious, maybe?"

John was puzzled. "Dooey Dolan deserted. You know that, Lew."

Wallace said steadily, "It isn't Dolan I'm talking about. I never got to know him at all. I'm talking about the friend who scampered up that tree with you just now but stayed there, so that only the good soldier came down. The one who, a while back, went off into the desert on a slow mule and came back on a fast horse. That friend. The one who comes and goes. The one who'd stick around, if you'd let him."

John stared at him. "It's no good, Lew. You don't understand. I was up in that tree and everything got frozen for me. I didn't care whether the Texans got away free or whether that whole damn citadel blew up, killing them and every last Mexican I was looking at."

Wallace swore softly. "For Christ's sakes, why *should* you care about what happens to a bunch of idiots? It's playing around in trees you like, isn't it?"

He turned and stalked off.

John stared after him. All of a sudden, he felt sad.

Worth's division left the walnut grove and swung westward. Up front rode the general himself with his Mexican prisoner in tow. Then came a few horse-drawn artillery pieces, followed by the marching army—three thousand men in all, half Regulars, half units of volunteers.

They started out at a brisk pace, almost as if on parade. The Indianans marched ten abreast about midway in the procession. John was in the third file, between Crossman on his left and a man named Joe Morgan on his right. Talk was at a minimum, ordered so for security reasons. The route Worth had chosen cut through a sloping forest of towering trees that had shielded the maneuver from the citadel from the outset. But Mexican patrols were known to be roaming this area, and the danger of alerting them was ever-present.

The brisk pace continued for two hours, during which time the division covered about five miles. Then it rained. The rain came suddenly, in a heavy downpour, as it had only threatened to do earlier that day. The forest floor quickly turned to mud. Men got drenched, slipped, stumbled and swore, mindless of any enemy patrol that might be lurking. Up ahead, an artillery battery, pulling out of mud, caught a rock and turned over. General Worth was seen barking commands at its crew to haul it upright so the division could move on. But even though that was done in the space of a few minutes, by then the going had become all but impossible. Orderly communications along the length of the division broke down. Some regimental commanders kept their men moving; other volunteer units took cover under trees until such time as the rain would let up. The disorganization that set in resulted in regiments becoming separated from each other, in some cases by as much as three hundred yards.

The Indianans became one such isolated unit. Wallace, shouting to be heard now over the wind and rain whistling through the trees, ordered them off the muddy track, as much to allow room for those who wanted to pass them as for their own protection.

Kentuckians passed by. Missourians passed by. The latter regiment's commander roared at Wallace, standing under tree cover: "What's the matter, Lew? Letting a little cloud pee bother you?"

Wallace grinned. "See you later, Tom."

They all went by, those who were going to. Worth,

his Texas scouts and the Regulars were far up ahead. John looked but couldn't see any unit on either side of them.

The rain kept coming down heavily for another hour. When it finally stopped, it was dark and the forest was more sea than land. The trees were still. In the blackness they retained a muggy green scent. They would smell like the trees of Connecticut, John thought, if the weather were cooler, if the stars were out, if. . . .

"What do we do now, Lew?" Crossman said.

Wallace shrugged. He had gone to test the forest track for footing and had stepped ankle-deep in water. Nor was the ground much firmer where they stood, under the trees. "Catch up, I suppose. Wouldn't want to miss our little party with the Mexicans."

"Lew?" It was Joe Morgan speaking, and he was nervous. "Slogging around in all this mud and being cut off from the others like we are, wouldn't we be hard put if we ran into a Mexican patrol?"

Wallace frowned. "Maybe so, but it'll take tomorrow's sun to dry things up. We'll chance it."

"Lew?" John spoke up. "I've an idea. Suppose I go on up ahead and scout the terrain for a mile or so? It isn't likely to take me long—a half-hour at the most to take a good look around."

Wallace said wryly, "More games, Bell? You'll probably run into one of our own units before you do Mexicans."

"Right," John agreed. "So, if I'm not back in a half-hour, you can figure that's what I did. I'll have whatever unit it is wait for you. That way, when you come up with the regiment, there'll be that many more of us to go on with."

Wallace thought. "Not a bad idea at that. All right,

Bell, take off. We'll give you exactly one half-hour by my watch. Stay in the woods where you can't be seen. One thing more: if by chance you do spot a Mexican patrol, it'll behoove you not to stand there and dwell on it. Just signal us with a rifle shot and run like hell. Got it?"

He gave John a pointed look and John grinned. "Sure thing, Lew."

John knelt, took off his shoes and socks and rolled up his pants to the knees, all so he could move more quickly through the forest's mud. Then he gripped his rifle tightly with both hands, so that it would make no inadvertent noise, and stole off into the darkness.

He went feeling sad, lonely, homesick—and intent on proving to Wallace that, when the chips were down, he could carry out a simple mission.

The trees got thicker and the darkness darker as he made his way through the woods along a route that, after five minutes or so, he could only hope paralleled the track he'd left. But he had problems at first with his footing and in maintaining a generally westerly direction, taking his bearings from an early greyish moon that had risen. There wasn't a sign of life where he trod, not even a snake; it was as if every living thing had scurried deeper into the bush during the rainstorm. The only sound he heard was water dripping from leaves into pools below.

He went on that way for another ten minutes, intently listening for sharper, more significant sounds. He must have cut further inland from the track than he'd thought. There was little he could see by now. As the trees got still thicker and the foliage overhead blocked out the dim light of the sky, he twice walked straight into trees without seeing them.

The first time he did this he got scared; the silent

tree, after all, could just as well have been an outposted Mexican, waiting silently with a bayonet for John to get close. He moved on, in a nervous, expectant manner. But it was soon obvious that no large enemy patrol could possibly be lurking in this area; it became, in short order, a jungle of tangled undergrowth with no clearing in it whatsoever. John swore the second time he walked into a tree. Going on in this direction was pointless. What he would only succeed in doing would be to get himself lost—if he hadn't done that already.

Irritated, he turned in the direction in which he figured the track lay and began hacking at vines with his bayonet to cut himself a path back to it. It took him another ten minutes to reach it. The road was bathed in grey light and from where John first saw it, it looked serene, with surface water glinting on it.

But it wasn't unoccupied; that was for sure. John heard voices—muttered, indistinct. They were coming from the direction he had started out from, about fifty yards down that way. He realized then that what he had done—not by design but by accident—was circle through the jungle around whoever the voices belonged to.

John stood stock-still and listened. He heard the neighing of horses. No American unit near the Indianans had had horses, which was enough to alert him to the probability that this force was Mexican. Still, they might be Texas scouts sent back by Worth to check on tardy units. John wanted to make sure. He ducked back into the woods and, staying behind trees, made his way down to a point where at last he could see the horsemen.

His eyes widened. They were Mexicans all right—not guerrillas, as he'd halfway expected to see making up a patrol in these parts, but a fully uniformed and armed force of dragoons. Unless he was mistaken, they were the same dragoons that he and the rest of the Army had seen riding up ahead of them during the long march from Camargo.

It didn't matter whether they were or not. What mattered was that there was a large number of them —perhaps two hundred—waiting by the roadside for some American regiment or other to come their way. They were between him and the Indianans.

John thought quickly. Alerting the regiment with a rifle shot alone wouldn't help them one damn bit; there were too many of these people to fight without Indianans getting killed left and right. And Wallace couldn't avoid them either, if he came on. Unless, John thought, he could draw the Mexicans off the road altogether. Suddenly he saw some point in firing a shot anyway, then running like hell.

He was well-placed for the scheme that came to his mind. The first thing he had to do made the blood pound in his head when he thought of it. Damn it, he didn't hate these Mexicans! He didn't even know the bastards! And they weren't shooting at *him* . . . but they soon would be. He had to show them he meant business, didn't he?

John lifted his rifle and drew a bead on a man who was sitting on his saddle on the ground, leaning against a tree. He was just waiting there, idly chewing on a toothpick. They were all just waiting there. John pulled the trigger. There was a deafening roar. The Mexican's head jerked up in surprise. He lifted his hand toward his mouth, as if to remove the toothpick, then dropped it toward his chest where the hole John's bullet had made was already bloodying his shirtfront.

John didn't wait to see more. He ran. He crashed into the underbrush, swerved back in the direction he had come from and kept running. Behind him he heard shouts, curses, horses being mounted. He had shot and probably killed one of them. They were coming to get him. That's just what he wanted them to do.

He made for the impenetrable jungle he'd dead-ended in before, zigzagging while there was still enough clearing in which to run from side to side. As he ran, he kept reloading and firing his rifle, from different points in the forest, turning each time to aim it at the road. The shots echoed loudly, bouncing off trees and rocks, he hoped with the effect of a regiment shooting. When he used up his bullets and there was nothing further to be served by his broken-field tactic, he raced straight ahead, plunged into the thick undergrowth and hid there.

He waited, his heart pounding, in a kind of cul-de-sac of matted vines that both hid him and kept him from running further. But there was no point in running further. Wherever he might run, horses could run too and he would have been overtaken soon enough.

He hoped he'd drawn all or most of the Mexicans off the road. He'd done what he could to break their ranks, to keep the regiment from blundering into them. If Lew came on—which he might, cautiously—there was a good chance he'd find only a patrol-size contingent left in his path, something the alerted regiment could handle.

On the other hand, John was where he was—in deep. He gripped his empty rifle.

Pretty soon he heard a neighing in the forest, about a hundred yards from him. He'd had a good lead on the Mexicans after his surprise shot and quick flight. He'd also caused some delay in their pursuit with his subsequent shots, enough of a delay to get him further into the jungle to his present cover.

But that's all he had created, a delay. He heard the clank of metal, like muskets against sabers, as the Mexicans dismounted. How many were out there, he didn't know. In the blackness of the undergrowth he couldn't see more than ten feet in front of him. It didn't seem possible that they could find him. Yet, as he held his breath, he heard low, muttering voices coming closer and closer.

He heard them beating the bushes. Not just those in his proximity—there were about a dozen of them, he soon judged—but other groups to the distant right and left of him. There was a long thin line of them advancing into the jungle, on foot, hacking at vines with their sabers.

Fear and hope warred within John. He did not stir. There was always a chance that they would give up and go away. But they didn't and, with a pang, he made a good guess as to why. In his hastily made plan, in his precipitous flight, he had overlooked the fact that he'd be leaving muddy prints of his bare feet. Fortunately, he'd splashed through deep puddles the last twenty yards or so. They didn't know exactly where he was; that's why they were spread out, widening the search, and why, it seemed, he had borrowed still more time.

Time to do what with? The hacking sabers came to within ten feet of him, at the level of his head as he crouched low. One of the Mexicans swore, "Carramba!" as his scything blade got stuck in a knotted vine; then the blade went back up—John could see it glinting—and came down again in a mighty sideswipe that slashed the vine in two.

It was too much for John to take—almost. Out in the forest, horses neighed. How many Mexicans had been left out there? he wondered. If he had to, could he dash out and capture a riderless horse before any mounted Mexicans there could stop him. . . ?

The scything Mexican bellied up to him. His belt buckle, a thing with a golden sunburst on it, was inches from John's frozen gaze. The blade swooshed up, out of John's vision but felt in the prickling at the back of his neck. He braced himself. With a roar, he dived from his hiding place, butted his head into the Mexican's midriff and kept going.

The man he'd butted fell away with a whump. Two other Mexicans immediately loomed in front, but John had his rifle by the barrel and was ready for them. He clouted one on the side of the head with the gun's butt. The man's skull cracked into the other man's cheekbone and both, with cries of pain, went sprawling in the mud.

John leaped through the pool at the jungle's edge and kept running. Shots followed him as the Mexicans recovered. They were off target, hitting trees far to either side of him. They couldn't see him any more than he could see the neighing horses he was running toward. Then, he did see them, in a clearing shafted with sky light, and his heart suddenly exulted. There wasn't anyone tending them—no Mexicans at all! His luck was incredible.

He had his pick of empty saddles. His feet fairly flew as he headed for the nearest horse, a big roan that stood with its ears twitching, its reins looped loosely over a tall bush. The trick was not to take time to mount but to leap over the roan's rump. He'd never done that before, but he knew that, under the pressure of pursuit, he could do it now.

He flung away the gun, now hampering him for such a mount. He ran the last ten yards at full, charging speed. He was about to leap when something—a bulky shadow, no more than that—stepped from behind the bush to which the roan was tethered and got in his way.

John thought it was a bear, so silently did it move. He crashed into it, unable to stop, and drove both it and himself into the ground. His head spinning from the impact, his vision blurred by spattered mud, John wrestled vainly with the thing that had fallen on top of him. From the hands clutching at his face and his mouth, he was sure that it was a Mexican and he began battling for his life.

"Bell, it's *me*—Crossman! Cut it out, will you?"

John went limp at the hoarse whisper. He opened his eyes. Sure enough, it was Crossman.

"Get back here, you damn fool. Quick about it!"

Crossman scrambled up and began tugging John by the hand, even as he lay sprawled, back behind the bush he had come from. It was help John didn't need. Quickly, he followed. There were three other Indianans behind that bush. John glanced up and down the line at several other bushes bordering this glade. Behind them was the rest of the regiment, holding bound and gagged Mexican horse-tenders under guard.

Wallace nodded at him. "Nice going, Bell."

"What did I do?" John said, perplexed. "How'd you get here?"

"Wasn't it you who fired six or seven shots back a while ago?"

"It was me," John admitted.

"Well, it was good thinking. We got the message. If one shot was to signal an alert, we figured that many meant a catastrophe. So we came. Quiet, now."

Hidden behind the bushes, they waited for the Mexican dragoons to return for their horses—which the dragoons did promptly enough, having lost their quarry in the darkness but knowing the direction in which he had fled.

The Indianans were ready for them. They opened fire as the first of them appeared, felling five, creating instant confusion among the others. There was return fire from dragoons who kneeled and poured shot at men hidden from them, but the skirmish was brief, the rout complete. Followed by volley after volley of the regiment's bullets, the surviving Mexicans mounted their horses and rode pell-mell away.

When the engagement was over, the prisoners the regiment had taken were questioned under the threat of death if they lied, and they informed Wallace that their brigade alone had been prowling this area and there were no other Mexican units up ahead to be faced. Lew finally turned to John.

"As I said before, you did well," Wallace told him. "If you hadn't fired all those shots, we'd have had no way of guessing what was going on here. We would have come ahead and stumbled into a superior force and would probably have been wiped out. You deserve a commendation, Bell. After we capture Monterrey, I'm going to see that you get one. Do you think you can stay alive until then?" He seemed amused as he asked the question.

John swallowed. He wanted to minimize his contribution toward saving the regiment. He wanted to confess that what he had done he had done impulsively, in an attempt to save his own neck, certainly without thinking that imitating a regiment might bring on that regiment. He hadn't planned to bring them on. He wanted to tell Wallace that, to square his conscience. But he could see that Wallace wasn't interested in lisening to him, that all he wanted John to do was accept his congratulations and say no more about it. Because *everybody* had to stay alive to get on with the job, and there wasn't any room for John to keep falling away inside himself with his private guilts.

"Thanks, Lew," was all he said.

Only Crossman had a cross word for him. "Could have stopped you easier, Bell, if you didn't come on like a damn lunatic circus rider!"

"Next time, leave me be and just knock the horse over," John retorted.

Crossman frowned. "Yeah, maybe I should have done that. Just given it a little whup with my shoul—"

John grinned. "Come on, Crossman. Let's move it out."

12

THE REGIMENT caught up with the rest of the division at around eight o'clock that night. Most of Worth's force had moved on through the rainstorm, it turned out, and was now camped at Monterrey's western outskirts, just off the road that led on to Saltillo.

The Indianans found several brigades already positioned on that road, facing Saltillo, ready to combat any reinforcements the Mexicans might send from that town. Most of the troops, however, were encamped on low ground bordering a narrow, shallow river, across which lay the rear of Monterrey. Looming directly before them on the other side of the river were the two hills they had come to take—Federacion and Independencia—a two-fold side-by-side barrier to Worth's planned attack on the city's back streets.

The Indianans' approach with Mexican prisoners in tow caused something of a stir, even in a camp nervously anticipating a battle to be fought the next day. Wallace had some explaining to do and did it principally to Worth. When he returned to the regiment he had a dry comment for them.

"The general compliments us on our victory and upbraids us for having been laggard in the first place," he said.

There was hardly any response. The Indianans had grown to expect some such comment from the Regular Army brass. Besides, having settled on the ground alongside the other units, they too were nervously looking at the hills that were their objective.

Wallace studied their faces for a moment, these men who had already proven their courage in skirmishes. He could see them trying to appraise the difficulties of this new and different challenge. The hills they were staring at rose on their near side to a height of five hundred feet in a forty-five degree angle most of the way. They were rock-strewn, making for a treacherous footing. At their tops were gun emplacements. Wallace searched for the right words.

"The best I can tell you," he began slowly, "is that if things go well, our action tomorrow will be limited to taking that small emplacement over there on the top of Federacion. There's a large fort halfway down the slope on the hill's further side. The Fifth Infantry Regulars are to circle around and take that fort while we go after the guns on the ridge."

The men gave him sharp looks. From where they were encamped, they couldn't see the fort Wallace was talking about. Various apprehensions stirred in their minds.

Wallace went on to explain Worth's overall plan.

The division was to subdue the fortifications on Federacion the next day and the two others on Independencia on the day following. They would then move into Monterrey proper. With Taylor's forces coming in from the northeast, the Army would have the city in a nutcracker.

The men tried to take in this comprehensive strategy. Some nodded; they understood. But there were others who were troubled by a more immediate matter. It was Joe Morgan who finally said, "Lew? That fort you've told us about? What if the Army doesn't have it when we get to the ridge? If the greasers are still holding it, some of them are sure as hell going to be firing artillery at us."

It was an awkward moment, the wrong question at the wrong time. A ridiculous question. A "what if" question impossible for any man to answer. All Wallace could do was spell out Joe's choices for him.

He said steadily, "Joe, if it comes to that, I guess you'll either be joining in an attack on the fort or running back down the hill the way you came. Suit yourself."

"I ain't gonna run," was Joe Morgan's sullen reply.

Wallace nodded. "Get yourself some sleep," he told the regiment, then strode off.

There were mutters of determination akin to Morgan's as Wallace moved away. There were also jeers heaped on Morgan for what was considered by some to be a vain-glorious remark.

"Joe, you may not even *get* to the top of that dadblamed hill. Didja ever think of that? Joe, you ain't got no trust, that's what's the matter with you. Why, them Regulars are regular sweethearts, ain't they? They ain't goin' to let us down, are they?"

The last came with an extra burst of derision, as if to torment poor Joe further.

John remained where he was for a while, taking in the aftermath of Wallace's briefing. He noted Joe Morgan's doubts, noted how Joe couldn't hide them from the others. He felt his own doubts, and it seemed to him his were deeper than Joe's. His doubts were more fundamental, whereas Joe seemed to be concerned only with what would or would not happen the next day.

John had come to the conclusion—half soberly realized, half still terrifying in its implications—that he had no business being in this war at all. He reached the conclusion about himself that someone like Lew Wallace must have seen all along: that he was a displaced person in this war, that he was *sick*—sick with a longing to go home.

Except for the life of him, John could no longer tell what home meant. And whatever it meant, he couldn't go back to Connecticut before taking part in Monterrey, for that would reveal his ultimate cowardice to all. Or was he a coward? Was that really it?

In this turmoil, John got up and drifted away from the rest. He went to the edge of the river to look more closely at the hills beyond, to steel himself for tomorrow's battle, but other thoughts intruded. The river was the Santa Catarina. John liked the name. Catarina was a girl's name . . . like Sally. John felt infinitely sad. He'd lost Sally, probably forever, for not being manly enough to fight for her when he'd had the chance—against whomever his unknown rival was. He'd quit, gone away like a dog with its tail between its legs. Mooning about Sally, always mooning about her, he thought.

He'd been looking at the silvery beams on the river.

He jerked his gaze up to the hills, as if to rid himself of his debilitating thoughts. Despite himself, the hills too—those fiercely guarded hills—took on a romantic character for him. Federacion and Independencia had the same sort of half-moon-shaped crests at the top that he had seen from the desert on distant mountains. But now their jagged peaks, jutting into the sky, looked sharp and menacing to him. Tomorrow he would die. It wasn't he who was romantic, he told himself; it was Dooey Dolan. Dooey could carry things off, with a flair. One day Dooey would come back to his senses and return to the army. One day the war would end. Dooey would go back to Connecticut. He'd beat that unknown rival silly, as a man should, and take up with Sally. They'd make a striking couple. John would bless them from the grave.

John choked up, nearly cried out in his anguish at what he was doing to himself. Now he had trouble even discerning the gun emplacement on Federacion, let alone appreciating the danger it posed. Fleetingly, he thought about how he was only twenty-two years old. He wished that he were older, wiser, knew more; he wished he understood *life* better!

He took a deep breath, then several more. What was a kind of panic in him—a dizzying spectacle of this hateful war, this world, himself, all in chaos—subsided and left him quiet, drained of all emotion save one that he could name and knew without a doubt that he felt.

He was standing that way, motionless, when he heard footsteps coming up behind him. He turned and saw it was Lew Wallace.

"Hello, John. How's it going? I've been talking to folks here and there. If you want to be alone, just tell me."

"I'm scared," John said simply.

He waited for Wallace to say, "We're all scared." He didn't think he could stand it if Wallace said that.

Wallace nodded. "You've been scared before. You'll be scared again."

John shook his head. "You don't understand—I don't know who I am."

Wallace nodded again. "I wondered when you'd realize that. I wondered when you'd be able to put it that succinctly."

John looked at the gun emplacement on Federacion and saw it now as pieces of cold iron. The hill was now stripped of the character he had given it. It looked empty to him, just a desolate configuration of rocks and rising land with pieces of iron at the top and a long, largely hidden slope on its far side.

He said absently. "How do I charge up that hill tomorrow if I don't know who I am?"

Wallace studied him. "Is it a philosophical discussion you want on the eve of battle, John? Or a pep talk?"

"Both. Either. Anything that would help me."

"I see. And it's *my* help you want?"

John looked at Wallace, briefly, but there was a flash in him. "Yes, your help, Lew. You told me this morning that those Texans who charged the citadel were idiots. That somehow made me feel better."

"Because then you could feel superior to them and for a while things were all right for you again?" Wallace shook his head. "You got me wrong, John. I didn't say they were idiots. I said that was what *you* were saying they were. As for me, I don't know the chaps."

John stared at him, taken aback.

Wallace went on. "You did a little better, in your terms, this afternoon, when you called us into the woods . . . didn't you? We came. Maybe there is a touch of the regiment in you. Something that's in you that just comes naturally when you let it. Something that cares about us."

"Do you think so, Lew?" John said, still doubtful.

Wallace waved him off impatiently. "Do you hear what I'm saying? I'm saying we're all scared. Joe Morgan's scared. Do you know why? I just had a long private talk with him. He's scared because he's a sharecropper's son and never got past the second grade. He thinks he can't come up to snuff with me because I taught school for a while and fool around writing stories now and then. Can you beat that? But Joe's going up that hill tomorrow, and so am I and so are you."

Wallace stood there for a moment, breathing hard. "You had your chance to quit, John. I gave it to you. You didn't take it. I guess something in you wants to be here. The closer you see it, the better off you'll be. But even if you don't see it, you'll be running up that hill with us tomorrow anyway. So ends our philosophical discussion. So ends my pep talk."

"And what about what's over the hill, the thing I can't see?" John asked. He wanted the philosophical part to go on.

Wallace said steadily, "I'll tell you what I just told Joe Morgan. You'll see it from the top of the hill—if you get there. It's a fort."

The Indianans got up in the morning, rolled sleep out of their eyes and saw that it was a bright, fine day for a charge, a glistening-dew day fit for a picnic. The air was clear. The sky was a cloudless blue. The gun emplacements on Federacion stood out in sharp relief under a hot sun.

There was nervous, idle talk at the breakfast fire among men who had brought their tin cups there for coffee.

"Do you think they can see us from up there?"

"Course they can, you damn fool! We can see them, can't we? They probably got their beady little eyes on the whole damn division!"

It was certainly true that the division's units had gathered, were making their final preparations in full view of the hilltop. Most of it was infantry, but John saw artillery pieces being rolled to the river's edge for an imminent crossing. The artillery was to back them up, the infantry had been informed. Shells flying over their heads as they ran were to soften up the Mexican emplacements before the infantry reached them. It could only be hoped the guns would be effective once they started rolling up the hill; there were impeding boulders and sheer ledges in view. The Indianans had been warned—indeed, could see for themselves—that they shouldn't count too heavily on the big guns' aiding their charge.

John went over to Joe Morgan. "How're you doing, Joe?"

"Jes' fine. How's yourself?"

"I'm about to crap in my pants."

"Me too."

"I'd rather get going, more than anything else."

"Me too."

"We live through this, I'm going to get my ass out of Mexico."

"Me too."

"Don't you ever say anything besides 'me too'?"

"Jesus Christ, Bell! I'm scared shitless—What do you want me to say?"

"Well, let's go over to the water and get our feet wet."

The two went to the river and became the first of the division to step in that day. The water seeped over John's boot tops and he found he had to pee.

"I've got to pee," he said.

"Me too," Morgan said. "You first, me never."

John looked at him. "What do you mean? Why not?"

"I'll be damned if I'll take my pecker out. One of them greasers up there might shoot it off."

"Morgan, that's the dumbest thing I ever heard in my life."

"Yeah, well if you're so smart, if you think you know so damn much, you go ahead and pee."

With trepidation, John unbuttoned his pants and began to pee in the river. He was nervous about it. Morgan had put the idea into his head and he was really afraid that the Mexicans on the hill would unleash a barrage of gunfire and shoot his penis off.

"You ain't got much of a pecker," Morgan commented.

"Yeah, well, I guess that's the way it goes with peckers."

Crossman, behind them, yelled for them to come back and get their gear. The order for the division to move out in force had been given.

As John was rebuttoning his pants, Morgan said, "When's the last time you had a hard-on, Bell?"

John shrugged. "Back in Camargo, I guess."

"Did you jerk off or what?"

"No, I had a girl friend," John said. "The Mexican lady I was staying with."

"Was it any good?"

"Sure. I mean, I guess it was. You forget."

"Yeah, you sure do, don't you?" Morgan looked worried. "You know, the last time I had a hard-on was in New Orleans, on the way down here. Don't know why I haven't had one since. You'd figure in the course of time a man would have his share of hard-ons. Don't know what it is. All this walking around you have to do out here in the desert. People getting sick and throwing up all over the place . . ."

"Yeah, well . . ."

"I just don't know what to do—how to go about having a hard-on again, I mean."

"The first thing you ought to do is pee in the river, like I did."

"Morgan! Bell!" Crossman was shouting at them.

"That ain't going to give me no hard-on."

"Of course not, dummy. But the way it was with me," John said, thinking about it, "was that the Mexican didn't shoot my pecker off, so I figure I still have a chance."

Morgan eyed him. "You funnin' with me?"

"Just go ahead and pee, Morgan. Get it over with."

Morgan did so, no more willingly than John had.

"That's not much of a pecker you got there," John said.

"What do you mean by—son of a bitch!"

John had started to laugh. Now Morgan started to laugh. Crossman came trotting up at that point.

"Bell, here's your gun," Crossman said. "Morgan, here's yours. And put your damn pecker away before one of them greasers shoots it off!"

John and Morgan roared. They were close to tears from laughter.

"And what's so goddamn funny about that?" Crossman said, glowering. "You want to lose your pecker

to soMorgan saw what he was about. His eyes came into
ain't no nd he nodded. He wouldn't be running away,
John garunning toward something.
When he camen left their cover and made a beeline
river. He got into ace. Shells whistled by them as the
across together. acement sought to destroy the
"Here's to the hard-on over He hadn't counted on
"Hope you're right," Morgan said. it was too
They came out of the river and ran across a narrow stretch of flat land to the base of the hill. Already, from the hill's top, its Mexican defenders had started cannonading those men who had begun the climb. Shot and shell came down in a wide sweep about halfway down the slope, too far from the nearest climbers to be of immediate danger to them but setting up a curtain of destruction for them to run into.

There were Indianans and other volunteer units all over the hill, some charging upwards with a kind of inflamed abandon, others proceeding cautiously. John, running side by side with Morgan, chose the latter course and steadied Morgan into taking it with him.

"Over there!" John shouted, as the sweeping fire came in their direction, closer now as they climbed higher. He pointed to a nearby configuration of large rocks, a natural barricade, and practically commanded Morgan to get behind it.

Morgan turned a white face, frozen in expression toward him, obeyed the order, stumbling toward the rocks. It occurred to John that the other man's earlier headlong rush up the hill might have been an effort to get himself heroically killed as much as anything else. There was a panicked look in Morgan's eyes as he fastened them on the men still charging up the hill ahead of him.

The shells now exploding around John's ears added impetus to his soaring rage. He tugged. Morgan tugged. Slowly but surely, with all four Regulars, now pushing it from behind, the big gun came up to the top of the ledge and got on relatively flat ground.

When the gun was free to roll on, John and Morgan stood to one side, breathing hard from their exertions. At that point, a Mexican shell landed nearby, exploding into fragments. Wincing, John shouted at the Regulars, "For God's sake, shoot the damn thing!"

"Not at this range, friend," one of them said. "Thanks. We'll leave the rope where it is. We might need it up ahead. Look to your man."

They left, rolling the gun swiftly now. They went uphill some distance and then, under John's intent gaze, did indeed operate the gun, lofting one, two, then a third shell toward the emplacement. The balls landed close enough to disconcert the Mexican defenders. There was a let-up in the shooting at the infantrymen in the field. Most of them took advantage of the respite by moving up closer to their goal.

John breathed a sigh of victory. At least, he and Morgan had contributed that much. He thought about helping to get other artillery pieces moved.

All of this happened before what the Regular had said finally registered on him. *Look to your man?* He spun around and saw Morgan sitting on the ground. He had an odd smile on his face, a sort of rueful pucker at the corner of his mouth.

"Bell, I think I been hit," he said.

"*Agh*, you're crazy. You look fine to me. Come on, I'll give you a hand up and we'll get us some more boom-booms."

He started Morgan's way, but Morgan waved him off.

"No, no, I been hit. That shell that landed before? Something whumped me in the back. I think it was a piece of it. I feel like I'm bleeding all over the place back there."

John went behind Morgan and took a look. There was a fist-size hole in the muscle area to the right of the spine, barely covered by Morgan's holed and tattered shirt. The raw meat blotch, imbedded with tiny pieces of metal, brought bile to John's throat. There was a small thick pool of blood on the ground near Morgan's rump and John took a look at that.

"How do you feel?" he asked.

He couldn't see Morgan's face but he heard his answer clear.

"Weak," he said. "Like I got nothing inside me. But you know, Bell, I don't think I ever had anything inside me. It was all out there, you know what I mean? I'm mighty glad we helped haul that gun up. I had me some fun. That fellow who told you to get out of the way when all you was doing was trying to help . . . wasn't he a pisser?" Morgan laughed, shaking his head.

"It's nasty, this," John said, crouching to examine the wound more closely. "I'd better see if I can get some help."

He was getting up to do that while Morgan went on speaking his thoughts. "The only thing is, I didn't get a hard-on. Felt strong as all get-out pulling up that gun, but it ain't the same thing. . . ."

"You wait right here," John said sternly. "I'll be right back."

"I ain't going nowhere," Morgan said irritably. There came a sudden look of fright in his eyes. "Hey, Bell! I'm getting awfully sleepy. I think I might be dying. Wouldn't that be something? Me dying now . . . ? Hurry back, will you?"

John started off, only to hear Morgan's tired voice call after him. "Hey, Bell, forget that. C'mere and hold my hand."

He retraced his steps and found Morgan dead.

This was the extent of John Bell's active participation in the Battle of Monterrey. Standing by Morgan's body, he saw the ultimate capture of Federacion's gun emplacement by men braver than he, aided by the bombardment of artillery that managed to get up the hill without his further help. He never saw the Mexican fort over the hill, which was called El Soldado. Hours later, he was to hear that it too had been taken, in what turned out to be a combined action shared by the Fifth Infantry Regulars, who attacked it from the further slope, and men who captured the hilltop emplacement and turned its guns down on the fort, decimating its defenders.

Three days later, John was to hear that the city of Monterrey itself had been taken, as planned, by the nutcracker forces put into play by Worth from the west and Taylor from the northeast.

John participated no longer because, standing by Morgan's body, he felt himself dissolving inside, bleeding in spirit as he had seen the other man bleeding in body. What he did was walk back down the hill, wade the river and report to a medical tent that had been set up in the camp the volunteer regiments had left. No doubt he had a peculiar expression on his face.

An American doctor, a civilian, greeted him. "What's the matter, soldier? You hurt? Climb up on this table and I'll have a look at you."

"I'm not hurt," John said. He pointed vaguely toward the hill from which came the sounds of warfare. "There's a man dead up there."

The doctor looked at him sharply. "You're hurt," he said.

"I guess I am," John admitted.

The doctor looked swiftly around the tent. Several wounded men had already stumbled or been carried down the hill. There would be scores more later. He was there alone to tend them.

"I can't help you much," he said. "I wish I could but I can't. War's hell. Does that help?"

"It's all in the mind. I put myself through hell."

"With no help at all from what you must have seen on the hill?" The doctor studied John a moment, then whistled. "I admire your arrogance. In any event, I can use a hand bandaging some of these people." He looked at John questioningly.

John shook his head. "I don't think I can do that now."

The doctor nodded. "All right. Go outside and take it easy. There are some cots out there. Lie down if you wish. As I say, there's not much I can do for shock, which is what you appear to be in right now, but I'll come out and see how you are when I can."

"Thanks. I'll do that," John said.

He went outside but did not lie down. He took a walk into the trees instead. At that time, the shelling of the fort El Soldado was taking place on the other side of the hill. He could hear the muted roar of the big guns, so far away now that he could all-too-easily imagine himself being there, a hero. But he hadn't taken that route; he'd taken another. He didn't know how he felt about what he'd done—which was to quit, despite his announced intentions to Wallace, to all and sundry, to himself.

All he could think of right now was that he'd lost

a friend. With a man named Joe Morgan, whom he'd hardly known, he'd briefly shared common fears, common concerns and, in the end, one simple deed that was of help and was at the limit of their capacities to perform. With Morgan dead, he hadn't wanted to do any more. He just hadn't.

He didn't go back to talk things over with the doctor; he didn't see the point of it. What was there to talk about? The confusion in his head while other men, true heroes, were coming down the hill with smashed bodies that really needed attention? No, he would go home now. Somehow, once there, he'd clear up his life, get his values straight. Nothing he'd seen of the war in Mexico made much sense to him.

He looked toward the distant roar of battle one last time. He wondered about this El Soldado, this fort he could not see, that was now being shelled into oblivion. He wondered if Americans of the San Patricio Battalion were there to defend it. He wondered if Dooey Dolan was there. Later, John was to be told by the Fifth Infantry Regulars who captured the fort that, yes, San Patricios had indeed been in the fort and had fought them valiantly to the end, but that nobody named Dolan had been among the killed or captured.

So John went home not knowing what had become of Dooey Dolan in Mexico. It mattered to him, not knowing. It mattered to him in a less passionate way than it was to matter to him later, but it mattered to him nevertheless. Because Dooey was his friend, a friend of long standing, almost a brother. If Dooey had gone astray, that was all right. He too had gone astray, lost his way in Mexico. He could only hope that wherever Dooey had gone he had made things better for himself than John had.

13

WITH DOOEY, TOO, it was a matter of finding a job in Mexico and trying to make good at it. The difference was that his job came naturally and easily to him whereas John's had not. Maria was a prize to Dooey. She was all the world to him. His job, as he saw it, was to love her, please her, play with her, lift her from the doldrums of the deep and obscure grievance she carried about wtih her wherever she went.

It seemed to him she had placed an impossible faith in the goodness and virtue of the Mexican overlords—notably Santa Anna—who, in the course of destroying the big, bad monsters from the north, would somehow redeem her.

But she was just an Indian girl, who was beautiful and all the world to him. He wanted to correct her misapprehensions about Santa Anna. Santa Anna was evil, a creature of greed and viciousness, a seeker after political power whose call to arms of the Mexican people was, first, the equivalent of dumping shit on them, then, second, certain to lead them to a battlefield slaughterhouse. If Dooey saw the American warlords—notably President Polk—in the same light, it did not enhance his feeling for the Mexican.

Dooey saw himself as Maria's redeemer—and her as his. She lifted him out of the bitter present of the war and out of the bitter memories of the past that had rankled him most of his life. She put him in the way of tenderness.

He was not defending El Soldado when John Bell thought he might be; he was nowhere near Monterrey. Despite John's fears, he was no pushover for some little Indian girl eager to use him as a hired gun in some ridiculous cause. He was fighting love's battle and, so far, he was winning it.

Maria had changed.

They were somewhere in the Sierra Madres, on a green-topped plateau, about a hundred miles south of Monterrey. They were camped for the night. Tomorrow they would move still further south toward Maria's village. Already Dooey was beginning to see that village as home, a permanent one for them both.

The "they" included Carlos, Juan and Florita, who had retired to tents they had set up against the weather, which here in the mountains was temperate, if on the chilly side. There was no war here. Dooey and Maria were alone together, poking sticks in the fire. But then they were always alone together in those early days, with eyes only for each other.

"Do you remember," Maria said, "when you went to Fort Texas that night and brought your gun back to Matamoros? And I said, 'Why do you have your gun if you do not intend to fight for us?' Do you remember what you said?"

Dooey smiled. "To shoot little birds with."

Maria giggled. "I suppose you meant me—if I didn't behave."

Dooey shrugged. "Maybe, but I like to hunt doves and quail too . . . that's to keep you guessing."

"I love you, Dooey."

"Why is that?"

"Oh, I don't know . . ." Maria made a gesture of helplessness. "I suppose it's because you're so bright and clever and . . . and so earthy and sensual." She looked at him, sloe-eyed. "My goodness, I never met anyone as earthy as you. The things you say and do when we make love!"

Dooey cocked his head at her. "Maria, where did you learn words like 'earthy and sensual'? In fact, where did you learn English in the first place?"

"Didn't I tell you?" she said with surprised innocence.

Dooey said wryly, "You told me *something* about it, and much else about yourself that I've come not to believe."

Maria bit her lip. "The nuns taught me—in Mexico City. We had American nuns teaching us when I was in school. That was when relations were good—were better, I mean, between our countries."

Dooey nodded. "That makes sense. And which family sent you to that school? I mean, which of all those families who adopted you?"

Maria blushed. "There was only one family, Dooey. The Rincons . . . the first family I mentioned. They were good to me."

Dooey looked at her. "You mean, you lied about the others? You made all that up?"

Maria looked away. "I—I didn't know you then, Dooey. I wanted you to think that I had had . . . well, many more adventures than was actually true."

Dooey snorted. "You mean you wanted me to feel sorry for you. Raped by this one, cast out into the streets by that one! Well, you know, it worked! I really did feel sorry for you. But you didn't have to go to all that trouble to—"

"Didn't I, Dooey?" Maria said softly.

"Of course not!" Dooey said. "Why should you pretend to be someone you're not?"

Maria smiled. "And you, Dooey? Why have you been pretending about yourself?"

Dooey looked at her puzzled.

"When I first saw you standing by the river in Matamoros," Maria continued, "I thought you were the gloomiest-looking man I had ever seen in my life. I did not want to meet you. I thought you would be ob—ob—"

"Obnoxious," Dooey supplied for her.

"*Si*, obnoxious."

"Well, I am obnoxious—or can be," Dooey said. "You just don't know me well enough yet."

"No." Maria looked at him; her features, in the shadows of the flickering firelight, looked soft and warm. "To me you are not obnoxious. You could never be. You are what you are, Dooey Dolan, a kind man and a gentle one."

Something caught in Dooey's throat, something akin to pleasure. He said, his voice husky, "Oh, go on with ye . . ."

"Oh, Dooey!" She mussed his hair.

"It's just something me sainted dumb father would have said," Dooey muttered. "But I ain't him," he added quickly, dropping the Irish brogue and the sentiment that went with it. "And whatever it is you're up to now, you can't get to me that way, Maria!"

Maria only smiled at him.

With Carlos, Dooey found the opportunity for some good hardheaded discussions about the war. Once removed from the shackles of his uniform and its never-wanted obligations (Dooey was now wearing lightweight white clothing and a straw hat borrowed from Juan) he had become a more-or-less detached student of the perfidy of war.

There were many villages along their southerly route. From their residents, Carlos got rumors and facts of the war's development and translated them for Dooey's benefit. It was clear that Carlos liked Dooey and enjoyed talking to him.

"*Amigo*," he reported one morning, on his return from one such visit to a town, "it is said we have suffered a disastrous defeat at the hands of your General Taylor. Your army has taken Monterrey."

"Fine. Try to keep the news from Maria," Dooey said drily.

"Ah, *amigo*, would I do anything to spoil our journey home?" Carlos grinned. Neither man relished the vision of the tantrum Maria might be expected to have upon hearing of the Mexican defeat.

Carlos grew sober. "There were many men killed on both sides, *señor*. It is a shame, a waste of life, for nothing has been gained through the American victory. There is no peace in sight. Your General Taylor has gone on to Saltillo, where it is said he once more does nothing. He sits and he waits. Waits for what, *señor*?"

"I don't know," Dooey said, "but I can guess. You

see, Carlos, General Taylor would like to be the next American president. But Mr. Polk, who is president, does not wish General Taylor to be the next president; he merely wishes him to hurry up and win battles. But every time General Taylor does win a battle—as you say he did at Monterrey—the American people are loudly informed of this victory by members of General Taylor's political party, which increases his chances of becoming our next president. So then President Polk orders him not to hurry up and win battles so fast. I suppose that is why General Taylor now sits and waits at Saltillo. In a manner of speaking, he does not know if he is to be promoted or fired from his job."

Carlos frowned. "What an unfortunate state of affairs, *señor*. This is the time for the Americans to end the war. If they do not, General Santa Anna will have his army formed, and then many, many more men will die."

"What's Old One Leg up to?" Dooey said. "Anything in these parts?"

Carlos hesitated. "To the town I have just come from, *señor*, Santa Anna has sent men to procure peasants for his army, as well as donations of money from the church. Many men have already left the town to join him in Mexico City."

Dooey nodded grimly. "Santa Anna is able to do this, Carlos, through the cooperation of our President Polk, who helped restore him to power in the first place."

Carlos looked puzzled, and Dooey went on to tell him what he knew about the secret deal Polk and Santa Anna had made—a deal which the latter had now, apparently, irrevocably betrayed.

It turned out that it was only the details of this private arrangement that Carlos was puzzled about. When Dooey finished, he said sadly, "Yes, it is the way with heads of states. They make arrangements between themselves by which they can hope to keep or get power. I am not surprised that Santa Anna has not kept his part of the bargain. There will be more glory for him in Mexico through continuing the war than if he had asked for peace."

The discussion left both men a trifle downcast. What Dooey and Carlos shared was the feeling that they were men without a country, renunciators and repudiators of their governments who had no alternative but to avoid the conflict altogether. Except that, in Dooey's case, he was not without guilty feelings—which compounded his frustration and led him to complain to Carlos:

"You'd think Maria would see it the way we do."

"Ah, Maria." Carlos shrugged. "She is a woman."

"What's that supposed to mean?"

"She does not see with her eyes, *amigo*. She feels the war—here." He pointed to his stomach.

"If that's the case, her stomach is pretty damned empty, if you ask me," Dooey said. "She hasn't the foggiest notion of what—"

"There is a way to fill a woman's stomach, *señor*." Carlos grinned at him. "Perhaps, if you do this, Maria would rest more content and we would all have more peace."

Dooey just looked at him.

The small procession moved on. The further south they got, the freer Dooey felt to enter the towns they passed, since the risk of there being any American scouts in them decreased. He also felt more and more expansive as they neared Maria's home, which he envisioned as a hidden, placid valley where—with Carlos's help—he might build houses for them all and learn to farm. He was good with his hands. Already designs for two houses were taking shape in his mind, one for Maria and himself, the other for the rest of the family. It would be good for Florita to be nearby; Maria would have someone to talk to while Dooey, Carlos and Juan were out working in the fields.

There was the prospect of excitement in these towns for Dooey, and he'd ask Maria along to share it with him. Which she did—up to a point. What stimulated Dooey was, perhaps, just the newness of the places they visited—new to him, at any rate. Most every day was a saint's day, or some other holiday, it seemed, with men and women in sequin-spangled clothing dancing in the streets at night amidst bursting firecrackers. Dooey felt like a boy again, just watching. Maria, more familiar with such Mexican recreations, was patient with him.

"You'd look great in one of those costumes," Dooey told her as they watched a dance one night. They didn't have any money to buy one. "I'll steal you one and we'll dance."

"Hmmph! You want me to be a strumpet and you a thief?"

But her eyes twinkled, and he could tell she enjoyed the flattering comment. "I'm just kidding," Dooey said. "Let's go take in one of those churches you like."

Dooey too liked the churches—up to a point. Their insides were encrusted with gold, which incited his awe and his greed. But ultimately he found the atmosphere in the churches oppressive.

Maria's eyes, however, shone with religious fervor. Once, when they'd left a church and were walking arm-in-arm down the town's cobblestoned street towards the *zocalo*, she said, "When I have a son, he will grow up to be a priest."

"A priest!"

Maria cocked her head. "Well, if not a priest, a general, an honor to his country."

Dooey groaned. "Maria, please, spare me. It's a beautiful night . . . let's just walk."

"And what is wrong with having a general for a son, pray?"

"I'd rather he start off just being a baby!"

They reached the *zocalo*, the same sort of promenade surrounding a park that soldiers like John Bell had marched past in other towns, under less romantic circumstances.

They found a bench along the promenade to sit on. Other arm-in-arm lovers paraded by. Two or three children were playing in the park, though the hour was late. On other benches, old men and old women, in couples or alone, were watching the children. This was the twilight routine in any Mexican town, and all was quiet and still as it played itself out.

Dooey was brooding, or pretending to. Actually, he was taking in Maria's presence, so throbbingly near him, while at the same time glancing around at the people about him, in their various generations. He was also thinking about the advice Carlos had given him.

"No son of mine is going to be a general," Dooey muttered. "He'd just grow up and boss me around. I wouldn't like that one bit."

Maria laughed. "Oh, I'd never let him do that."

"You wouldn't, huh?" Dooey grinned at her. Suddenly he felt as if something had been resolved between them. He went on, keeping the light bantering tone. "Look, if we have a baby, will that shut you up once and for all? No more boring me with your wild-eyed talk about the war?"

"I do not know what you mean," Maria said, a bit stiffly. And then, quietly, "Do you want to have a baby, Dooey?"

"Well, yes, sure," Dooey said. "See, then we'd have something of our own—just you and me. What more do we need if we have each other and a little tyke to care for? We'll stay at home and raise him and leave this war far behind us."

Maria considered the proposal. "If it's a boy, I want him to be a *fighter*."

"I'll *teach* him to be a fighter," Dooey said. "I'll box his ears when he wets his pants. Anyway, maybe it'll be a girl, in which case I already have a name picked out for her."

"What name is that?" Maria asked.

Dooey looked at her. She was not only at her most beautiful in the soft twilight but looked, with an innocent, expectant expression on her face, as sweet as candy.

"Maria," he said huskily. "Your name."

The upshot of this was that Maria did indeed become pregnant—something that, had it not been for their "understanding," would most likely not have involved any sense of commitment on Dooey's part. It was late in December, some three months later, when Maria told him she thought she was going to have a baby. By then they were living in the outskirts of Maria's village—which was called Juztexco—on just the sort of farm Dooey had dreamt about.

She came running into the fields, ecstatic with the news, and Dooey stopped plowing to listen to her.

"Florita says it will be a boy!" she cried. "Oh, Dooey, I am so proud."

"That's ridiculous," Dooey said. "How can Florita—?" He stopped. You did not argue with Maria's convictions—he'd come to accept that as a maxim for getting along with her. Besides, he was in love with her, perhaps more than ever, and happy for her . . . and for himself. So he stopped questioning Florita's ability to determine the baby's gender and beamed at Maria. Briefly.

"I am going to call him Antonio, after our president!" she cried.

Dooey set up a howl. "You're *what*? After that son of a bitch Santa Anna? Maria, what in God's name is wrong with you?"

Maria looked bewildered, and close to tears for having been yelled at during her moment of joy. "But . . . you didn't say I couldn't! You—you said only what we would name the baby if it was a girl!"

Dooey shook his head wearily. It was true. He hadn't ordered her specifically to eliminate the name of the man she worshipped, her country's leader. How could he have done that? She wouldn't have, couldn't have obeyed him. Dooey knew that much. Instead, he'd avoided the issue altogether, hoping it would just go away.

"I don't care what you call him," he said sarcastically. "You can name him Jesus Christ for all I care. I'll call him for dinner that way."

It was the first argument between them in a long time that did not have a bit of humor in it—at least, none that Maria appreciated. "You are a—a sissy!" she shot at him, then turned and strode back toward their house.

He stared after her, unsmiling. By sissy she meant that he didn't have any balls, that he was a coward. Sissy was a word the nuns had taught her, or that she had found in a book somewhere. She had been calling him that frequently of late. Never mind that he had fathered the child she was bearing. He was a sissy because he hadn't done what he never said he would do: he hadn't gone off like an idiot to fight in Santa Anna's legions. On the other hand, she had done what she had never said she wouldn't do.

Their "understanding" hadn't held up much longer than the romantic twilight they'd had it in. Thinking back, Dooey figured it had lasted about as long as it had taken them to conceive a child. Women, he figured, must know they're pregnant about a second and a half after they get that way. It must be just about three months since she'd started suggesting to him—with a little hint here and there—that he take up arms for her country. Then she'd started baiting him with little stinging remarks about his cowardice. Now her taunting was in full flower.

He hadn't laughed at her choice of the word sissy because he knew that with her it was no joke. It was a way of backing off from the ultimate charge: that not only did he not have balls for her, but that he might have a secret yen for other fellows, like Carlos.

Dooey swore inwardly. The trouble with Maria was that she wasn't just being serious, she was in earnest. God save him from women who were in earnest.

He left the fields to seek out Carlos and talk to him about the predicament they seemed to share. Also he could use a *cerveza* to loosen him up a little bit. It was about noon of a hotter day than usual for December in the mountains. He figured Carlos would likely be in the village's one bar-cafe, on the one dirt highway that passed through it, so he headed that way.

Walking through the countryside, he passed only elderly farmers and a few women and young girls. Most of the younger men had left the village, cajoled southward by Santa Anna's promise of steady army pay given with fervent appeals to their patriotism. Santa Anna, give the devil his due, had a way of saying, "Mexicans! Hear me!" so that they actually stopped and listened to the crap he dumped on them. Posters headed "Mexicans! Hear me!" followed by inflammatory recitals of American wrongs—some of them accurate enough in substance, Dooey had to admit—were plastered all over the village. Even Juan had gone south, for the money offered. Just like his U.S. counterparts, Dooey thought grimly, Santa Anna had something to offer to everybody.

Still, Dooey could not help feeling self-conscious, tight inside, as he passed the oldsters and was largely ignored. One woman did stop him. "Ah, *Señor* Dolan, *buenas dias . . . y hoy com' esta Maria*?"

"She's fine," Dooey said shortly. "She's going to have a baby."

The woman clapped her hands. "Oh, how wonderful!" she said, in Spanish. "You must take good care of her, *Señor* Dolan. She is so small, so fragile—she will need much nursing through the months from you!"

Automatically, Dooey nodded. It would give him great pleasure to gentle Maria through her months of pregnancy—if it turned out that that's what she needed. But then he reacted to the woman's beaming, which was not unmixed with a certain condescension.

"Yes, well, Florita will be doing most of the nursing," Dooey said. "I thank you for your kind wishes, *Señora* Martinez. *Buenas dias.*"

By the time he had the rusty-hinged sign of the bar cafe in sight, Dooey had reset his resolve. For a minute or so after leaving *Señora* Martinez, he'd walked along loose-limbed, almost as if he were wearing a skirt instead of pants, and he hadn't liked the feeling at all. But then he'd found his courage, the courage to hold out against both sides in this war—no matter what Maria and the villagers thought of him, no matter if he was caught and shot by the U.S. as a traitor. It was just going to be tough, that's all. It wouldn't hurt to get a little moral support from Carlos, who alone in Huatexco seemed to wholeheartedly share his views.

As Dooey came up to the bar-cafe's swinging door he stopped, suddenly rigid. From inside came loud laughter and unfamiliar voices raucously demanding barkeep Miguel's attention. The requests were in American-accented Spanish. Dooey stepped quickly to the alley at the side of the place and spied a half-dozen horses, a couple with U.S. Army insignia on their saddles.

He didn't know what to do. He could run, though the laughter he heard somehow didn't seem appropriate to a U.S. posse looking for deserters. Besides, Huatexco was too far south and off the beaten track for such a posse. You always imagined things when you were on the run. On the other hand they could be scouts. The word from Carlos was that Taylor had scouts all the way down to Mexico City, feeling out the territory for what might come from it in the way of a massive enemy troop movement. It would be safe for scouts to have a drink here; there was no Mexican military and hardly an able-bodied man around to interfere with them.

Scouts or posse, Dooey saw himself in equal jeopardy if he didn't leave and hide out before they saw him. In the end, however, his curiosity got the better of his judgment—or maybe it was just his longing to see an American face again. Anyway, he was equipped now with an easy way to disguise himself. He'd grown a thin black mustache, was deeply tanned and had on a straw sombrero. He pulled the sombrero down over his eyes and slouched into the cafe.

Miguel, with a cheerful greeting, blew Dooey's disguise the moment he set foot in the doorway. "*Señor* Dolan, it is you. You are just the *hombre* these *gringos* are looking for."

A flash of fear stabbed through Dooey's temples. He cursed Miguel for a fool or, worse, his wilful betrayer. He turned on the instant, ready to bolt.

A dark face at a table, one of several Dooey hadn't seen clearly, emitted a chuckle. "Hey, slow down, there. We ain't gonna eat you. We ain't even gonna nibble at you."

The man's tone worked wonders on Dooey. One minute he was fleeing for his life; the next, he had stopped and was muttering inwardly, "Oh, shit." He knew now, if not who the men were, what they were and even what they had come for.

He turned. The man who had called to him from the table, who Dooey could see now had a livid scar on his right cheek, was still laughing.

"You run like a bat out of hell, boy. But not nearly so fast as I would have run if I was you and thought I was someone I ain't. Name's Riley, Dolan. Good to meet an Irish *gringo* like myself."

Dooey shrugged. "I've heard about you."

Riley nodded. "Sure you have. I'm famous. Do they still talk about me up Matamoros way?"

"Don't know. Haven't been there in a while," Dooey replied.

Riley said, "From the looks of things, you weren't at Monterrey either. Well, that's all right. In fact, that's fine. No sense getting yourself killed for nothing. Come on, sit down and have a drink with us. This here's Gallagher. That's Ryan . . . O'Brien, and McShane. The last one down is Knecht. We sort of let Knecht hang around with us."

Dooey nodded at them all. He took note that they were wearing civilian clothes, western style. "Somehow, I thought that if I ever ran into a bunch of San Patricios, they'd be wearing Mexican uniforms. You're in their army, aren't you?"

"Mmmm-hmmm." Riley lit a cigar and puffed it before speaking. "At least, you know who we are. We're kind of on vacation, Dolan. Things are at a standstill right now, and we thought we'd just come up here and—"

"Uh-uh," Dooey cut in. "You're on no vacation. If you rode all the way up here, it's because you heard there was a *gringo* here you might be able to enlist. I can tell you right now you've got the wrong *gringo*."

He sat with them nevertheless. He thought he might just have a conversation with them, that it wouldn't hurt him to do that. It had been a long time since he had spoken American to anybody. He never thought of himself as speaking American to Maria or Carlos; he spoke English to them—there was a difference.

Only when he sat did he notice Carlos at a far table, sipping a *cerveza*, watching him, as if wondering what he was up to with these soldiers. He wasn't up to anything. He winked at Carlos.

Riley didn't seem to notice. "Hell, we ain't come that far. We're in San Luis Potosi now. Santa Anna and us, we'll be up this way in no more'n a month." He dropped the conversational tone now and leaned forward: "You're right, Dolan. We do want you. Some peons came down from this village and told us you were the best damn shot they ever seen. We want all the good shots we can get. Besides, there's more to it than that—"

"What do you mean?" Dooey said.

"There's yourself," Riley said. "And us. I don't know how you feel about us, Dolan. Maybe all I want to do right now is sound you out about that. I hate to see a good Catholic confused about where he belongs."

Dooey didn't say anything; he was amused more than anything else.

"You ain't saying you're not a Catholic, are you?" Riley said. "You ain't saying you're an Orangeman Protestant, are you?"

Dooey shook his head. "Get to the point, Riley."

"That *is* the point," Riley said. "You don't think I came over to the Mexican side just for a handful of pesos, do you, Dolan? I ain't no mercenary. I put in fifteen good years with the U.S. Army and would've stayed where I was exceptin' my eyes got opened. Didn't it blast your gut to see what they were doing to us up in the States? A man's a Catholic, he can't get a good job. He tries to set up in his own neighborhood, live in peace there—like we did in Philadelphia couple years ago—and they come at us with brickbats and burn our houses down. I saw what happened in Philadelphia, Dolan; I was there on leave, visiting a sister, when those damn Protestant bastards came at us. I busted a few heads on me own. But I figured it was an isolated thing, you know? Or even if things were just about as bad in New York and other places, I figured it would blow over. Then I came down here to fight this damned war, and I seen what Polk and them others wants. They want to blow away a whole Catholic country that's on their border. That's the plan. Well, I ain't standing for no such plan, and you hadn't ought to either."

Riley spoke with a passionate intensity. All the time Dooey had been listening, he'd been thinking.

"What you mean, Riley," he said slowly, "is that if I'm not with you, I'm against you, isn't that it? You're making a point that doesn't happen to be my point, but that doesn't matter to you. If I don't join up with you, then you think I might find me some U.S. scouts and sign on as a spy for them. I might count up your troops when they come through here, or take a pot-shot at Santa Anna . . . something like that."

"No tellin' what you'd do," Riley growled.

"And if I tell you I want no part of either you or them, you're just not going to believe me," Dooey went on. "So this is a threat. Show I'm a good little Catholic by traipsing off to war with you—or else. You'll take no chances, right?"

Riley eyed him coldly. "You are one smug bastard, Dolan. I ought to put a bullet in you just for that. You got us wrong. You've come this far. You're not with Taylor's army, you're here. How you got here I don't give a damn. I think you're running—just running. I'm giving you a chance to quit running, to act like a man and join up with us, because, like I say, we can use your gun. It's up to you. Think about it."

Dooey shook his head. "I've thought about it."

"Think about it some more. Take a good look at yourself, the way you came shambling in here before, all scrunched up with that hat pulled down. You know who you reminded me of? A deserter we called

Old Trapper Luke, up by Matamoros. He didn't want no part of this war either, just thought he'd hide out. Last time I saw him, he was just running plumb loco in the desert. Could happen to you. A man's got to make his choices."

Dooey remembered Old Trapper Luke. A picture of the fellow's meaningless death in the desert came to his mind. He didn't see fit to mention it to Riley.

"Thanks," he said. "Thanks for the warning."

"That's not good enough," Riley said. "Look, I've had my say. We'll be back up here in a month. You can join us then, or not, as you see fit. Forget about it for now. Let me buy you a beer."

14

DOOEY THOUGHT ABOUT IT some more in ensuing days. But he remained at sixes and sevens. He'd liked Riley, had found him tough, cagey . . . enviable even, in that he had a cause he believed in. The trouble was that it wasn't Dooey's cause. All he wanted was to be left alone to love Maria. But not even Maria would leave him alone now to love Maria.

Dooey wondered if he wasn't going loco at that. He went home to Maria after the San Patricios had left town and made the mistake of telling her they'd been there, soliciting his enlistment.

"Good!" Maria beamed at him. "That's because Juan told them how good you are with a gun. And you joined?"

Dooey frowned. "Wait a minute. Juan told them? You mean you told Juan, before he left, to tell them I was—? You mean *you* sent them after me?"

"I did," Maria said proudly. "You don't speak well of yourself. You never speak well of yourself. I had to do it for you—through Juan."

Dooey swallowed hard. "Maria, you must be out of your mind. You had no business doing that. You know how I feel about this war. I don't want to fight in it."

"You did not *like* the San Patricios?" She sneered at him. "Just as you like no one else, except old women like Carlos?"

Dooey took a deep breath. "Maria, I liked the men who came here. They were fun to have a beer with. But I don't want to go off and fight with them. I want to stay here with you. I love you."

"Ha! I doubt that you are capable of loving anybody! If you loved me, you would fight for me—for me and our son!"

It was a battle Dooey could not win. He wanted to slap Maria and kiss her at the same time. They were equal impulses; he barely controlled himself from doing either. They stood and glared at each other.

"There's something wrong here," Dooey said finally, his voice faltering. "We're behaving badly."

A gleam came into Maria's eye, either out of a sense of victory or out of the desire that he continue to challenge her. It was as if she liked this fight. Dooey didn't. He felt saddened, rejected by her.

He roused himself as she continued to glare at him. "I'm going to stay with Carlos until you calm down," he said. "There's got to be a way we can work things out between us."

It still felt like a marital spat to Dooey, something that would blow over. It was the way his parents used to fight when he was a small boy—his mother savagely, unfairly, his father buckling under the strain, withdrawing in his anger, yet coming back sooner or later to renew their bitter love. It was a terrible way to live, yet it was the way Dooey knew. Things would blow over; they always did.

Until the bitterest of ends.

There was something in Dooey that wanted to ward off the ultimate catastrophe, like the one that had overcome his parents. Something wrong had to be made right. He sure as hell wasn't going to go out and get drunk. If he got drunk, he might go back and belt Maria. His father had never belted his mother, to the best of Dooey's recollection; he had other ways of "getting even" with her. But there was such a rage in Dooey that he thought he might belt Maria if his temper were loosened by alcohol. So he wasn't going to get drunk.

He went over to Carlos's place—and got drunk.

"Carlos," he said, midway in their consumption of a keg of beer. "There's got to be a revolution. Everybody's got to change—me, you, Maria—everybody."

"*Si, amigo*," Carlos nodded. He had an anything-you-say look on his face.

"We're all slaves, don't you see that? Me, you, Maria—everybody. You know what we're slaves to? Something that's old and rotten."

"*Es verdado, señor*."

Dooey, nodding, went on. "Don't make any difference what you call it. Call it Polk, call it Santa Anna, call it mama or papa. It's anything that's evil 'n ignorant 'n old 'n gets us to do what we don't wanna do. Had this fight with Maria . . . didn't want to have it, had it anyway. Coulda killed her . . . coulda killed the baby. . . ."

Carlos shook his head. "You would not do that, *señor*. But I am sorry."

" 'Sall right," Dooey said importantly. "I'll straighten things out with Maria. First, I'll piss. Then I'll straighten things out with Maria. Don't go away, Carlos. Be right back."

He went out back behind Carlos's shack and emptied his bladder. Standing there, looking out at the fields, he got dizzy. The fields were green, rolling and empty. Most everyone had gone away . . . to the war. It was evening and it was cold in the mountains, cold enough to make him shiver as he peed.

When he came back, Carlos changed the subject, or seemed to.

"Are you going to join the San Patricios, *señor*?" he said quietly.

"No," Dooey said shortly.

"Maria will not give you any peace until you do. You speak of change. It is not that I do not understand you—I understand you, for I know of oppression and live with it. But it is you who must change, *señor*. Maria will not."

He spoke as if he knew.

"You're wrong," Dooey said doggedly. "There must be a way to reason with her, to show her where her true interest lies. We're going to have a baby, Carlos. . . ."

He wanted to hold onto Maria, at all costs; he didn't want to let her go.

"No, Maria will not change," Carlos repeated. "The power to change may be in you, *señor*, but it is not in Maria. Not now, perhaps never. It is the man who must hold the power for Maria, for she does not have it in herself, and you are not that man, *señor*."

"Who is it, then?" Dooey shot at him.

"That is not important, *señor*. It is not you." Carlos looked sad. "We drink now," he said, "and the drink loosens my tongue. I told you before that I was sorry, and now I will tell you why. I made a mistake, *señor*. When you first came to us in Matamoros, when I saw you fight your own people on Maria's behalf, I—and Florita too—thought you would be able to take care of Maria. She is the child in our little family—you must understand that. We wished her to be cared for and protected by whomever she might choose as a lover. We thought that you would wish to do that."

"I do!" Dooey exploded. "That's why I came here—to care for and protect her."

"No." Carlos shook his head. "We were deceived into believing that was so. You can be quite charming, *señor*, quite the *caballero*. Please, let me continue. You see, it was not even our Maria that you came here with, it was the Maria of the moonlight—of your imaginings. You do not love Maria, you wish to own the moonlight. This you cannot do, *señor*. It will slip between your fingers."

"Carlos, I don't know what you're talking about," Dooey muttered thickly.

"I think you do, *señor*."

Dooey remained silent.

"You speak to me of oppression, *señor*, of this war you hate so much. Many times you have told me that we are ruled by people who do not care about us, who would see us die for their betterment. I listen. I say little. I believe what you say, *señor*, but you do not have to tell me this. I have told you I know oppression, yet the oppression I know is not the oppression you know. I do not enjoy sitting in Miguel's bar and being viewed as an old woman afraid to go to war. I do not enjoy suffering indignities in silence. Yet, what else can I do now? I would like to be stronger in myself than I am, then I would like to find friends with whom I might seek a way to free us of our oppressors. Santa Anna is not the first, as you know. He is only the latest.

"But, you, *señor*—" and now Carlos finished what he had to say "—you are oppressed differently. You are oppressed by your need to possess the moonlight." He smiled. "You are a romantic, *amigo*. I am a peon. It is not easy for us to speak with each other."

Dooey looked morose. His mind was wandering. "Maria said I couldn't love anybody."

"Perhaps that is true. I do not know. Perhaps it is Maria who cannot be loved. Perhaps one can be fond of her—as I am fond of her, as we are all fond of our *chicita*—but perhaps she cannot be loved."

Dooey gritted his teeth. "I don't believe that. All I wanted was to have a drink with you, Carlos."

Carlos studied him. He recognized, finally, someone who could not be saved from great hurt.

"Be of good cheer, *amigo*. We are drinking. All's well with the world."

It was, ultimately, Santa Anna himself who figured in Dooey Dolan's joining Riley's San Patricio Battalion. Not Dooey, not Carlos in his wisdom could have predicted the incident that followed a few short weeks later. Not in its enraging detail.

But it was as if the event, with its thunderbolt force to shatter Dooey's moonlit vision of Maria, had been there all the while in his destiny, needing only to be played out for Dooey to be driven in cold, empty fury to fight for any damn side in the war that wanted him; to become what it had always been in him to become—given the right triggering circumstance—a hired killer.

Dooey tried to patch up his argument with Maria, continuing to think of it in the terms of a simple marital misunderstanding.

"I love you and I need you," he told her. "Why are we fighting like this? It's foolish—we're both being foolish. Maria, listen to me. If I thought a Mexican victory in this war would help you and your people, I'd do what you've been asking me to do—I'd join the San Patricios in a flash, wearing your banner on my sleeve. I mean it. But win or lose the war, your lot will be the same. The lash on the poor will go on. I say let the army come and go. It'll be gone in a day and I'll keep working the farm for the good life we have here in the mountains—for you, me and the baby we're going to have."

She taunted him. This was after Dooey returned from his brief stay with Carlos. Florita had gone and the two were alone in the house Dooey had built for them, hardly speaking to each other until Dooey tried breaking the ice.

"Florita thinks you are so clever with your talk," Maria sneered. "She calls you Zorro, the fox. I call you Zero. If you love me so much, why don't you show me that you do?"

She stood before him, hands on her hips, challenging him with her sex.

Dooey swore. "How the hell can I make love to you if you stand there hating me? You're beautiful, you're desirable, is that what you want to know? Only I don't want you right now—I want to straighten out our lives."

"I do not hate you," Maria said coldly. "I feel sorry for you, as I would for any weak and spineless thing.

But I do not hate you. You are beneath my hatred."

As ugly as this little scene had been, Dooey clung stubbornly to his belief that he could win Maria's heart again. The villagers had arranged a fete to honor the arrival of Santa Anna's forces, due in a matter of days now to break their journey northward with an overnight stay in Huatexco. Already the high road had been festooned with green-and-white Mexican flags and banners, and the local padre was having a special stand built in front of Miguel's bar-cafe from which to bless the general and his staff with holy water. It had been arranged that the troops would camp out in the fields; General Santa Anna himself would sleep in a private flag-draped tent erected for him near the church. There was also to be a midnight Mass celebrated at the church with Santa Anna in attendance.

Dooey hadn't planned to attend the welcoming ceremonies. Now he decided he would. It was a complicated thing with him. He wanted to see Santa Anna if only to hate in person rather than as an abstract the man who had become a major irritant in his personal life. At the same time he told himself that Maria, after all, was entitled to whatever feelings of glory her idol's proximity might afford her. Besides, maybe just the sight of Santa Anna might pacify her, get her off the one track she was on in her mind, so that she'd let up on Dooey for a while. But to achieve the last required a special effort on his part. Accordingly, he made that effort.

"I've changed my mind about not going with you to see the army," he said. "There's no need for you to suffer embarrassment because of my not being there. I like a good parade. I'll cheer along with everybody else. Here. I thought you might like this."

Abruptly he handed her a sequin-beaded white veil he'd bought from a peddler who'd come from San Luis Potisi, in the van of the army, to supply the village women with costume jewelry and the like for the honoring ceremonies. "I thought afterward we might go to the Mass together," Dooey said, by way of explaining the purpose of his gift.

Maria took the veil, her eyes gleaming. Obviously she liked the gift, but her feelings about accepting it remained—just as obviously—mixed.

"Thank you, it's beautiful," she said. "But you do not have to come with me if you do not wish to. I am perfectly capable of going by myself."

"I know you are," Dooey said steadily. "But I'd like to go with you anyway."

Maria sighed. "I cannot stop you. But please don't spoil the day for me, Dooey, promise me that."

She said it as if she were speaking to a small skirt-clinging child she would have preferred to have out of her way. Dooey, in his devotion, chose to ignore the tone.

"It's all right," he said. "It'll be fine."

It was a strange day all around. There was snow on the ground when Dooey awoke and more flakes falling. It was December 11, 1846. It was the first time Dooey had seen snow in Mexico. Awaking groggily, seeing it through the window—noting that the evergreen just outside was already blanketed with it—reminded him that Christmas would soon be here. He felt sad somehow, without knowing why. Maria was still asleep beside him. It took him a few moments to rouse himself, to realize that not Christmas but the Mexican army was due to arrive in Huatexco that day and that he should be thinking of how much

Maria was looking forward to the spectacle rather than dwelling on his own sadness.

So he nudged her awake, though it was still dawn. "Hey," he said, forcing some gaiety into his voice. "Time to get up. Santa Anna's coming! Santa Anna's coming!"

The moment he said it, he regretted it. He hadn't been able to keep the condescension, the mockery out of his voice. Yet he hadn't wanted to hurt her—he swore to himself that he hadn't wanted to hurt her. He'd only been taking a little nip at her for taking this day so God damn much more seriously than he could.

Supercilious, arrogant Dooey Dolan. He cursed himself for a fool.

Maria got up. They treated each other as if they were walking on eggshells. He watched her put on her best dress, the one dress she saved for going to church in, and the beaded veil he had given her.

"How do I look?" she asked. "You look gorgeous," he said grudgingly. "You always look gorgeous, no matter what you wear. I'll go get Carlos. It's a long walk to the village. We should get started soon."

Something was very wrong, Dooey knew. Maria had had such a determined air about her that morning, something that left him out completely. He felt very insecure without knowing why. Something was in the wind that he didn't know about. The wind itself, with the snow in it, was very cold. It was also numbing. He got to Carlos's house and found both him and Florita ready to take the long walk in to see the Mexican army.

Carlos winked at him as if they were conspirators of a sort, a couple of outcasts who would watch the passing military parade with a shared cool detachment.

Florita, however, had a word for Dooey. "Do not mind what you may see Maria do today, *señor*. She is only a child. She needs someone to adore."

"Jesus Christ, what's she going to do—kiss Santa Anna's feet?" Dooey exploded. "I don't care if she kisses his feet, I just want this damn day over and done with!"

Florita looked at him sharply. "Say nothing, *señor*. This day let Maria be."

It was advice that, later that day, Dooey was to find hard to follow.

They returned to get Maria, then all four trudged down through the mountain snow to the high road. Towards noon all the villagers were lining the road, craning their necks, looking expectantly south. Dooey looked with them. The road came uphill and Dooey was as curious as everybody else to see what would loom up out of the snow-flaked mist.

The cold, snow-enshrouded setting added a sense of drama to the villagers' expectations. After an hour's restless wait, a young boy was sent to ride down the road on a mule and vanish into the mist—the hope being that he might see the army in the clearer air of the valley and bring back a report on its progress.

Meanwhile, the padre sat on his ceremonial stand to rest his feet, and Dooey turned to Carlos.

"It's bad, my renunciation of this war," he said, none too coherently. He'd been in the cold too long; his teeth were chattering. "There'll be thousands of troops coming through here. Taylor may get slaughtered. I have a friend with Taylor's army. He could get himself killed . . . and I'm just standing here."

Carlos looked at him stonily.

"I know, I chose it," Dooey said. "I'm just feeling a little guilty, that's all."

He regretted saying that, too, even though it was the way he felt. You needed courage to do anything in this war, even to take no part in it. But Dooey felt his courage oozing out of him. He felt as if he needed Maria to remain strong. She just had to understand him, support him in his intentions to remain exactly where he was—in Huatexco, working their farm, raising their child, loving her. . . .

But this wasn't the time to try to claim her attention. One glance at her flushed, excited face as she waited for the army told Dooey that.

The boy on the mule came back through the mist and raised a cry that snapped all the onlookers alert. "They are coming! They are coming! Thousands! Millions!"

The padre jumped to his feet. A serape-wrapped band began playing the Mexican national anthem. There were murmurs and shouts from all quarters. Carlos peered silently into the mist. Dooey, too, peered into the mist.

The first to came through it were Riley and his bunch, their hats and saddles snow-caked. They rode straight through the village, stone-faced, headed for Miguel's bar. On the way, Riley spotted Dooey.

"Dolan!" he called out. "How's life treating you? Come have a drink with us later. We'll be drinking it up all night!"

They were followed by the army's mounted advance guard in full regalia—plumed hats, gold-braided epaulettes lightly dusted with snow, sabers clinking at their sides. Next came four horse-drawn cannon, lined up in an even row across the road as if on parade. But they *were* on parade, that was the point; and the crowd of villagers, so far from any scene of battle, cheered mightily at the spectacle.

Foot soldiers went by, many of them Indian conscripts, some of them out of step, but each carrying a brand-new musket, proudly, the beneficiaries of their new president-general's ability to raise money for uniforms, arms, new boots—from churches, landowners, wealthy citizens, poor citizens, common citizens, everybody.

But where was Santa Anna himself? After the pitiful succession of sneak-thief leaders who had preceded him—Centralist Party leaders, Federalist Party leaders, but all thieves filling their own pockets, buckling under the pressures of the American army—where was Mexico's redeemer?

The crowd waited. Dooey waited.

Finally, Santa Anna appeared, on a white horse. Dooey took a good look at him. He came through the curtain of mist preceded by a fanfare of trumpets blown by a half dozen foot soldiers caparisoned in red, as opposed to the green-and-white uniforms that had come before them. The crowd raised a great cheer on seeing him, then went silent in response to Santa Anna's commanding presence. His stern set face said that, despite these theatrical doings which he had permitted to take place to honor him, there would be no trifling with *him*.

Santa Anna did not lift a hand or look any way but straight ahead. He made no special demands on the villagers' attention; he merely appeared and they fell silent.

Dooey, silent too, saw a face that was less than awesome. What he saw was Santa Anna's smugness, in a tight, thin-lipped mouth slightly turned down at the corners and in narrowed eyes agleam with a personal triumph he was not otherwise expressing. Dooey found himself not hating what he saw but being bemused by it. Santa Anna, in a cocked purple hat, was putting on a show of aloofness that Dooey recognized, could see for what it was: the charm that charmed by not charming, or by not seeming to want to charm. There was a cold, reptilian look about that face, an insincerity. But Dooey wasn't disturbed by this aspect of Santa Anna.

What did disturb him, even though he had been prepared for it, was Maria's adulation, the burst of enthusiasm she gave vent to as soon as the general came into view.

"He is magnificent, is he not? He is *magnificent*!" She said it to Florita, by her side, and not to Dooey.

Jealousy, not unmixed with disgust, ripped through Dooey's gut. How could she call this cheap showman "magnificent"? What did Santa Anna have that *he*, Dooey Dolan, didn't have? The man was a snake charmer, nothing but a snake charmer!

He didn't lose control of himself then; that came later. Then he said nothing, only seethed.

It came time for the padre to sprinkle Santa Anna with holy water and proffer him and his army the good wishes of Huatexco in their heroic undertaking to drive the American devil out of Mexico.

This was a sober ceremony that deepened the attention of most of those watching, touching as it did on both their patriotic and religious feelings. Even Riley and his San Patricios, tough, unsentimental soldiers all, came out of Miguel's bar to watch it, removing their hats as the padre solemnly invoked Mary, Mother of God, to protect all those on this righteous venture. Again, this was something Dooey stood apart from, lacking all such convictions, not condemning those who felt them but puzzled—as he was always puzzled—that they should put up with such passionate intensity with the destruction of human life.

Dooey looked around. Was here anyone present who shared his sense of alienation from these proceedings? He looked at Carlos. Carlos looked interested. Dooey wasn't even interested. He turned his head toward the stand again and looked at Santa Anna, the recipient of all this homage. Dooey swallowed. For the briefest of instants, with deep revulsion, he glimpsed the one person who did seem to share his views. He saw a bland look of total cynicism on Santa Anna's face as his forehead was touched by the padre in the motion of the cross.

The blessing completed, Santa Anna raised his hand. Snow fell. All was still. Santa Anna spoke:

"Mexicans, hear me. I am humble before your accolades. It is not I who deserve them, but you yourselves. This mighty army you see here with me today—the mightiest that has been assembled in our country's history—has been raised by me with your indulgences, born of your pride, your clear view of the issues at stake in this war brought invidiously to our borders by American greed for our land.

"From our eastern coast to our western coast, they wish to take from us our farms, our ranges, our mountains, our rivers. Water, the holiest of waters, has touched my face today. Now, see, the snow falls steadily. But I promise you that this flow from God in heaven, in the persons of your priest here in Huatexco and his angelic messengers in Mexico's clouds hovering above, shall be as nothing compared to the enemy's blood once we reach our destination."

The snow was falling more heavily, but the villagers stood mindless of it, hypnotized by Santa Anna's words. Dooey had to admit the man could hold an audience. He had an admirable facility with words, and he spoke with a stern, commanding visage. But the words, in Dooey's ears, were empty, cheap, ultimately self-serving.

Santa Anna went on. Playing on the word "nothing" he had just used, he pointed to his left trouser leg, cut baggy to make room for the artificial leg he wore.

"As you know, my friends, I lost this leg in battle against another enemy, the French, when they too sought to invade us. But the loss is as nothing to me. I will gladly yield up my life before I will permit dishonor to stain our beloved country. . . ."

Still he went on. Maria's face began to take on a fervent look that made Dooey's blood run cold when he glanced at her. It wasn't simply a look of devotion. As she gazed at Santa Anna, oblivious to all else around her, what appeared on her face was an expression of pure, naked lust, all the more startling for its total lack of self-awareness, its . . . innocence.

Dooey was sickened by what he saw. He felt himself being wiped out, nullified by that look. He didn't want to believe what he was seeing; he refused to believe it.

The scene that followed had a blurred, nightmarish quality for him, though none of the other onlookers seemed to see anything amiss. Santa Anna finished speaking and was greeted with wild applause. A half dozen women, five of them mothers of Huatexcan conscripts, went out into the road to kiss Santa Anna's hand. The sixth woman was Maria, who broke from the crowd, her face flushed, her eyes glistening.

When Maria's turn came to pay her obeisances, Dooey saw her kneel on the ground, press Santa Anna's hand to her lips while at the same time she nestled her cheek against his wooden leg, that symbol of his service to his country. Or was it just that to her? She rubbed her cheek against the trouser leg. For a moment, Santa Anna looked surprised, then he looked amused. Then, as he glanced down at Maria's head bobbing at his wooden knee, an expression of lasciviousness, of an answering lust, flickered in his eyes.

It was a passion play, over and done with in an instant. After a moment, Santa Anna raised Maria's head by the chin, looked into her eyes and said, as if humbly grateful for all of the homage that had been paid him, not just hers, "Bless you, my child. Bless you all." But now the look on his face was both amused and thoughtful. "I hope you will attend the Mass tonight. I shall look forward to seeing you," he said.

Still trying to believe that he had imagined the sexual nature of what had transpired, Dooey walked home with Maria afterward, saying little. He was raging inside. It seemed to him that Maria had been taunting him, yet he could not be sure that the advances she had made toward Santa Anna had anything to do with him, which made him feel somehow worse. It could be he had ceased to exist for her.

Sulking, he said, "I've changed my mind. I'm not going to that Mass tonight. It's not my church."

Maria, looking straight ahead, shrugged. "That is your choice to make."

"So it is," Dooey said, but he could not resist adding: "Can't you see that Santa Anna, your hero, is trifling with you? He's trifling with your whole damn country and you're all letting him do it. What he wants is the gold out of this village's teeth, nothing more."

Maria gave a short laugh. "Who are you to speak of trifling?"

Dooey gave up; it was no use. But when Maria had gone off to attend the Mass that night and he was alone with his thoughts, jealous suspicions began to gnaw at him. He wanted to remain calm but found he couldn't. The open, personal invitation Santa Anna had extended to Maria to attend the Mass bothered him. Maria's behavior at Santa Anna's feet and, later, her cold dismissal of Dooey, more than bothered him. He began to think of the rejection, if that's what it was, in another way. If Maria had said he was a trifler, maybe that's what he was—somebody who was not allowing her to be the person she was, somebody who wanted to own her, to bend her to his will. For this he could make amends; he could go down to the Mass after all, show her his nature was more generous than he'd so far given her reason to believe.

After wrestling with his grudges and grievances, this was what Dooey ultimately decided to do. He would be big; he would forgive and forget. When spring came their baby would be born, and they would come closer together just in caring for it. All would be well. But first he would go to the Mass to be by Maria's side.

Jealousy gnawed at him all the way back down the mountain.

By the time Dooey reached the village that jealousy had turned into a kind of dread. So long had he been debating the pros and cons of going to the Mass that when he got there it was over. The church was dark. Hardly anyone was about. From Miguel's bar, a block away, came an occasional raised shout from Riley's drinking bunch, but the rest of the village was still. At Santa Anna's private tent, near the church, an army private stood guard before the tent's closed flap, a musket on his shoulder.

Dooey looked away from the tent, up and down the road in front of it. He told himself that he was worried about Maria's safety. She hadn't returned home after the Mass, he hadn't passed her on the mountain, and he looked around for some villager who might tell him if she had suffered some mishap or other.

He knew somehow that she hadn't. Still, seeing no one on the street, he walked over to ask the guard at the tent. He said, in careful Spanish, "Have you seen a girl about this tall? *Pela longa y negra . . . muy bonita*?"

The soldier looked at the hand estimating Maria's height. He grinned. "*Vamos, señor.*"

Dooey stared at him a moment; the private didn't have to say any more.

"Get out of my way," Dooey said thickly. The soldier stood there, a slight frown replacing his lewd grin. He reached for his musket. Heedless of the consequences, Dooey swore and crashed a fist into the man's face, flinging him to the ground. Then he raised the tent flap and stepped inside.

A lantern lit the scene. Santa Anna was sitting on a red velvet chair, nude, his head thrown back in ecstasy. Maria, in her church dress, the white beaded veil still on her head, was kneeling between his open legs. Half the length of Santa Anna's cock was in her mouth.

The moment froze for Dooey Dolan. Then time started again, in agonizing slow motion. So impassioned that she was hardly aware of the disturbance, Maria turned her head ever so slightly. Dooey saw her eyes agleam and thirsty, unwilling to yield up what she had in her mouth until the last paroxysm of joy was given Santa Anna. She saw Dooey, frowned, but did not stop. Santa Anna had no idea he was there.

Dooey felt sick. He closed his eyes and turned his head away. A black numbness seized his brain. A rage to kill was in him, but it had no object in either of these two. He stumbled blindly out of the tent and vomited on the ground. From inside the tent he heard "Oh!," a murmur, a grunt, a sigh of satisfaction. The sounds meant nothing human to him now; they were the expected aftermath of the coupling of animals.

He lifted his head and stared blearily at the tent guard, who by now had regained his feet and was stepping toward him, his musket aimed at Dooey's middle. Dooey gave him a look, as if to say, "Go ahead, shoot," and the guard stopped. He seemed to understand.

"I am sorry, *señor*," he said sympathetically. "It is the weakness of the flesh—nothing more. I myself . . . you yourself—"

Dooey walked away. He did not know where he was going or what he was going to do. He was filled with self-loathing. Nothing in life held significance for him—perhaps it never had. He could not remember a time when life had held any meaning for him.

It had stopped snowing. The village road was white. The mountain looming over the village was white. Even the night sky was whitened with the threat of more snow to come. Everything Dooey saw was devoid of color. He felt chilled to the bone and wished there was some place he could go to get warm. But there was no such place; it seemed to him there never would be.

He kept walking, leaning into a cold wind. His feet

took him past Miguel's and he heard laughter from inside. Riley's bunch, Dooey thought. What were they laughing about? What *was* there to laugh about? He was irked by that laughter. If he could, he would smash all the laughter in the world into bits of grief to match his own. In that black mood, he veered from his aimless course and peered into the cafe's front window.

He saw a damnfool game of some sort going on. A wine bottle was perched on the sill of an open side window. Riley and his men were all seated at one table. One of them—Knecht the German, it was—had just lifted and aimed a Colt pistol at the bottle. The bottle was tied to the sill, for some reason, via complicated loops of the men's ropes.

Knecht was drunk; they were all pretty drunk. As Dooey watched, Knecht fired and the bottle broke into pieces. That's it? Dooey thought comtemptuously. Hell, at ten yards range anyone could hit a bottle with a Colt, drunk or sober. But apparently Knecht hadn't done what he'd set out to do; he looked disconsolate. He handed some money over to Riley, who laughed and slapped him on the back while another of the men went over and set a new bottle on the window sill.

Dooey started to turn away. He felt cut off from such high-jinks. The touch of curiosity he felt he was willing to forego. His misery suited him better; he wanted to stay cloaked in it.

Just then, Riley happened to glance up at the window. Dooey moved off into the shadows, but he'd been seen. A moment later, Riley was sticking his head out the door, calling after him: "Hey, Dolan, come on in and have a drink—you look like one cold bastard."

Dooey shrugged. "I'm all right." He stood hesitating a moment. "Thanks, I will," he decided.

He followed Riley inside. "You know these fellows," Riley said by way of reintroduction. "Where you been keeping yourself, Dolan? Didn't see you at the Mass, or anywhere else after the little show we had for the boss this afternoon."

"Wasn't at the Mass," Dooey said. "I was just walking." He roused himself. There was a way, he thought, of acting like a man—even though you felt like your balls had been cut off. All it took was paying attention to what was going on in front of you, not what had happened ten, fifteen minutes ago. Like he didn't have any argument with these fellows. Like Riley had invited him in. Like there was this shoot-the-bottle thing they were doing. Little things all, maybe, but if you couldn't handle the big things in your life, what else was there?

Dooey looked at the Colt on the table. "What sort of mischief are you guys up to?" he said.

"Mischief is right." Riley grinned. "This dumb German says he can shoot the cork out of that bottle without breaking it. He can't. Hell, no one can. He's had five tries at it and he's busted five bottles. He don't understand much English. We've kind of been goading him on and he keeps paying up. Now, sure as hell, he's about to bust the sixth."

"Oh, the cork." Dooey looked over at the bottle on the sill.

He saw the little cork sticking up; he saw it sharply. He seemed to have preternaturally sharp vision when it came to that cork. If you held a Colt absolutely steady, you might hit it. You just might. And if you didn't—what then? It wouldn't mean a damn thing.

You might hear a cackle, you'd pay for a beer, but you wouldn't lose a damn thing that mattered.

Dooey shrugged. "I think I can hit it," he said. "I'll take over Knecht's wager, if it's all right with him."

It wasn't, but Riley, in his glee at finding a new sucker, was able to persuade the reluctant German to yield on the next shot.

Dooey took aim. He seemed not to have a nerve in his body, nor any sensation that he could identify. He was as still inside as death.

He fired. The cork flew from the bottle and the bottle remained perfectly still on the sill. Riley stared at the bottle, then at Dooey.

Dooey put the gun down. "Humph," was all he said. He was pleased with what he'd done. He was also amazed. He hadn't expected to hit the cork. As Riley had said, it was a near-impossible stunt. It flashed through Dooey's mind that, had he been the man he was earlier that day, caught up in the jangled throes of things with Maria, caring so much about her, about himself, about their lives together, he would have missed that cork. But now that he was dead, numb, nerveless dead, it turned out that he could do anything . . . anything at all.

It was amazing.

Riley was speaking to him. "Dolan, there ain't a man here, myself included, who can shoot like that. I heard about it, now I've seen it and believe it. It's one hell of a shame you ain't coming along with us, 'cause we could damn well use you."

It was then that Dooey said it.

"You've bought yourself a gun, Riley. When do we leave?"

15

TWO MONTHS BEFORE Dooey Dolan, in his reckless despair, threw in his lot with the San Patricios, a past fling had already begun to catch up with him.

John Bell had murder on his mind.

It wasn't, of course, anything Dooey could have known about, this righteous wrath of John Bell's directed at him. And had he known, would it have made any difference? John Bell, Sally Middlebrook, they were far from Dooey's mind as he waited in the San Patricio camp just north of the village the next morning. Maria . . . Maria and Santa Anna. It was these two and what he saw as his cowardly flight from a confrontation with them that occupied his mind.

Already he was having second thoughts about his impulsive decision to join Riley's bunch. Why had he done it? For the crumb of ego-salvaging praise they'd offered him? It hadn't worked; already the effects were wearing off.

He hadn't gone home from Miguel's bar. Instead, he'd asked Miguel to find Carlos and have him bring to the San Patricio camp the few things Dooey had in the house he'd shared with Maria, including his gun. Miguel had complied, happily, glad to see the *gringo* finally take up arms for Mexico. Dooey knew the truth, that he was running away like a dog with its tail between its legs.

That morning while waiting for Carlos, he lived in fire and ice, as he would many a morning during the long trek northward. The vision of Maria and Santa Anna burned in his brain, yet in his gut was only the cold numbness of his impotent rage. It amused him, briefly, to think that had he been man enough—as he put it to himself—to beat Santa Anna to a bloody pulp and most assuredly die for it, he might have gone down in American school history books as a hero, the slayer of a hated despot, the details of the scene and his motive for the act hushed up for the sake of a lesson in patriotic martyrdom.

They did him no good, these fancies of his. He knew the truth, the truth of his shame. And he would not shame himself further. He would honor the commitment he had so recklessly made to Riley. What that would entail, he did not know. Deep down inside, Dooey still didn't want to shoot anybody—American or Mexican. But he figured that when somebody started shooting at him, he'd shoot back. That was the way of things.

He was in this savage mood when Carlos came. The night snow had turned to morning ice and Carlos, walking stiffly, looked cold. He came by a path that avoided the other San Patricios, who were hunched over a breakfast fire. He made his way directly to Dooey, who was not hungry and had not joined the others. Besides, he felt that he owed Carlos a private goodbye.

"You asked for these, *amigo*," Carlos said, handing him his Springfield and a bag of clothes.

"*Muchas gracias*, Carlos. It was good of you to bring it."

Carlos nodded, absently. He stood shivering in the cold. "You cannot do this, *señor*. You know that."

Dooey snapped, "I can do any damn thing I want to do. Here, put this on."

Carlos caught the heavy shirt Dooey took from his bag and tossed to him. It was something Maria had made for him. Carlos only held it in his hands and said, "You cannot do this because it is not fair to *them*." He nodded toward the San Patricios by the fire.

Dooey grunted. "Since when do you care about them?"

"Perhaps it is you I care about, *señor*. They have a cause they believe in. You do not. How can you fight with them, as one helpful to them, if you are not of a mind with them?"

"Who says I have no cause?" Dooey shot at him. "I'm getting three times what the U.S. Army paid me, and there'll be a hundred acres of land for me out west when this war is done."

"*Señor, señor* . . ."

Carlos's tone had been compassionate, but when Dooey looked up at his broad Indian face, he saw it void of expression. "Carlos, why don't you just go away and leave me alone?"

Carlos shrugged. "I came to say goodbye, *señor*, that is all." Then he added, "Maria had no message for you."

"I didn't know I asked for one," Dooey said testily.

Carlos went on as if he hadn't heard. "She told me . . . something. She told me you had no business being where you were last night. But she had no message for you, not even good bye. It is I who will miss you, *señor*."

Dooey, head down, said nothing.

"Can you not look at me when I tell you this, *señor*?"

"No. I know what you're going to say, Carlos."

"I shall say it anyway." Carlos was stubborn; he would not give up. "Was it not you, *señor*, who spoke to me of the need for revolution? What has changed? It remains true that Santa Anna and other rulers we have had before him have lain waste our country. He is not our champion, he is our enslaver. If it remains true, as you have said, that *no* government today cares about its people, that they want only to put us to use in their aim for power, then—"

"Then *what*?" Dooey shot at him. He was getting nervous, uncomfortable. Carlos was boring him; he didn't want to think about what the Indian was saying, only to get on with what he had committed himself to do. "Carlos, I was full of hot air when I said those things. I don't know anything about revolutions. What do you want me to do? Stay here and form some sort of conspiracy with you to blow up Mexico, America, the world?"

"That is foolish, *señor*. No. I would wish only that you would stay in Huatexco and talk with me more about slavery and freedom. There is no one in the village I can talk to about this matter. They think me either an old woman or a fool, not to be bothered with."

"And me? What have I been?" Dooey shook his head. "Carlos, it's cold. Go back to your house. Slavery, freedom, they're empty words for me. They have no meaning. There's only killing. You don't talk about it, you just do it . . . until someone kills you."

"Such a pity. Such a waste." Now Carlos did look sad. Then, as if determined to make one last effort, he said, "*Señor*, I have come to believe that you know more about slavery even than I do. Has it crossed your mind, *señor*, that in joining the San Patricios, you are doing exactly what Maria has always demanded of you? Is it in any way for yourself that you will now fight and kill? Or is it in obedience to Maria's will? *Señor*, I have never been a slave to love. I am unacquainted in my heart with that form of slavery, but you know it well. And if you were content with this condition, I would say nothing, for there would be nothing for me to say. But you are not content. Therefore, you have the seeds of rebellion in you. You *do* know something about revolution, but what you know you have hidden from yourself.

"I do not know why you have done this, *señor*, but I feel there is a connection between the slavery you know and the slavery I know. I want to know more about this, to see it more clearly. Perhaps there is a wider brotherhood in slavery than we think. If that is so, perhaps one day there can be a wider brotherhood in revolution too—not just those who are kept poor in body, but those kept poor in spirit as well. I—"

Dooey looked up. Riley was coming over, and Dooey was thankful for the interruption.

"I am sorry, *señor*," Carlos said. He saw Riley too.

"Perhaps one day you will come back to Huatexco. I hope you do. *Señor* Riley, he will say to you now, 'Where you been keeping yourself?' If you return, I shall say that to you. Perhaps then we can drink beer together and talk some more." Carlos smiled. "Goodbye, *amigo.* I wish you well."

He left just before Riley arrived.

"Where you been keeping yourself, Dolan?" Riley said. "Come on over and have some grub with us. I ain't taking no for an answer."

"Sure thing."

Dooey got to his feet. As he walked beside Riley, the latter said, "What'd that old Indian want?"

Dooey shrugged. "To say goodbye. He's a friend of mine."

"Then he's a friend of mine," Riley said. "Come to think of it, they're all friends of mine, these Indians. Simple folk. All they want us to do is protect their churches, and that's exactly what we aim to do."

"That Indian's not so simple," Dooey said.

John Bell had arrived home in late October. His mother, his father and almost everybody in Wethersfield were at the station to greet him. John and Dooey had been the only two town boys to actually to go off to the war in Mexico and a great deal of enthusiasm prevailed at the return of one of them.

Even before John could locate his folks in the crowd, someone was shouting at him: "How did it go, John boy? Did you give it to them good?"

John, glad to be home, had a broad smile for his questioner and everyone else. "Heck, Jim, I thought you were *against* the war."

"When one of our own has been fighting in it? Not

now, Johnny, not now. Wait 'til you see the parade we have fixed up for you!"

There was a brass band playing and more than a few hand-held flags waving. In the din and clamor, John finally spotted his parents, midway in the crowd. He looked for Sally, too, but did not see her.

He made his way to his folks. "Hi, ma. Hi, pa. Gee, I'm glad to be home."

His mother was the first to notice his wan look. "Are you all right, John?" Abigail Bell asked anxiously.

"Sure, ma, I'm fine." John kissed her on the cheek. "It was a long trip. I'm just a little tired, that's all."

"Of course he's tired," James Bell said, beaming. "He's got a right to be tired. After being in on that battle at Monterrey, taking the place in spite of that huge army the Mexicans threw against us, John has a right to be tired. Why, Abby, do you realize that we were outnumbered three, maybe four to one."

"Well, pa, I—" John began and stopped, puzzled. "Pa, what's going on around here? When I left you were dead-set against my going. Now, all of a sudden . . ."

"It's not so sudden, John. We've been seeing things a little differently the past couple of months. Do you know that Scott has taken over command from Taylor? No more of that fooling around up north. Scott's leaving Old Zach up there to mop up, or stew in his own juice, whatever he wants to do, but Scott's taking an invasion army down to Veracruz for an assault on Mexico City that will end this war fast!"

John, who'd read and heard of the turn of events—it was in all the papers by now—still pursued the question that was troubling him. "But, pa, what about the principles you held against the war? You said Polk was trying to carve Mexico up into slave states. You—"

"Well, I see now that I was wrong about that, John. All sorts of things are going on. It's not just Scott who's on the move. We have a fellow—name of Fremont—out in California winning *that* territory for us. With just sixty, seventy men they say. Now, nobody's going to try to grow cotton in California, so that's one place that will never be a slave state. Neither will the rest of that land out west, up to the Oregon border and east to the Rio Grande. Land the Mexicans shouldn't be holding because, heck, they don't even *live* there!" James Bell slapped his son on the back enthusiastically. "Point is, John, once Scott gets through teaching the Mexicans a lesson and we buy that land from them at the right price, we're *all* going to be a darned sight better off!"

"Oh, I see." John, who'd winced under his father's hearty whack, now put a grin on for his benefit. "Pa, can we go home now? I guess I'm more tired than I thought I was."

John did see. He saw that even in a man like his father, whom he respected and loved, principles could go begging when fast, aggressive action was promised and you found yourself with high hopes of being on the winning side in a war. If a war got stalemated, as this one had been almost from the beginning, you could get to feeling frustrated personally. *That's* where wrong entered in, that's when presidents and generals were seen as unjust in their aims, cowards, shady dealers—any number of things. Maybe they were, maybe they weren't, but that wasn't the point. The point was *winning*, the feeling that through some new dramatic action you just might be able to work your way out of whatever mess you'd gotten yourself into.

So it was with his father. And if not quite in the same way, so it was with him.

But when the Bell family got home and John put his bag down, he suddenly wasn't tired anymore. "Ma, if you don't mind, I think I'll go over to the Middlebrook farm. I . . . I want to tell Sally I love her. It's maybe something I didn't do the right way when I left."

There was a moment's silence.

"You won't find Sally there, son," James Bell said quietly.

"Sally's staying with her aunt in Litchfield," Abigail Bell added quickly. "Otherwise, of course, she'd have been at the station to meet you."

"Oh," John said. "Well then, I'll just go up to Litchfield and see her."

"You might try one of your mother's biscuits first," his father said wryly. "That and a good night's sleep. You can always take the coach to Litchfield tomorrow, you know."

John stood undecided.

"Sit down, son," his father said, smiling. "There's so much we have to talk about. I'm sure we can fill the time."

John sat. His mother went to get the lunch she'd prepared.

"What would you like to know, pa?" John began tentatively. "How did Danny work out in the factory?"

"Good, good . . ." Again, James Bell smiled. "And you . . . how did you work out, as you put it, in Mexico?"

"Pa, I'm glad I'm through with it," John said bluntly. "I did my duty—or tried to—but it was a foreign war to me. That's the best way I can explain it. It was as if I had to go there to find out I didn't belong there. All I want to do now is go back to work in the factory and get my own life in order."

"Your own life. That includes Sally, I take it," James Bell said quietly.

"Yes, pa, it surely does." John hesitated. "Pa, I don't want to talk about the war, but maybe we have to. Here I've come back less than enthusiastic about it to find you all in favor of it. Pa, I have to tell you this. I wasn't any hero at Monterrey, as you seemed to be telling ma I was. I left the battlefield before the main action started. I got fed up and just walked away. What I want to know now is, do you consider me a quitter?"

James Bell waved his hand. "Why should I, son? You didn't desert, did you? In fact, you overstayed your enlistment. I told your mother what I did because your last letters were unhappy ones, filled with self-doubt. I've been doing my best to keep her from worrying about you. It's been damn hard on me, I'll tell you that!"

John was taken aback. "Pa, I'm sorry—"

Again, James Bell waved his hand. "Sorry for what? For doing your best at a job you'd set out to do even though your feelings about it turned out to be less sanguine than you thought they'd be? I don't call that quitting! I call that true, honest-to-God, day-to-day courage!"

"That's just your opinion, pa," John said.

"You're damned right it's my opinion!" James Bell exploded. "What else did you ask me for? John, have I failed you in some way? I want to see you with more confidence in yourself. It wasn't you who was the quitter! It was your so-called friend and champion DeWitt Dolan. *He* deserted—you didn't! *He's* that pathetic weakling, not you!"

John winced. "I was wondering when you'd get around to Dooey, pa," he said slowly. "You still don't understand. There were times I envied Dooey for having walked out on a war he didn't believe in, something I couldn't do. He met a girl; he fell in love. He wanted to live in peace—what's wrong with that? I thought about Dooey a lot, always kind of hoping that he could stick to his guns—I mean, well, you know what I mean. I never thought of him as a weakling for doing what he did."

James Bell regarded his son silently, with a flickering pain in his eyes that John did not notice. "Do what you can to forget DeWitt, son," he father said kindly. "And do what you can to forget the war. You've done your part—let others finish it. You are a fine young man; Sally is a fine young woman. Just don't forget that."

John looked up in some surprise. "I know that about Sally, pa. She's why I came home, why I never should have left home in the first place."

John went up to Litchfield the next day. James Bell had let him go in ignorance, knowing that John must learn about Sally's situation for himself and deal with it himself. There was no other way, James Bell thought, for his son to grow up. But he was worried; how would John behave when his illusions about Dooey collapsed, when the roof fell in on him . . . ?

John knocked on the door of the neat white farmhouse and knew something was amiss the moment Sally's Aunt Clara opened the door. The woman's face blanched at the sight of him. "John! It's you! We didn't expect you. We didn't really expect anyone from Wethersfield."

"Why not?" John asked. "What's wrong, Mrs. Middlebrook? Sally's ma usually visits when Sally's staying here, doesn't she?"

"Well, yes, she's been here, but—" The woman got even more flustered. "Please, John, don't come in. You'll only hurt Sally. In a month or two, she'll be back home, and then—"

"I don't understand," John said. But he did understand something. His face got red even as he spoke.

"Let John come in, Aunt Clara," Sally said from behind her aunt. "He might as well."

The woman nervously opened the door wider.

Sally said calmly, "I wanted to come to town and greet you yesterday, John. But, as you can see, it would have been difficult for me."

She wore a loose-fitting white dress that did not disguise the fact that she was close to giving birth.

John felt sick; he was close to tears. "I guess it's a case of my wooing you too late," he said inanely. "I meant to come back and show you that I—that I would—" He stopped; he didn't know what else to say. Miserable, he turned to go.

"That you cared for me and would fight for me?" Sally said. "It wouldn't have helped, John, not then. Please, though, don't go yet."

John stopped and turned to look at her again. Rage swept through him. She looked beautiful to him—and she looked older, too, more mature than he was, as if she were in possession of some wisdom he could not attain, no matter how hard he tried. That, too, made him furious, this secret wisdom of hers. He did not see the shadows of grief in her eyes; in his fury, he was oblivious to them. He tried, knowing he would fail, knowing he was failing even as he asked the question, to make things better for himself.

"Was it—was it someone who took advantage of you?" he said stiffly.

"It was Dooey, John."

John frowned slightly.

"It's Dooey's baby I'm having, John. At first I thought I would kill myself rather than have it. Then I decided I wanted to live. When the baby is born, Aunt Clara will see that it's properly adopted. I'll come home then."

John hadn't even heard her. "It couldn't have been Dooey," he said. "Dooey told me . . ." He tried to remember what Dooey had told him when he was still trying to make up his mind about leaving Wethersfield. "He told me you were just a girl—"

Sally's poise wavered, but she recovered quickly. "He told you the truth. I *am* just a girl, John, just human . . . like Dooey, like you—"

"No, no, no, that's not the answer," John said. His voice sounded thin and dangerous to Sally; it did to John's ears too, like someone else's voice and not his own.

Sally said quietly, "John, stop. Don't do this to yourself. Don't do it to me. It's you I love, not Dooey. Whatever happens now between us, John, I've lived in darkness for months now, searching my heart and soul, and I *know* it's you I love."

In that voice he did not recognize as his own, John snarled, "How did he do it, Sally? Did he get on top of you and just drive it in up to the hilt? Did you eat it up? Was it good, Sally? You're goddam right it was good! Dooey does everything well, doesn't he? He ruins your life, betrays our friendship, becomes a traitor to his country—not by taking half steps but by going the full measure."

Sally's eyes had widened. She saw John was beyond hearing her, beyond hearing himself. She heard in John's diatribe only his envy of and hatred for the loved friend who had betrayed him, and knew that his rage had little to do with her.

"That smug bastard! That son of a bitch!"

Aunt Clara was standing beside Sally, her mouth open in shock. Sally took her hand, turned on her heel and left John in his darkness. . . .

In the following days, John slowly saw what he had to do and, as events developed, what would make it possible for him to do it. What he had to do was somehow get back to Mexico, find Dooey Dolan and kill him.

It took cunning to shield his need for vengeance from his parents. When he got back home from Litchfield, his father, after surveying him carefully, limited himself to the comment, "So now you know. I'm sorry, John." Then he said, "Why don't you go off fishing upriver for a couple of days? I've already asked the town to delay the parade in your honor. I thought you might want to have some time by yourself to sort things out first."

"Thanks, pa. I believe I will do some fishing."

"John?" John had started for his room, but stopped and turned at the sound of his mother's voice.

Abigail Bell's face showed her concern. "John, I do not ask you to forget what Dooey did, only to find a way to forgive him for it. So desperate for affection he always was, it's understandable that—"

"Thanks, ma. I'll think about it," John said quietly.

He was halfway up the stairs to his room and could

hear his mother murmuring. "Oh dear, I believe I said the wrong thing!"

"There's no right thing to say, Abigail. Leave John alone. He's fought in the war, hasn't he? He's a man. Sally's shown herself to be a brave young woman. They'll work this out between them."

John flung himself down on his bed. "Oh, shit!" He slammed his head down. "Oh, shit!"

He went upriver at a time when more and more rumors about Scott's assignment to Veracruz were being circulated daily, exciting everyone. Toward the end of the second day, John stowed his fishing gear in his tent. He hadn't fished much, had mostly sat on the bank and watched the river boil up on its rocks, the way his rage boiled inside him. He wandered into the nearby village of Bathford. Walking aimlessly, he came across a tavern and was drawn inside by the vigorous clamor being raised by several young workers homeward bound from the mills. They were discussing the war.

"Are you signing up, Sam?"

"You bet your boots I am!"

"Not me. Sounds like the same old malarkey to me. If I'm going to stand and sweat and, sooner or later, fall down in one place, I'd just as soon do it right here in the mill!"

He was hooted down.

"Josh, you're wrong about that. This Winfield Scott ain't like Ol' Zach at all. Let him land in Veracruz, inside a month he'll be in Mexico City, bootin' old Santa Anna in the tail. Mark my words!"

"Mark *your* words," Josh countered. "Shucks, you can't even read somebody else's words straight. See what it says in this paper? Santa Anna ain't anywhere *near* Mexico City. Says here, Ol' Zach's up north, place called Saltillo, waitin' for him to come up *his* way."

"Well, that don't make no never mind. What'll happen is, Ol' Zach'll kick his tail back down to Mexico City. Then Ol' Scott'll come in from Veracruz and kick it in for good!"

The argument broke up in guffaws. It was evident that none of the participants was going to be swayed from the feelings and opinions he already held about this new development in the war.

John, in his brooding state, sat alone at a table and ordered an ale. He drank it immediately and ordered another. A couple of the workers gave him curious looks, possibly because of his sun-tanned face and haggard expression, maybe just because he was a stranger in town. At any rate, they soon picked up their discussion again.

Josh, turning a page of his paper, said grudgingly, "Guess this Scott's a tough old bird at that. See where he says he's going to round up all those traitors and hang 'em on the spot. Going to get every danged one of 'em that deserted the Army since the war began. Guess that's somethin' I can see my way clear to agreein' with."

There was a general assent to that. Someone muttered, "Papist bastards most of 'em. They ought to hang 'em just for that."

John's interest had picked up at this. Made bold by the ale he had drunk, he called out, "How's he planning to find them?"

The workers reacted in various ways. There was no answer to the question, at least not in the paper Josh was reading. More than that, the question had been asked in so hostile a tone that some were inclined to ignore the man who asked it. One, however, attuned to John's tanned looks and something in his demeanor, asked, "Have you fit in the war, stranger?"

"I have."

"Whyn't you come over here and tell us something of what you've seen?"

John walked over, swaying just a little. "The trouble with you fellows is that you don't think positively," he said.

"Huh?"

"He's right," someone said.

"The war stinks, but we've got to win it," John said.

He was quite drunk now. He was talking to himself; others just happened to be listening in.

"Hear, hear," one of the others said.

"I was at Monterrey," John said. "We took a long time getting there, and once we did, it was rough. I was plenty scared. But . . . you know what made it worse for me? Just the sort of things you fellows have been talking about. All this carping about generals and things . . . I did some of that, we all did." He climbed higher on his soap-box. "But what's really at stake in this war is . . . honor, our honor as a country. We can't let the Mexicans push us around—no. Nor the nay-sayers in our midst either. As for those traitors, well . . ."

"Yes, what about those traitors?" one of his listeners prodded. He and the others had been impressed by what John was saying. For some, his heated words struck a blow at their consciences. "Did you come up against that there San Patricio Battalion in Mexico?"

John shook his head. He was just drunk enough to tell the truth—his truth, as he saw it. He lapsed into his listeners' manner of speech. "Do you know what one of them traitors did to me? Ruined my girl, that's what. A friend of mine—a *so-called* friend of mine. Went off to fight in Mexico with him and all along he'd been screwing my girl. Just didn't want me to find out what he'd been doing, that's all. Left her in a hell of a mess. I came back to marry her and—do you fellows know what I'm saying?"

One of them whistled. "One of them deserters did that to you? And you're just standing here jawin' about it? Christ, if it was me, I'd be in Mexico right now, lookin' to blast his head off. I'd get him before Scott got him, that's for sure!"

John nodded vigorously. If he had needed any support to act on the murder that was already in his heart, he was getting it now.

"You talk about honor," Sam said. "I'm enlisting next week, but if I had all your reasons for getting to Mexico, I'd be doing it tomorrow!"

John's point of honor was one they could all agree on. Any lingering doubt about his rightful course of action had vanished. What did his parents—who spoke of forbearance, who fed him sop—know of a man's need to fight for his honor? These men—young men like himself, his peers—they knew!

John made the leap in his mind that made personal betrayal synonymous with betrayal of a much wider scope. He'd fought for his country, hadn't he? Dooey had *deserted that country*. Dooey Dolan was a monster of betrayal.

"That's just what I'm going to do," he said.

John came home from fishing and told his parents he was re-enlisting. It came as a shock that soon wore off.

"Up there on the river, pa, I came around to your way of thinking," John said. "There's a job still to be done, and with Scott moving the way he is, I want to be in on it."

He sounded very sober-minded and James Bell seemed to understand. "I take it you've come to a decision about Sally?"

"I can't face that situation right now, pa. I need more time. Besides, there are more important things in life. Right now, it's getting the war won that counts."

"That's so. It's a good way of looking at things." James Bell added a little hesitantly, "If that's your decision, I approve. But I wish you sounded more enthusiastic about it."

"I've been to the war, pa," John said. "I know what it's like. It isn't enthusiasm that's going to win it—that's for the folks at home. It's persistence, tenacity, slogging it out on a day-to-day basis. I'll manage."

"With a will, you mean. Yes, I imagine wars can be won that way too." James Bell smiled. "Odd. We'll be having your homecoming parade, and soon after you'll be leaving again."

"The town will have to put off the parade until I get back," John said. "I'm leaving today, pa."

John went back down to Fort Hamilton in New York. Welcomed as a combat veteran, he had no trouble getting himself reassigned to Mexico. As to which battle area he would be sent to—the one up north being held by Taylor or the one about to be opened up by Winfield Scott on the Gulf Coast at Veracruz—it turned out he had no choice. As of late fall 1846, the War Department was sending all volunteers to join Scott, and transferring to that general most of Taylor's forces as well. Scott was Polk's new choice for getting rid of the Mexican thorn in his side once and for all.

North or south, it made little difference to John what part of Mexico they decided to ship him to. He didn't know where Dooey Dolan had gone. All he knew was that he was determined to find him sooner or later, on a battlefield or in that Mexican girl's hut—somewhere, anywhere. And when he did, he would have his moment of bloody reckoning.

What did appeal to John, when he found himself assigned to the Scott-led army, was Scott's avowal to seek out deserters and hang them. John figured that he might—just might—get a chance to volunteer for one of those seek-out missions.

At Fort Hamilton, the delay in shipping men and supplies out to the Veracruz area again seemed interminable. This despite the promise to the public of a speedy victory. Navy ships had to congregate first for a planned sea bombardment of the Gulf Coast port. There were limited billets available for soldier-passengers on these ships. Besides, Scott's priorities were for Taylor's battle-hardened troops and those recruits already in Louisiana, and other southern staging areas. To get things moving took time—lots of it.

John bided his. Close to three months he waited at Fort Hamilton with a patience born of practice, a patience that grew even stronger with the desire for vengeance in his heart.

In all this time, only one chance encounter, during his third week at Hamilton, lifted his spirits out of their dark and murderous prison. He met again Captain Robert E. Lee. Wandering into the engineers' area, John saw Lee busily emptying out his desk and stopped to say hello.

Lee looked up and smiled. "Getting ready for the big fight, soldier?.."

"Sure am," John said. "Do you remember me, sir?"

Lee gave him a closer look. "Can't say that I do."

"John Bell," John said. "You wouldn't remember the name. It was back in June, and I don't think we were introduced. You mentioned something then about how you didn't relish your desk job, how you'd rather be in Mexico."

Lee grinned. "Well, I got what I wanted. General Scott has asked me to join his staff. I leave for Veracruz tomorrow. Truth is, I can't wait. Better late than never for a forty-year-old codger like myself. And you? If we met in June, I take it you've been to Mexico and back."

"I was with Taylor for a while, sir."

"Then I envy you the head start you have on me," Lee said, smiling.

"That's about what you said the first time we met, sir."

"I did?" Lee frowned. "Wait a moment, weren't you with another volunteer, a chap who gave me what for about being with the military?"

John nodded. "Dolan was his name, sir."

Lee snapped his fingers. "Dolan, yes. Whatever happened to him?"

"He deserted in Mexico."

Lee frowned again. "Too bad, though I somehow suspected he might. Too bad," he said again, shaking his head. "Seemed a nice enough chap, a bit headstrong perhaps, misguided, but—"

It wasn't what John wanted to hear. "He's a traitor, sir, a black-hearted villain."

"Yes, well . . ." Seeing the grim look on John's face, Lee got an uncomfortable expression on his own. "Well, no doubt he'll be rounded up with the others.

It was good talking to you, soldier. Now, if you'll excuse me—" He returned to packing up the contents on his desk.

John stood there a moment, feeling anger sweep over him like a cold wind. He didn't like being dismissed so casually. He didn't like Lee's remembering Dooey Dolan and not remembering him. The least Lee could have done was agree on Dolan's villainy, but he hadn't even done that!

John wasn't sure that he liked Captain Lee anymore. He wasn't sure—no, he *was* sure that he wouldn't be getting along with anybody in the Army who backed off from recognizing the injustice that had been done him.

Well, so be it then. Let the Army go where it would. He'd follow along . . . he'd do his bit . . . his day would come. . . .

16

ON FEBRUARY 22ND, the day John Bell arrived at hot, steamy Lobos Island north of Veracruz, Dooey Dolan was far from him in mind, spirit and intent—not to mention geography.

On February 22, Dooey was up in the cold, bitter mountains again. Descending from Huatexco, the Mexican Army had had to cross hundreds of miles of desert before once again ascending a six-thousand-foot-high Sierra Madre range for a rendezvous with Taylor's army near Saltillo.

It was night. An icy wind and a heavy rain had the San Patricios and fifteen thousand Mexican soldiers shivering and fretful. They weren't on the move now. They'd made camp at a point just a couple of miles from the American position on the Saltillo road and were waiting the return of an emissary sent to demand Taylor's total surrender.

Dooey didn't want Taylor to quit, but five miles back, at Agua Nueva, the Mexicans had come upon stores burnt by U.S. troops. Santa Anna assumed Taylor's small army—made still smaller after its depletion by Scott—was in full retreat, so he'd moved up swiftly and sent Taylor his ultimatum: surrender or be annihilated.

But Dooey itched for action. He saw value now only in throwing himself into battle—any sort of battle, so long as the guns blazed and helped him forget Maria forever, so hard did his love for her die in him.

He got his murderous wish. Toward morning, the emissary came back with Taylors' reply. Riley came back from Santa Anna with a copy of it—for the San Patricios' amusement as much as anything else.

"Listen to this. We have Old Zach saying here: 'I beg leave to say that I decline acceding to your request.'" Riley grunted. "Can you imagine that old billy goat actually saying that? More likely he said, 'Fuck 'em, Bliss—now you put that in English.' So we're up and at them. Let's move it, men."

The battalion moved out, along with the Mexican infantry and its cannon support, to confront Taylor on his left flank. They stopped at a plateau east of the Saltillo road, defended at its closest point by an American volunteer regiment; Dooey did not know which one.

There had been laughter among the San Patricios at the way Taylor's rejection of the surrender demand had been transcribed, even some expression of affection for the tough old general, despite the choice the ex-U.S. troops had made to fight him. Riley's men had their convictions—political, religious, whatever. Dooey had none. He gripped his rifle and went forward, waiting for that first shot from the American side that would thaw the cold feeling in his gut and send his blood coursing with excitement. Just for the excitement of it: to live in a whirl of fear, maybe, but with every instinct of battle alive. To live!

Two divisions of Mexican infantry advanced at a fast pace, with cannon support behind them and the San Patricios in their midst. Dooey kept up the pace, running effortlessly now toward clouds of smoke being sent up by three American field guns in the van of the plateau's defending regiment.

Seven thousand Mexicans charged in that attack and the field guns' projectiles erupted in their midst. It was all Dooey needed—the sight and sound of the whistling shells falling, exploding in his path of advance. He stopped, kneeled, fired his rifle . . . joining the other San Patricios, of a piece with them. Mexican cannon fire roared from behind them. Two of the three American field guns were smashed by Mexican shells, their gunners swept back or felled by rifle fire. The third gun stayed in action a while longer. Dooey ran in closer, stopped, kneeled, fired. One of the American gunners went down—shot by Dooey or by Ryan, next to him—or by any one of hundreds of Mexican infantry in their area. Then, while the attackers were still at a hundred-yard range, men of the defending U.S. volunteer regiment ran up from the American rear, bravely stood their ground beside the last remaining field piece and poured rifle fire back at Mexican forces now veering in at them from all sides. Dooey recognized the defenders' uniforms and blinked: they were the Second Indianans, his old outfit. But . . . what did it matter? They were firing into his face.

And yet it did matter; somehow, it did—even if briefly. Dooey sprawled headlong, kept low. Rifle fire passed over his head. Something kept him from shooting back. Someone screamed. Dooey jerked his head around in time to see Knecht the German fling his hands up to his face, see the blood oozing between his fingers before he screamed again, "*Nein! Nein!*" and fell in a heap.

Confused, Dooey started to run to Knecht's side. Ryan grabbed his arm and growled: "Forget it, he's done for."

"Yeah, yeah, you're right." Dooey's teeth were suddenly chattering. He swung around again to face the Indianans' fire.

"Come on!" Ryan shouted at him. "Let's get 'em!"

From the fallen Knecht's direction now came hundreds of charging Mexican infantry, like a stampede. Dooey couldn't have plowed his way back through them even if he'd wanted to—and he didn't want to. He was in it now, up to his ears in it. The sound of the guns firing at him and at the men around him were the sounds of enemy guns—the enemies of life. They had to be silenced. Dooey, charging with the others, now saw the enemy as faceless—not as the Indianans, not as people at all, but as a machine of destruction, his and everybody else's. There was a scream in Dooey's throat not unlike Knecht's cry of horror . . . his last "No!" to senseless death. Except that Dooey's scream didn't come out; he was still there, alive, with the illusion that he was fighting for life, intent only on breaking the death machine.

It was the guns he wanted to smash now, not those who held them. It was an impossible dream: the guns and the men who carried them were indissolubly one. But then, as if God had taken pity on Dooey Dolan in his madness and granted him one small favor, what was impossible to realize because unnecessary to attempt.

At the approach of the Mexican horde, the crew manning the last field gun and then the entire Indiana Volunteer Regiment of riflemen simply broke and ran. A feeling of glee, a feeling that at this moment he had neither to kill or be killed, that through desire alone he was controlling his destiny, put wings on Dooey's feet for the pursuit. It was sport now, a race—no more than a race, like hounds and hares—to rout the back-up American forces. And the image held for awhile; it measured up to the reality that immediately followed, for the hares were fast afoot. After the Indianans fled, the Second Illinois and another volunteer regiment behind them also broke and ran as the charging Mexicans crashed into them.

The American forces, vastly outnumbered, were in full retreat, some holding on, breaking more slowly than others, but all ultimately fleeing from the plateau to form a long stretched-out line down in the valley beyond it. Now Dooey's breath caught in a new moment of doubt and anguish. He could see what was happening, could see order being restored and distant men kneeling with rifles pointed, could anticipate again—with horror—having to smash into their toy-soldierish array, having to kill, be killed . . . and for no damn reason! None at all! Everything he had hoped to gain from battle, the pulse-pounding lift of spirits, was coming up in him again as a savage denial of it. The bastards, the dumb bastards! Why didn't they keep on running? Did they, like Knecht, need the ultimate bullet to scream "No!" to? Did he? In God's name, what did he think he was doing? What had he gotten himself into?

And then a startling thing happened. The Mexican cannon fire hadn't stopped; nor had fire from an American battery that, as the smoke cleared from its cannonade, suddenly loomed before them. They had reached the last American strongpoint on the plateau. From a range close enough to constitute a real threat to the Mexican attackers if they advanced any further, the U.S. battery lofted a new round of shells in Dooey's and Ryan's direction. As menacing as the battery was, it didn't halt the Mexicans, most of them conscripts, for an instant. They came up running, eyes unfocused, guns waving, charging straight into the guns.

Damn fools! And yet, Dooey might have charged with them. He had no head left, wasn't thinking, had no allegiance—least of all to the self he'd just found he'd betrayed. There was a goddamn-everything, goddamn-me feeling in him that took form now in a compulsion to charge into the teeth of those guns along with the Mexicans, at one now with the lemmings they all were. He took one quick step—

Ryan, who'd thrown himself flat on the ground as the first artillery shell landed near them, grabbed Dooey at the ankles and yanked him off his feet.

"God damn it! When the shit flies, you duck!" Ryan roared at him. "What are you—a stupid greaser?"

Dooey lay where he'd come down, hard, on his stomach, clutching rain-cold dirt, steadily digging at it with his nails. Up ahead, he saw the sickening decapitation of one Mexican, the bodies of others blasted to bits by the American shells they had charged into.

Dooey didn't say a word, but he stopped clawing the dirt; he was spent. Something had gone out of him—he didn't know what—and suddenly he felt lonely.

None of the Mexican infantry had reached the American artillery piece to destroy it. Now the Mexican cannon began to zero in on the piece, getting closer to it with each round.

"Just lie here," Ryan said softly. "It'll soon be over."

It was. Dooey could see the American major in command of the battery coming to a swift decision once the heavy enemy cannon began finding the range. The officer waved his arms in a signal for his men to withdraw. They proceeded to do so—on the double.

Ryan grinned. "Know that major from the old days. Feller named John Washington, cousin of old George. Guess good sense just runs in that family."

The plateau was cleared now. The cannon ceased firing. Ryan and Dooey got up and walked over to join Riley and the others, who were regrouping for the next stage of the attack.

Ryan pointed to the soldiers in the valley as they walked. "Dolan, did I see you worrying about those fellers back there? Well, don't." He gave a short, derisive laugh. "Take it from me, we ain't going anywhere near them. It's Taylor himself we're after. He put up some volunteers to stop us, but he and his supply train—according to what I happened to listen in on between Riley and Santa Anna—are over thataway. Some ranch called Buena Vista."

Dooey looked where Ryan was pointing. A road stretched to the northeast, bypassing the valley by a wide mark.

"No, sir. Those fellows ain't going to bother us—nor us them," Ryan went on confidently. "It's the greaser cavalry that'll finish off Taylor. They ain't much but numbers, but then numbers is what Zach ain't got. You and me, we won't have to do much from here on in. Just sort of set and wait until Taylor's done in. Then, prob'ly, we'll go back down south and face up to Scott."

Dooey hadn't said anything and didn't now.

Ryan gave him a swift glance. "You did good, Dolan, for one who ain't ever been in battle before. Right sprightly shooting you did at them field-gun boys. We'll make a soldier out of you yet."

Dolan did say something then, quietly. "And if I've changed my mind again? If I want out from the San Patricios? What then?"

He wasn't unprepared for the answer, but he wanted to hear it.

"Well now, flip-floppin' around like that wouldn't sit well with Riley, nor me neither," Ryan said thoughtfully. "Us with heads to be hanged if it comes to that, you knowin' so much about what we done, where we're going—things like that. You'd be a hard man to trust. Like, you could whip into the American lines, say howdy-do, here's your long-lost boy home again and there's *them*, meanin' us."

The notion seemed to amuse Ryan more than anything else. He slapped Dooey on the back and laughed. "Hell, you was skeered, that's all, like I was. Bein' skeered and throwin' myself down on the ground like that is why I'm here an' them blown-up Mexies ain't. Like I say, you'll get used to soldierin'. Come on, let's see if we can get some coffee."

Dooey let it go at that. Ryan's half threat alerted him to the danger he'd be in if he tried to leave the San Patricios now. On the other hand, Ryan's neat conclusion about him—that his expressed fears during and after first-time battle were more or less natural—suited Dooey fine. It was convenient; it bought him time to think, to reappraise in a cooler light what he had just put himself through.

He'd put himself through a crazy hell.

His head had been stuffed up with fancy ideas.

His impulse to run and save Knecht even though Knecht couldn't have been saved—maybe that was something real about him. He would have had that same impulse, he knew, had Knecht been a Mexican, or a U.S. trooper. Anyone at all who had shown evidence of wanting to live, he would have wanted to save.

It was himself he had not wanted to save.

He'd been trying to kill himself, had taken a near-fatal step toward it. Wasn't that what Maria had asked him to do? He'd been trying to go out in a blaze of imagined glory—a sacrifice on the altar of an uncaring love.

Something was wrong. He'd wanted to save Maria—from what?

Dooey had a blinding image. He saw himself, at eight, tucked in his bed while his parents set fire to their house. He wanted to save them, except that it had been too late; it had always been too late. What else had they done, from the moment he'd been born, but tell him to die?

And he *would* have. He would have gone down in that other blaze of imagined glory, gone down with his parents—*ma, pa, don't leave me—wait for me! I'm coming!*—except that he hadn't. He'd crawled out on a fire escape and lived.

Maybe it wasn't Maria who told him: "Go die." Maybe it was Catherine DeWitt. Anyway, he hadn't done it; he'd crawled out on that fire escape again. He'd *let* Ryan stop him, because if he'd really wanted to charge that gun, he would have.

Whatever he'd made wrong, Dooey now wanted to set right. He *had* been a traitor, he saw that now.

A betrayer first of all of himself—all his life that. And then—through his general moral spinelessness, his arrogance, setting himself up as untouchable, never to be hurt again, his ultimate equivocations—a betrayer of just about everyone who had placed any trust in him.

Dooey didn't want to be a slave to an ancient passion anymore; he wanted to be free, truly free. Henceforth, he wanted to live upright—honest with himself, honest with others. He wanted to make amends, to clear the air he had dirtied.

But Dooey had gotten himself into something of a pickle. The first thing he wanted to do was clear up the mistaken idea the San Patricios had about him. He wasn't going to put the finger on them, but he also didn't want to fight with them anymore; he'd made a serious mistake joining them. What he wanted to do was go back to Huatexco and clear the air with Maria. And he wanted to talk to Carlos too.

He found step one easier wished for than done. In the first place, his private concerns were dwarfed by subsequent events.

Soon after Dooey and Ryan joined the rest of the San Patricios in the camp they'd made on the plateau, all hell broke loose. The San Patricios were preoccupied with the hopeful expectation that the Mexican cavalry—gone on ahead with the vast majority of the army—would annihilate Taylor's army at Buena Vista.

"Make yourselves to home, boys," Riley said absently when Dooey and Ryan came up. "Cold as a bitch, ain't it? Take it easy—and stay on your toes." With that, he looked towards the east.

The San Patricios were intent now on the unseen fray in the distance. They doubted that they'd be called into action again, but they could be. Anything might happen. There was little data for judging; up ahead in the valley, those American volunteers who had fled the plateau to make a stand against an expected attack that never came, began to move at a steady marching pace along the same road the cavalry had taken, toward Buena Vista.

"What're they doin' that fer?" someone asked Riley. "It'll be over by the time they get there."

"Don't know," Riley said. "Don't know anything. Just sit tight."

"I ain't movin'," the man said.

And so it went . . . for hours, as the San Patricios awaited word of what might or might not be happening at Buena Vista. Santa Anna had ordered them to remain behind; he was up there with his army, confident of victory. Some said they'd been kept from the action because Santa Anna had easy pickings and wanted the full glory of Taylor's defeat and surrender to redound to Mexican credit alone. Riley didn't know anything about that; he just took orders from the boss.

Dooey got caught up in this nervous anticipation. It remained bitter cold and when Ryan, unasked, brought him a cup of coffee from the fire, Dooey said, "Thanks," and drank it. Ryan wasn't a bad sort. That was part of the problem: none of these people were bad sorts. The other part of the problem right now was that Dooey was a good deal less confident than they were that the battle was all but over. He looked for Ol' Zach to come riding out of the blue—their way. He tried to tell himself it was just another fantasy of punishment he thought he deserved for being —or not being—Dooey Dolan, the man who had never stood up and still had it in him to get flattened.

But, really, he had seen too many Mexicans of the sort who had plunged heedlessly ahead, and he knew they were not men of mettle like Taylor had in his regulars—Grant, Bragg, and other officers and men like them. If they came en masse and captured all those in San Patricio uniforms, where did that leave him?

It left him nervous and waiting, just like the others.

It didn't come as a bolt from the blue. In fact, it didn't come until the following evening. And it wasn't Taylor's galloping, avenging army that appeared on the darkening horizon; it was one young Mexican lancer, riding hard towards them on the road from Buena Vista. A messenger, bringing near-hysterical word of a commingled victory and defeat.

The boy jumped from his horse. Riley was waiting for him, but even he had trouble understanding the words that poured from the messenger's lips.

"We have won, but we must leave—*pronto,*" the boy announced. "You must not stay here, *Señor* Riley. I have been told to tell you to go back to San Luis Potosi and wait for our army to join you there. You must do it now!"

"Wait a minute," Riley growled. "What do you mean, we've won? If we've won, why the hurry to go south again? Don't we get no spoils?"

The boy could repeat only what he'd been told to repeat. "We have destroyed completely the American army, and General Santa Anna has decided to go quickly to defeat the one in the south."

"Oh," was all Riley said.

Dooey for his own private reasons, breathed a sigh of relief but remained silent. Someone said, "Sounds like a full-scale rout to me. Only, the other way."

" 'Tain't either," Riley said flatly. "If it was a rout,

they'd be on our asses. Sounds like a tactical withdrawal to me, like it didn't go one way or the other and the boss has made himself some other plans. Ain't that what you're telling me, boy?"

The messenger, under threat to deny it, hung his head. "All is confusion, *señor*. Many were killed on their side; many on ours. We did great damage. We drove them all to a hacienda and surrounded them. This was last night while it snowed. We might have defeated them in a final attack, but we could not see them in the dark and did not know how many were left. So the general—" The messenger hesitated.

"Decided not to risk it," Riley finished for him. "Well, that's all right. It's a decision the boss made and, if you gave 'em a good walloping to begin with, maybe it was the right one." He glowered. "Only one thing, boy. If there's ever a next time, don't lie to me—just tell it plain. If the boss wants to tell the folks in Mexico City he won big here, that's fine with me. But you hadn't oughta have lied to *me*. What you done was just a waste of my time."

Riley turned to the other San Patricios. "There ain't no real rush, looks like, so we'll do this easy. Ryan, Dolan—you go back to Agua Nueva and get us our horses. We'll do like the boss says. It's a hell of a lot warmer down south, anyway."

Dooley saw the glimmer of an out. Riley didn't like being lied to and Dooey didn't want to lie to him. It made for a bridge between the two of them.

On the way south, first day out, Dooey waited his chance, then rode up and caught Riley alone.

"When we get to Huatexco, I want out," he said. "I made a mistake coming up here with you, Riley. I hate the war."

Riley looked sideways at him sourly. "That ain't no way to act."

Dooey didn't say anything.

Riley, frowing, said, "Found you got no guts, Dolan?"

Dooey answered steadily, "I said I hate the war, Riley."

"I heard you." Riley spat. "What you didn't say was that you was holding us cheap from the time you signed on with us. I thought maybe you were, but figured you might come along. I see it plain now. In and out—that's holding us cheap."

It occurred to Dooey to deny the charge, to tell Riley he thought them fine fellows all in all. It was not without truth, and might help ease his predicament. He said instead, "All right, I held you cheap. What's it going to cost me?"

"Don't rightly know," Riley said. "You're no good, Dolan. You don't like anybody—including yourself."

Dooey could see Riley working his anger out and did not interrupt him.

"But that ain't the point now," Riley said finally. "Point is, you deserted the U.S. Army, Dolan, just like we did. If we drop you off at Huatexco, some of the boys are going to think you'll turn coat again—give evidence against us save your own neck."

"That's not my plan," Dooey said.

"How do I know what your damned plan is?" Riley flared.

"I'll tell you what it is," Dooey said. "There's a girl in Huatexco. I was living with her, long before you came. I guess maybe I held her cheap too. It's hard to explain, but I want to go back and see if I can patch things up with her. No more betrayals, Riley, of you or anybody else."

Riley's eyes narrowed. "I think I get it. You're talking about that Indian snatch who went down on the boss."

Dooey flushed.

"Word gets around." Riley thought awhile. "You know, it makes a kind of sense at that. You were using us, Dolan. You got yourself all cut up inside and used us. Now there's this change come over you, you say, and you want to go back to this hot-pants little greaser girl and—Dolan, you got shit for brains."

Dooey didn't say anything.

"Ain't up to me anyway, whether we hang you or let you go make an idjit of yourself," Riley went on. "It's up to the boys. Guess what we'll do is hold a trial. Tonight. You don't get a free ride on desertion, Dolan. No more from us than from the other side."

The San Patricios held court on Dooey around a campfire that night. He wasn't going to be given a chance to speak for himself, it turned out; that was Riley's dictum, one that Dooey—still believing it behooved him to bite the bullet, to be a man in the face of their judgment—agreed to abide by. But from where he sat, excluded by some distance from them, he couldn't help feeling that they were about to judge the fate of someone else: the man he had been but no longer was.

Riley put the issue to them: to let Dolan cut out from the battalion, or to take no chances and hang him from the nearest tree. That much got home to Dooey. He felt his neck prickle, went cold with the clarity and brevity of Riley's presentation.

But for the rest . . .

At the start, it didn't bode well for Dooey, this trial.

"Hell, Riley, I say hang him." The speaker was emphatic. "It ain't just what he *might* do, it's what he didn't do when he had the chance to do it. Those Indiana volunteers? He didn't shoot at them at all. Now that's a fact. I saw it. And it's a damn bad sign. A man can say he hates war all he wants, but if he won't shoot back when his life's at stake, I don't trust him. Unless . . . unless it wasn't at stake. Unless he had reason for believing they weren't going to shoot at him."

Riley said, "You think the U.S. Army planted Dolan with us, Tom? That he's an undercover agent?"

Tom got indignant. "Hell, *I* don't know. But I can see a case for maybe believing it." He looked around at the others for support. There were grumbles of dissent with his hypothesis, but over and above these, a continuing dark disapproval of any defense at all that might be put up in Dooey's behalf.

Riley nodded. "That's all right, Tom. I just wanted your feelings about it. That's what I want from all of you—your feelings about Dolan. I don't want him left alive if he's going to keep us nervous about him."

Now Dooey became alarmed. Their *feelings* about him? Their general feelings about him? Jesus Christ! What Riley was doing was manipulating them, pulling their strings. Dooey had been string-pulling in his time. If it was up to feelings, he was a dead man!

"He's a shifty son of a bitch," someone else said, following Riley's lead.

Ryan spoke next, hesitantly. "It's hard to figure. I got to ask this. What I saw Dolan do in battle was—well, it was a little peculiar, but it wasn't for hanging. I mean, if we're going to hang a man, I think we ought to have more evidence."

Well, that's more like it, Dooey thought; some use of reason, at last.

Riley kept looking at Ryan. "What's the question?"

"Huh?"

"You said you had a question."

Ryan was stumped. "Don't rightly know."

"Maybe it's—can we afford to take the chance?"

"No! We can't!" someone yelled. Another added: "String him up, Riley."

This was more than Dooey could take. He leaped to his feet. "Listen, you dumb bastards!" he shouted at them. "Even if I did ride all the way from Huatexco to Veracruz, what in the hell would I have to tell them that they don't know about you already? Riley, Ryan—all of you. They've got the book on you! There isn't a man here I didn't hear about when I was at Matamoros. It was a goddam litany they were singing. Get Riley, O'Reilly, O'Hara and Ryan—get all the damn Irish traitors! Now, what am I going to add to that? And as for you, Riley, what the hell are you doing setting up a kangaroo court on me? I got a good mind to punch you in the nose!"

Riley had turned to him. He was grinning. "He loves us, the son of a bitch really loves us." Then his face got dark. "Listen, Dolan, you had it coming to you. Any man who tries to make a fool out of me for some twat is going to get put through the wringer until it hurts. And it ain't over yet. Put up your dukes, Dolan! I'm personally going to beat the tar out of you!"

He charged Dooey, his fists already up in a boxer's pose, his right drawn back for a smash at Dooey's chin. Dooey's mind went blank. Enraged by the sudden attack with no thought of defense, only of beating Riley to a pulp, he had his own charge going before Riley reached him. Riley drew back, measured him as best he could and let go the right at Dooey's lowered head. The punch crashed into Dooey's ear and deafened him; a follow-up left boomed into his right eye.

But Dooey, now hearing little, seeing less, could not be stopped. His need for revenge—after having been humiliated, tricked, whatever it was—was too powerful a force in him for Riley to counter. A red blur in his right eye, then sudden pain again and blackness in his left as Riley flicked a sharp jab at it. Dooey kept coming and bulled into Riley's chest, total fury unleashed. Riley, clutching the head that had whumped him, was lifted off his feet and driven backward until, arms and legs flailing, both men went down in a heap at the edge of the campfire.

Dooey, on top of Riley and pummeling him, didn't hear the commotion behind him, ignored the hands trying to pull him off Riley, trying to stop the fight.

What they were trying to tell him—and Riley—got through to Dooey finally when he heard a bugle in the distance, a sharp sound in the night marking the appearance of a Mexican army division, the first to regroup after the Buena Vista debacle and now making an orderly retreat.

Dooey didn't know who they were when he first heard the bugle. He lifted his head sharply, alert for the approach of an American unit ordering them to lay down their arms and surrender.

He got up when he saw Mexicans. Riley got up. There was an unspoken agreement between them. It went something like: "Don't let the Mexicans see us fighting among ourselves." Just a tinge of pride and dignity on Dooey's part. He'd beaten the hell out of Riley. He felt good about it. It was over.

Riley was rubbing his cut chin, looking towards the advancing Mexicans, waiting to greet them with a friendly hello and exchange battle news and future plans.

"You can go, Dolan," he said. "Do what you have to do in Huatexco. If things don't work out for you . . . well, hell, we'll still be around."

A few days later, they rode into Huatexco. Riley and the others went immediately to Miguel's cafe. Dooey rode up the mountain trail, then down into the valley to the house he'd built for himself and Maria. The weather here was warm again, with more than a hint of spring in it. The snow had melted, and the wetness that remained added a compelling tang to the brown earth and growing grass. Even the earth wants me reborn, Dooey thought.

But he was troubled and anxious. He had an idea of how he wanted to conduct himself with Maria but he didn't know if he could carry it off.

He knocked on the door and Maria opened it. Dooey winced inwardly. Standing there bare-legged, in a brief halter, she was even more breathtakingly lovely than he remembered. A gleam came into her eye when she saw him, and a trace of scorn raised the corner of her lips. It seemed she still hated him.

Or was it his hatred for her that he was feeling?

"Hello . . . I'm back," he said, not saying, "Me, the bad penny," but only *just* not saying it.

"I see that," she said. "What is it that you have come for?"

"To tell you how I feel," Dooey said. Not saying, "This is my home, too, you goddam bitch. I built it," but only just not saying it.

Maria waited.

"There are many things I feel," Dooey said. "One

is that I'm angry with you about what you did, but I feel you had a right to do it."

Maria flared up. "I do not need you to tell me what I have a right to do."

Dooey drew in a deep breath. "Mostly what I feel is that I've never really known you, and I'd like the chance to do that—get to know you, I mean."

"*Know* me?" Maria laughed softly. "You have known me from the moment you met me. There is nothing more of me than what you have already seen."

"I don't believe that."

She looked at him in doubt for a moment. "Come in," she said.

He followed her into the front room of the house. In her lithe walk and the less-than-subtle swaying of her hips and bottom, he saw a flaunting and taunting of him that brought the blood of desire rushing to his head—along with a feeling of resentment.

He said nothing, made no move toward her. In the middle of the room, she turned. "Why don't you say what you really feel?" she taunted him. "Why don't you slap me, beat me? Why don't you rip my clothes off and take your vengeance on me?"

Dooey only listened. "How's the baby?" he asked.

The baby she was carrying had not affected her figure or brought any lines of concern to her face.

"The baby is fine," she shot at him. "I am fine."

"You seemed so happy when you found out you were going to have a baby," Dooey said, studying her. "What is it, Maria? Tell me. Was it the baby? Just something you felt you had to own? You and me, if we felt we didn't have much of ourselves, did we have to try to own someone or something else? I know I tried to own you, Maria—that much I know. It didn't work because you didn't want to be owned, no more than I did. I think what we tried to do was keep a perpetual war going, between what was free in us and what was slave in us. It helped us to go on thinking we were alive. But I ducked out on that war, didn't I? Quit on it, ran away from it. Maybe I thought it wasn't worth fighting. . . ."

That was a new idea to Dooey. He frowned as it came to him. Momentarily, it lifted him out of the sense of hopelessness he felt, standing there in his San Patricio uniform with Maria not even listening to him.

She said, "You confuse me, Dooey."

Dooey looked at her. He could have said he confused himself and looked sheepish about it; that might have charmed some warmth and tenderness out of her. But instead he struggled to get his ideas across, as if he were fighting for his life.

"Look, Maria, if I'd beat you when I saw you with Santa Anna—if I beat you now—we could have kept that war going. You didn't want me to join the San Patricios, did you? What you wanted me to do was keep the battle going with you, for me to act like a man—your notion of a man—a man who would curse you, revile, debase you, anything so long as it hurt and got you mad so you could rise and do battle again. It's when you saw me quitting on that battle that you went off with Santa Anna, to find someone else who would debase you, isn't that it?"

Maria shook her head slowly. "Poor Dooey."

And the life started going out of Dooev then.

"Why are you wearing that uniform, Dooey?" Maria said quietly.

"I tried to go off and kill myself," he said. "It was a damn fool thing I did."

"For me you tried to kill yourself?" Maria kept shaking her head. "That is nothing I ever wanted you to do."

"I guess I know that now," Dooey muttered.

"But what you don't know is what was always there for you to see. I love my country, Dooey. Many times I have told you that. The Americans are trying to take our lands away from us. I do not wish for that to happen. You led me to believe you would fight for my country—not die for me."

She was repeating a lesson in the simplest of words, as if he were a backward child.

Which he was . . . or had been.

Dooey passed his hand over his forehead. He'd heard her for the first time; he'd controlled his passions and listened to her. Of all the things he could feel, this one—the love of a country, Mexico, America, any country—was not his to feel. Feelings for individuals, yes; feelings for a country, no. It made no sense to him that anyone should love his country, for what was there to love in sheer faceless multitudes? It was beyond him, yet *she* felt it—strongly, beyond reason. It was an unbridgeable gulf between them.

"Goodbye, Maria," he said and left the house he'd built for them for the last time.

Dooey stopped off to see Carlos. Their meeting was brief. He told Carlos something of his experiences—his inner and outer ones during the battle up north near Buena Vista and the one he had just been through with Maria.

Carlos listened gravely. "Yes, *amigo*, and now?"

Dooey had a sadness in him about letting Carlos down. "I can't make a revolution with you, Carlos. Not now. I wouldn't know where to start."

"Perhaps you have already started, when you said goodbye to Maria. Even before."

Dooey listened. He heard, but he shook his head. "I have more to learn, Carlos, lots more. I'll never learn it by talking, not now. There's something I want to do now. After the war, maybe, if things go well with me and you, we can sit down and talk more about oppression—you and me and the others who feel enslaved one way or another."

Carlos smiled. "I will be here, *señor*. There is always time for the revolution. The true one, it will not happen today or tomorrow. Perhaps it will never happen. But you, *señor*, I do not lie to you, you have made a beginning. What will you do now?"

"I'm going back to the war, Carlos, with the San Patricios—if they'll take me on my terms."

Dooey rode down to Miguel's cafe. Riley saw him hitch up his horse and came out to greet him, a little high on the beer he'd drunk.

"Dolan, you old *numero,* you old *bastardo,* it's welcome back to the army, is it?"

"Maybe," Dooey said. He looked Riley in the eye. "Get this, Riley, I'll never shoot a gun at any man again."

Riley belched. He swayed forward precariously. "Well, now, what're you plannin' to offer us if it ain't your gun?"

"Somebody gets shot, I'll take care of him, best I can. You don't have anything like a doctor or a nurse with you. I'll stay in the lines with you. If I can save someone's life, I'll get in there and do it. That's what I'm offering."

He waited. Riley's beer-fogged brain digested this slowly. "That ain't the kind of dose I figured you'd get from that Injun gal. Finally found yourself some religion, Dolan?"

"I can pick up bandages and medical supplies on our way through San Luis Potosi. What do you say, Riley?"

Riley smiled broadly. "I say all right. I say fine. You're all right at that, Dolan. It's something we sure could use—and it's nice to have you join the human race."

17

THE WAR WENT on at its own pace, disappointingly slow for all those Americans who saw in Winfield Scott's thrust inland from Veracruz a quick, decisive victory. The fighting was to last another six months, into late August days that made for an almost universal climate of heat and frustration. After the initial hope faded that the demands of national honor might be quickly satisfied, James Bell and other decent men like him in the country cursed the war's dragging length.

The continuing national tension disturbed President James Polk. Midway in Scott's advance on Mexico City, in which several battles were fought and won, Polk thought it best to start prolonged negotiations with the Mexicans to accommodate growing anti-war sentiment and insure, if he could, victory for the Democrats in the presidential election of 1848. (Despite Polk's efforts, the war was ultimately to catapult the Whig candidate, General Zachary Taylor, Old Zach the gut-fighter, into the White House on a new wave of patriotic sentiment.)

Dooey Dolan and John Bell were lost to the issues being confronted by graver men than they.

What the months' long continuance of the war did for Dooey Dolan was to help him realize some purpose in his life at last, by lending a hand towards life's preservation in the company of men he had made himself a part of. He was a San Patricio whether he liked it or not, a wartime traitor to the U.S. from the moment he had joined the group, doomed to be hanged if caught. Why not, if he had to die, die fighting for life? Besides, he liked the San Patricios; they'd become friends of his. The way Dooey put it to Riley on the trek south was the way he felt it: "I may not save my neck, doing this. But it sure beats the kind of death I've known." And he only said that much because Riley remained a bit curious about the change in him. After that, Dooey said no more and Riley asked no more.

What the drawn-out, day-to-day struggles of the war did for John Bell was delay his confrontation with the man he wanted to kill. In late April, John finally learned of Dooey's whereabouts, learned enough, that is, to know that he was on the right track. But the events leading up to his discovery actually began with the battle for Veracruz.

Veracruz was largely a naval battle. In early March, when John arrived at the Lobos Island staging area, ships of the U.S. invasion fleet were already massed off that island's coast, ready on command to convey their heavy naval guns and 11,000 infantry troops down the coast to a port of entry defended, Scott believed, by 20,000 Mexican troops as well as the formidable stone fort of San Juan de Ulua in the Veracruz harbor.

Scott was wrong. Veracruz was actually defended by just one Mexican garrison whose commander thought it best not to send men en masse to man the beaches. The port lay completely vulnerable to bombardment from the sea. From a mile offshore, with the infantry as spectators, the U.S. Navy's guns lobbed shell after shell over the target's 15-foot-high waterfront walls.

It was a spectacular sight, the fall of Veracruz. Yet for the infantry, it was scarcely more than that. John was one of the first into the landing boats, one of the first of eleven thousand men to race onto Collado Beach and secure it unscathed. While brigades of Regulars took off to surround and bottle up the three thousand-man garrison, John and other volunteers pitched in to get the heavy guns ashore.

The only resistance the infantry met on the beach came from a 50-mile-an-hour norther that roared in almost at the same moment that the troops came ashore. The storm pelted sand and biting fleas into the men's faces, repeatedly knocked them off their feet, delayed their efforts to get even the ten-pound guns ashore. The storm, which lasted for seven days, made their labor almost unendurable and sometimes impossible. During its worst, men quit moving altogether, lay down and wrapped themselves in canvas sacks for protection against windblown, darting and—as it was soon discovered—disease-bearing fleas. As for the larger 24-pound guns, the ones Scott felt he needed to force Veracruz into surrender, they couldn't be brought ashore at all, nor could emplacements be sited and built for them as long as the storm raged.

All this time, to the constant apprehension of some

of the newer recruits, Mexican gunners in redoubts along the city's walls were lobbing lead at them—rounds of bullets and mortar that did not reach their distant position but came close enough to turn new recruits sick with fear that the enemy would soon get the range.

John found himself steadying the others. He'd been through enough of the war to judge the enemy's intentions against what it could possibly hope to effect. Though he remained alert to the splintering shells behind him, it was the fierceness of the storm and the voracious fleas that he saw as giving them their only real trouble.

In the end, when the storm died down, not an infantryman had been killed or wounded, but many were too haggard, too enervated by the storm's lash and the bleeding bites they had suffered to be of further assistance. John pushed himself to get the job done, the job he had been ordered to do. When a gunboat carrying a 24-pounder finally managed to make it ashore, he and some others like him trotted painfully to the water's edge.

"Where does it go?" John shouted.

A sailor shouted back at him cheerily: "You look like hell, man. It goes to a Captain Lee—over there someplace. He's to site it." He pointed south, down the beach.

John nodded, the name Lee making a flickering impression on him. At least he knew him; he'd find him. He and the four infantrymen with him unloaded the piece and started tugging and rolling it through the yielding shore mud. It was a tough job.

"Seven days and seven nights and this is what we come up with," one of the men muttered wearily. "Seems to me the Lord did better than that."

It made John grin. He felt lighthearted with an accomplishment in the making. Soon enough he spied Lee and directed the others: "Over there—that way!"

Lee and a younger officer with him were so far from the city's walls they couldn't be reached by anything the Mexicans might bring up on short notice to hurl at them. They already had an emplacement site picked out. John and his crew brought up the gun.

Lee, busy with the other officer, at first acknowledged them only as a group with a terse, "Thanks, men. You can leave it right here. I'll get some of my people to do the rest." Then he recognized John and smiled, and John forgave him for not remembering him at Fort Hamilton. "Bell . . . good to see you. Shake hands with P.T.G. Beauregard. I'm sure he appreciates this too."

The curly haired Beauregard, a man in his late twenties, smiled. "I'll appreciate it more if you go back and get my gun, soldier. All I'm doing is helping this old duffer line up his."

John grinned at him. "I'll help you set up if you like, Captain Lee. Just tell me what to do."

Lee nodded. "You might at that. The more hands the better. We've been held up long enough."

In the press of his own work, Lee now ignored Beauregard, who realized he was no longer needed and departed with the infantrymen who had come with John. They headed back towards the boats bringing more big guns in.

John stayed. With the engineering personnel Lee quickly rounded up, John did what was necessary to get the 24-pounder ready for firing. Then he stood back, as did Lee, and the artillerymen took over.

In due course, all the other big guns were brought ashore. From up and down the beach, 24-pounders blasted the city of Veracruz. A church in the distant *zocalo* was torn from its foundation. Houses were demolished, hundreds of civilians were killed. The Mexican garrison—what was left of it—broke through the encircling Americans and fled into the hills.

In the end, after a two-week siege, Scott had what he wanted: the city's total surrender. It was thought the price had been small; in all, just thirteen Americans had been killed in battle during the taking of Veracruz.

But it turned out the price wasn't so small. In the days that followed, Scott—like Taylor before him—found that he couldn't move inland as rapidly as he wished. Now the suffocating sea-level heat came on, and with it infections, diseases, lassitude. Maybe the American army was laid low by fleas—the poison they injected into non-immunized, vulnerable bodies used to more temperate climes. Or maybe it was the bad water . . . or the bad food. No one knew for sure, but the men were laid low by the hundreds, by the thousands—with no cure in sight, or even amelioration. The medical staff could do no more than they had been doing throughout the war: let men lie and groan, or ship them home.

For a while, Scott did not know what to do with an army suddenly now so largely on its back. So he remained in Veracruz, waiting, growing more and more irritated by the delay, but still waiting.

John Bell was one of those who took sick. It was an undeniable sickness with him, as it was with so many others. A heavy dreariness, a burdensome weight on the spirit, yet in his case with a gnawing in the pit of his stomach telling him that he must not lie there . . . he must not, he must not. He must get up and . . .

He lay feverish in the Veracruz hospital, one of the few large buildings left untouched by the American bombardment. As had happened to him more than once in the war, he hardly knew where he was, or even who he was. He had a dim memory of feeling vastly excited when Captain Lee's gun was first fired, and of all those guns going off and the whole city going up in fire. God, what a booming glorious sight! Victory, smash 'em, victory! He was on fire with it! But then, all those people being killed, those civilians; he'd seen the burials still taking place two days later when he'd finally given up, had come to the hospital, half stumbling with his illness. Why did they have to kill all those civilians? What in God's name was the point of it all? And he sweated with that, the water pouring out of him.

It took John three days to come down from anguished thoughts befogged by fever, anguished thoughts in which Dooey Dolan had had no place. But when he did come down, when his fever left him, there was Dolan again. He was the gnawing in his stomach that would not leave him, that was with him still, cold as ice.

It was what made him get out of bed when he might have stayed there, as others in his ward did when an orderly came through the hospital some days later and made an announcement. General Scott had come to a decision about what to do with his army.

"We're moving out the day after tomorrow," the orderly said. "It was just posted. The general seems to think you fellows are only down with the heat and once you get into the mountains, you'll be all right again. There's no direct order applied to hospitalized patients, but the general expects to be in Jalappa—that's close to a mile above sea level—very shortly.

That might be better for your health than anything we can do for you here. You'll have to decide for yourselves on whether to go or not."

Over half the men in that ward were too sick or had too little confidence in the iffy nature of what they had been told to find the will to move.

John was one of those who got up, dressed and checked out of the hospital.

He'd already learned that the San Patricios had come south with the Mexican army and knew that, sooner or later in the course of the invasion, Scott's troops would likely confront them. What he didn't know was whether or not Dolan had joined them. John was taking the chance that he had, and that Scott might see fit to form a special unit for rounding up all deserters, wherever they might be hiding.

There was good reason to believe Scott might. Deserters had become his pet peeve, something concrete and specific of a military nature that he could fix his mind on during the general harrassment from Washington on political matters. Everywhere in camp were posters listing traitors' names and descriptions—Riley, Ryan, all those Regulars who had deserted before the war. Scott wanted to hang them.

John didn't care about those men; he just wanted to get to one certain deserter before Scott did, and would have volunteered for any mission sent out to find any of them.

As it turned out, though one such deserter-hunting unit was indeed later organized, John didn't have to join it.

He got the information he was seeking just prior to a battle at Cerro Gordo, a sleepy little hill town on the road to Jalappa that—on the basis of advance scouting reports—took on the aspect of an exceedingly dangerous obstacle in the American army's path. And though the information about Dooey reached John at secondhand, its source was unimpeachable: it came from the one man in Scott's army who knew both Dooey Dolan and John Bell.

What happened first was that the road-weary army was brought to a sudden halt in a mountain pass some fifty miles inland from Veracruz, with Jalappa still twelve miles off. Rumors of the reason for the stop soon filtered down through the ranks.

"Santa Anna's up ahead . . . He's got twelve thousand troops with him . . . They say he's got the high ground on both sides of the road covered with cannon . . . Yeah, three-gun batteries, seven-gun batteries —they're all over the place . . . Who knows how we're going to get through? Damned if I do!"

John caught such remarks from junior officers in his and other regiments. There was nothing for it but to join the rest of the troops in plunking his weary bones down in the chaparral, his canteen and rifle beside him, to await developments . . . and wait some more.

For a day and a half the army sat where it was. Then a decision was reached. It was made by General Winfield Scott himself. The general, who had remained behind in Veracruz while his field commanders advanced the army, now came riding up the road to settle the argument that had arisen among them. Alongside Scott rode Captain Robert E. Lee.

John's spirits picked up when he saw Lee. He had no idea what Scott had in mind for dealing with the situation they were faced with, but he had faith in Lee. He'd formed an enormous respect for the captain's abilities and judgment and coolness under fire. If Lee figured in Scott's plan—and it seemed pretty clear to John that he did—it could be they wouldn't have to sit there much longer, hung up and blistering in the desert sun.

As it turned out, Scott's plan was for Captain Lee to go on a vital mission that very night, into the deep ravines and dense forest that lay far to the left of the Mexicans' hilltop guns guarding the road. He was to look with his engineer's eye to see if a trail could be cut through the woods allowing the army and its guns to outflank Santa Anna and come up behind him on the Jalappa road.

It wasn't until the following afternoon, long after Lee had returned and reported on the success of his mission to Scott, that John heard of the adventure Lee had encountered. Word came down the line that Lee was up ahead, regaling listeners with the previous night's exploits. John got up from where he was sitting and waiting, and walked up the road to join a sizable crowd of officers and men gathered around Lee.

Lee was still intoxicated with the dangers he had faced during the night. John thought he looked twenty years younger than he had at Fort Hamilton.

"I could have reached up—like this—and grabbed the rifle of one of them, he was that close," Lee was saying as John squeezed into the group around him. "So I just lay there, under a log no bigger than the one I'm sitting on now, and I swear I thought I'd had it. Six of them, mind you, within inches of me—having a fine old time gabbing—and me with my nose buried in ferns, not daring to breathe. And the ants and spiders crawling all over me! Darned if that didn't turn out to be the worst part. Because when those six left, more came. I tell you, it was the damnedest thing! Seems like every patrol they had out in the woods was using the log I picked to hide under, to sit on. I had those ants and spiders making a good meat dish out of me for hours!"

"And nobody saw you?" someone said.

Lee grimaced. "Soldier, if they *had* seen me, you'd have had a dead Lee to bury!"

He was about finished with his yarn; there was another staff meeting for him to attend, this one principally concerned with which troops would take the outflanking trail he had scouted and which, during that maneuver, would keep Santa Anna's army occupied with a diversionary attack.

The captain got up to go and the crowd dispersed. John lingered behind. He wanted to put in a personal word of congratulations.

He didn't get the chance. Lee happened to glance John's way, saw him and suddenly frowned.

"Bell, come here a moment, will you? I'd like to talk to you—in private."

John went over. Lee confided to him briefly: "I'm afraid I have some disappointing news for you, John. One of the patrols that came my way while I was under that log was made up of San Patricios. Your friend Dolan was with them—I recognized his voice. I reported this to General Scott. I want you to know that I'm sorry your suspicions about Dolan have been confirmed."

John heard him, and then for a moment heard and saw nothing in the red blur of renewed rage that swept over him. The ways, the innumerable ways in which the Dooey Dolan he had worshipped had betrayed him and now his country buzzed in his head like gnats.

Lee was speaking to him gently. "Don't take it so hard, son. We have to learn to accept these things, no matter how it hurts."

But Lee didn't know, that was the point! He didn't know half.

John drew himself up. Something went click in the breech of his brain. He was stiff and cold with his thanks. "I appreciate what you've told me, sir. It isn't anything I can't handle."

He left to rejoin his regiment while Captain Robert E. Lee—as had Lieutenant Lew Wallace on other occasions—stared after him in wonder.

John Bell didn't kill Dooey Dolan during the Battle of Cerro Gordo, because his prey was no longer there to be searched for and found.

This battle, fought over two days in mid-April, 1847, resulted in a decisive victory for Scott's forces. It all but broke the back of the Mexican army. It drove the remnants back towards Mexico City for a series of last-ditch stands at Perote, Puebla, San Antonio, Chrubusco and Chapultepec, among other places along the national highway from Veracruz. Valiant as the rank-and-file defenders were, these stands could not stop Scott's relentless advance or dull his desire to take Mexico City by force. Only fumbling peace negotiations, hampered by political whim, could do that—and not before the Mexican countryside lay bathed in the blood of Mexico's champions.

Except for the soldiers of the San Patricio Battalion, most of whom were doomed to die in another way

It was all still to come, of course, along with the fate of the man among them whom John Bell, as relentless in his way as Scott was in his, swore he alone would kill.

* * *

The San Patricios, Dooey among them, were lined up with a Mexican division, answering bullet for bullet the expected attack from the front at Carro Gordo, when all hell suddenly broke loose behind them. For a moment, not even Riley could believe what had happened. He twisted his head around: two full American divisions had come out of the woods a half-mile back and were in full charge at the Mexican batteries defending the promontories, taking them completely by surprise.

"Christ almighty!" Riley swore. He turned to the front again. He saw the trap he was in and knew in an instant that there was no way it could be fought out of. Riley hung on grimly. He started shouting at the other San Patricios, some of whom were looking askance at what appeared to be—and was—a catastrophic onslaught on their main line of defense.

"Forget 'em! Stay with what we have!" Riley yelled.

But it was impossible to do that, because if the San Patricios didn't panic, the vast majority of the Mexican infantry with them did. They saw doom facing them; they saw not only their batteries going under in the attack, but the road to Jalappa and all possible reinforcements being cut off. Confusion spread through their ranks and with it flight—into the same woods the Americans had come out of, into the gullies, then into the hills on the other side of the road.

Dooey saw all this happening. He saw the Mexicans running away even before the battling San Patricios saw it because he had been keeping low some distance behind Riley's men, holding no gun, holding only himself in readiness to give aid to the wounded if he could. Now he could see there would very likely be no San Patricio wounded. With no back-up support, there would likely be only San Patricio dead.

He ran up to Riley through a hail of lead and grabbed him by the shoulder. "You got to pull us out of here, you stupid son of a bitch!"

Riley tugged away from him savagely. A San Patricio beside him had already been killed. Riley grabbed the dead man's rifle and tossed it to Dooey. "You'll get your fool head blown off if you don't use that! They're coming right at us! We can get out if we can hold 'em down long enough!"

It could work, Dooey saw. An American infantry brigade was running up both sides of the road toward them at that very moment, still two hundred yards off but coming fast. If they could be made to stop, to take cover in the ditches . . .

The other San Patricios were firing steadily. Dooey flung himself down on his belly with the rifle and started shooting. It was all instinct, no thought, and his aim was perfect. He saw a man go down and heard Riley grunt approval.

And then it was done. What they had to do was done. The barrage of San Patricio fire slowed the one brigade that was the most immediate threat, drove it for cover into gullies still at some distance from them.

Riley growled, "All right, now! Let's get out of here!"

They got up from their own protected positions and sped into the woods. American artillery was following the infantry brigades up that road. The woods were deep and there wasn't any point in Riley's men sticking around simply to be captured, court-martialed and hanged. Alive, their necks intact, they could fight for Mexico another day.

18

So it wasn't over yet, neither the larger war nor the two personal struggles it dragged along with it on the road to Mexico City: John Bell's determination to find and avenge himself on his best friend, and Dooey Dolan's ongoing search for—what? Himself? Some new way to live in the world with resolve and clear purpose—his own—and devil take the hindmost?

Perhaps he had already found that, or was well on his way towards finding it.

Dooey retreated from the battle lost at Cerro Gordo with a clear awareness of what he had done there and a new deeper sense of commitment to the San Patricios.

Riley never brought up the matter of Dooey's having shot a rifle in their defense while under American attack. It was Dooey himself, during the ride west to Perote, who mentioned it.

"I guess I might as well be hanged for a sheep as a lamb," was the way he put it.

But Riley shook his head. "You don't have to fight in the line with us, Dolan. One shot don't put you in it. You can go back to being a sawbones—same deal we had."

Dooey thought about it some more. "You're a good bunch of guys, Riley. I'll do my share."

And he meant it at that point, was convinced he meant it. Determined to make a choice, he'd made it. If the choice was based entirely on the flushed warm feeling of camaraderie, what was wrong with that? Camaraderie was life-giving. A man had to be part of *something*, something ongoing, something *now*, in the present, and moving towards the future—toward whatever that future might hold. Dooey wasn't trying to kill himself, not now. Since he'd cut himself free from Maria, there wasn't a suicidal impulse left in him. There wasn't, by God, a damn thing holding him back from living and fighting alongside men who liked him and whom he considered—all he had to do was admit it—not just good but about the greatest bunch of fellows he had ever met!

The only reason Dooey had to keep arguing with himself this way was that now and then, at night while lying on a blanket and looking up at the moon, he would, in spite of himself, bring the sense and image of Maria to his chest and brain and lodge them there, as if he were a kind of temple of eternal peace, sheltering them both. She was a Maria of infinite tenderness. They had no age but were young and sorrowful, as if they lay with the world's grief as well as their own in their arms. At such times he could not leave her, never would. The fighting of a war had no place in this picture and did not exist.

These were moonlit fancies, Dooey knew that now. The Maria of his romantic imaginings was not the Maria he had finally gotten to know, but a dream creature calling him back to some other time, some other place. He could and did shrug these fancies off during the day. He *would* go on and fight the war, damn it. What the hell else was a man to do?

Yet, these imaginings gave him his share of troubled self-doubt.

It was the dramatic re-entry into Dooey's life of the real Maria which brought his and John Bell's destinies into tragic confrontation.

It was an August day. Dooey was in his billet in Mexico City, cleaning his gun. He'd fought in many battles by now, was inured to the killing he had done and the carnage he had seen. The Mexican army had given ground, slowly but inexorably. It was a beaten army—even Santa Anna knew it. He had left the army's command to other generals, had withdrawn to Mexico City's palace to ponder, draw up and tender to the American peace negotiator—a lower-echelon State Department official now traveling with Scott—a proposed settlement that would not be unfavorable to Santa Anna's retention of power once the Americans had left Mexico.

Yet, while Santa Anna bristled with indignation at having to deal with a "clerk" in the first place, and the militant Scott fumed, feeling encumbered by that same "clerk," there remained still another battle to be fought.

Five miles outside Mexico City's gates was the village of Churubusco. While the negotiators hemmed and hawed, Scott had finally decided to move his army on and storm the capital. It was now approaching Churubusco from the east. Dooey's San Patricio battalion was getting ready to go out and help in the attempt to stop the U.S. Army's progress.

There came a hesitant knock on Dooey's door at about eleven that August morning. During the week-long interruption in the fighting, he'd been having a passingly satisfying affair with the daughter of the woman who owned the house. He thought it was her at the door and said, "Come in, Carla."

It was Maria. Dooey's heart jumped when he saw her. She was carrying an infant in her arms, but for the moment Dooey had eyes only for her. He felt something like a stab in his chest from her loveliness, from the stricken look of hesitation and bewilderment he saw on her face as she stood in the doorway. All thought fled him. He went to her, quickly, and crushed her in his arms.

"Maria, for God's sake, Maria. . . ."

She began sobbing against his chest, cradling the baby awkwardly away from his savage embrace.

"Dooey, I need you! I love you! I did not know how much I needed you until you left!"

He stood there holding her. He didn't understand what she was saying, didn't get the full sense of it. He felt himself drowning in this dream of his come true, and he yielded to it—to a sea of forgetfulness, a river of time, to the long-ago yearnings he'd had as a child.

But it couldn't last. Slowly, Dooey came back to himself. He let Maria go.

She seemed to grow frightened again. She held the baby toward him. "This is . . . Maria, Dooey. She is what you wanted, a little girl."

Dooey looked at the infant and saw it as a sacrificial offering to him. Perhaps it wasn't, but he saw it that way, forcing himself to be colder now in his thoughts. Yet he didn't reach out and take the baby; he wasn't sure of what holding it would do to his resolve.

"How did you get here, Maria? How did you find me?"

She said quickly, "Carlos brought me from Huatexco. Everyone in Mexico City knows where the San Patricios are. Oh, Dooey! I do not want you to fight with them any longer. You will be killed if you do! Dooey . . . please . . . we have lost. Come home with me!"

Dooey looked at her as if from a distance. He saw a girl he didn't know. He thought he had known her, but it turned out he didn't. And it was too late now to go into this new puzzle of her. Maybe later, but not now.

He said, "Maria, I love you. I always have, I always will. But things are a little complicated here right now. I want you to take the baby and go back home with Carlos. There may be fighting here before long. I don't want you to get hurt."

She stared at him.

"You were a damn fool to come in the first place," Dooey said. "Now, go away. I have work to do."

He said it more coldly than he had meant to. It was for her own good that he told her to go, but it was for his, too, because he felt he would weaken if she stayed. He was going out with Riley and the others, as he had at Perote, Puebla, San Antonio—all those lost causes. It was just something he had to do.

Maria looked at him as if she no more understood the change in him than he understood the change in her. He thought: Was I wrong? Has becoming a mother made her need me—really need me? Has she finally found something in me to love?

He didn't know, and now she said:

"All right. I will go. I love you, Dooey, I love you . . . but I will go."

And she did, leaving Dooey to try and put her out of his mind again.

The Battle of Churubusco was fought on August 20, 1847. Except for the convent-fortress of San Mateo—a towering brickworks which was to be defended in part by 67 valiant members of the San Patricio Battalion—the terrain was mostly flattened cornfields, the road of the American advance cutting through them.

What the American troops saw, coming in, was the San Mateo fortress looming ahead on the left side of the road and Mexican troops in the cornfields on the right, at least 10,000 of them ready to deliver a barrage of grapeshot, canister, musketry, round shot and shell. Over four thousand Mexicans would be killed or wounded in those cornfields that day, another three thousand taken prisoner. And on the American side? Roughly the same sobering sort of casualty list in proportion to a far smaller force going in: 133 killed, some nine hundred wounded, another forty missing and presumed dead.

That was to come.

What the San Patricios in the redoubts of the San Mateo convent saw marching towards them was the same tough, disciplined American army that had forced them into so many retreats before, and below them that same Mexican army—now weak and emaciated—which might panic and flee even earlier than in previous battles, leaving them with no support. On the far side of the cornfields, a local hill road streamed with civilians leaving Mexico City by this unfortunate route.

At least one of the watching San Patricios took careful note of these departing civilians, stumbling in their fearful uncertainty as to which way to turn so as to get away from the random dangers of the impending battle. Riley, standing beside Dooey, saw him studying the civilians and said, "You know someone out there, Dolan? That kid Carla you been humping, maybe?"

Dooey shook his head. "I know someone who may be out there. The road goes where she's going."

He didn't say who it was who might be there. He knew what Riley thought about Maria, that Indian whore.

There was another feature of this general landscape that was of importance at this point to General Winfield Scott. It couldn't be seen with the naked eye because it was up ahead, three miles past Churubusco, on the approach to the gates of Mexico City. But Scott had it in his mind's eye and spoke of it. What he had to say about it just naturally got passed down through the ranks until every last man in the army heard it.

Two nights before the infantry reached Churubusco, the volunteers were marveling at the dramatic nature of what Scott intended to do with the San Patricios he caught. A man from Tennessee explained it to others around a campfire:

"See, there's this hill—Chapultepec—we're going to take after we blast 'em out of Churubusco. The one they say's got a castle on it flying a big Mexican flag?

Well, seems there's a bit smaller hill close by. What Ol' Fuss n' Feathers is gonna do with those bastards is put 'em on a scaffold on this little hill so's they can see us take the bigger hill. He wants 'em to see the Mexican flag come down and the Stars and Stripes go up. Then, *whup*, ther're done for—just like that. They get their horses kicked out from under 'em and hanged—just like that. Ain't that somethin'?"

"Jee-sus Christ!" A Pennsylvanian thwacked his thigh. "It sure is something. It beats all, that's what it does. Damn me if I don't want to be there to see 'em get it like that!"

"Maybe, Jack," someone said slyly, "you can be the one to put the flag up."

"Hell, I don't mind doin' that neither if it comes to it," the Pennsylvanian said. "Won't be no skin off my teeth if what I do makes 'em bastards swing in the breeze."

In the general support of the sharply vindictive terminal lesson in national honor Scott had it in mind to teach the San Patricios, one man in that circle of volunteers stood somewhat apart. John Bell didn't really care about Scott's plan; he had stopped listening. All that interested him was that the deserter battalion was right now at Churubusco.

And with it was Dooey Dolan, who had retreated from his vengeance so many times before.

"Here they come!"

Riley said what didn't have to be said.

Dooey put his rifle barrel over the high fortress wall and waited. They all did, tensely. The Americans came on, at first like blue flies shimmering in the distance. A division of infantry up front. Mounted dragoons behind them. Then the artillery, despite the ominous silence still too far away to hear the creak of its wheels.

But coming closer. And behind the San Patricios at their positions along the wall, higher still in the convent's towers, seven Mexican cannon—waiting, as were the Mexican musketeers in the cornfields.

Then the American infantry and dragoons stopped, up the road out of rifle range. The artillery pieces were rolled to the front and their barrels aimed directly at the convent.

"Christ, they're going to try to blast us out of here first," Riley said.

He had no sooner said it when a barrage of shells came their way with explosions that wracked the countryside like thunder. Shells smashed into the brick walls and were lofted over them. Swearing, the San Patricios pulled their rifles in and ducked down as the Mexican cannon behind and above them replied, adding more thunderous explosions to the landscape.

At first, the Mexican balls fell short of the American position, then they went over it, then they began to hit—into the midst of an army that had perhaps taken them too lightly, had not expected accuracy from them at so great a range and began to scatter into the cornfields to take up new positions and await the softening up, if not the total destruction, of the convent by their own big field guns.

The San Patricios cheered at the sight of the fleeing American infantry, not recognizing it as a hollow victory. But Dooey knew; he could feel in his bones that there was nothing to cheer about. He looked at Riley's grim face and saw that he knew too.

"Can't shoot those bastards unless they come this way," Riley muttered. But it wasn't the infantry he was concerned about; it was the American artillery.

Dooey knew the remark about the infantry—so hopelessly far from them—was only Riley's way of trying to keep his mind focused on his own proper work.

Soon he couldn't do that any longer; none of them could. The American artillery kept up a steady barrage while its infantry waited, secure enough now from what the Mexican cannon kept throwing back at its opposing big guns. Then the American artillery began having the far greater effect.

Still keeping low behind the wall, the San Patricios turned as one man when they heard an explosion followed by screams, turned in time to see one Mexican cannon with its crew blown completely from its tower position to crash down onto the stone walk beneath it. A moment later, another gun crew was wiped out by shell fragments exploding in their faces. Cries of anguish filled the convent. Cannoneers fled their guns. Three guns were silenced because their crews, having remained at their positions as long as they could, were now running down the tower stairs, then down another flight into the upper courtyard where the San Patricios were positioned.

The gunners' screams were horrific; they nearly tore Dooey's heart out. Still, a worse predicament faced him, Riley, all of them. As they watched the Mexican defense crumble, the San Patricios saw the Mexican commander on the wall above unfurling a white flag, preparing to surrender the convent.

Riley swore. "Christ, we can't let them do that! It's our necks if they do! Dolan, come on!"

The two ran up the stairs. Dooey, faster afoot than Riley, reached the commander first and grabbed the white flag from his hands. Then Riley was there. They overcame the Mexican's protests with threats of immediate death if he tried showing that flag again.

But the convent was done for anyway. There was no point remaining there after the American guns had taken their toll of Mexican cannon and Mexican will to fight back.

"Come on! Let's go out and get 'em!" Riley roared. "We ain't got a thing to lose!"

And they didn't; Dooey knew they didn't. Caught up in the moment, feeling the cause not yet lost if they kept fighting for it, he was right behind Riley, running out of the convent and taking a belly-down position in the cornfield, in the van of the Mexican infantry spread out behind them.

And now the American infantry, no longer in danger from convent guns, rose en masse and came forward to meet them, aided by a new barrage of artillery support.

Dooey waited, rifle ready. Shells dug into the field all around him, but he waited quietly, licking his lips. He thought he saw everything, because all there was to see was the American infantry coming straight at him.

But something else was happening too. The exodus of civilians on the road to Dooey's left had been interrupted. The barrage of cannon fire from both sides had stopped it in its tracks. The people with their donkeys and possessions had been afraid to go on. Some had been further terrified and come into the cornfield, more exposed to shell fire there than they would have been had they stayed on the road.

Dooey finally shifted his eyes and saw these wanderers. It was impossible to judge what they were trying to do. It occurred to Dooey that they might be trying to get back to Mexico City, and because the road behind them was blocked by people still wanting to go the other way, had come down into the cornfield with the idea of going around them. That might have been the case, but Dooey would never know.

He was peering into the midst of these wanderers and, as he did, his heart nearly stopped with dread. He imagined he saw Maria there. He saw a girl, a slim, shapely Indian girl. He was only imagining it was Maria—or so he told himself. He couldn't really see well enough at that distance to *know* that it was Maria. It must be some terrible vision he was having, that this Maria, who was not Maria—was going to get killed, that she was killing herself, deserting him, leaving him forever.

It was crazy.

Dooey blinked. It was *not* Maria—he was going mad again. The American infantry was coming, two volunteer regiments now no more than a hundred fifty yards off and ready to charge. He had to snap himself out of it. . . .

A girl had run into a cornfield for God knew what reason. And then, as the American artillery blasted out a new round of shells and the American volunteers charged, the girl was running straight at him. Dooey had roused himself and turned his eyes to the front. He was shooting back at that first infantry wave and so did not see that it *was* Maria, really Maria . . . until it was too late.

He cried out at her, horrified: "Maria, get back! Get back!"

He'd stopped firing the moment he'd seen her, but then the American volunteers had too. All thirty-six of them in that first wave had hit the dirt fifty yards off, unwilling to shoot a young girl who—God knew for what reason—had come running into their line of fire.

But the artillery, far back, had not let up. A shell

exploded a few feet from Maria as she ran. She was lifted off her feet and was dead when she landed.

Letting out a howl of anguish, Dooey ran to Maria's still body, knelt, took her in his arms and, huddling her face against his chest, peering at it, began sobbing uncontrollably.

His back was to the American infantrymen who, perhaps believing the girl was still alive and about to be dragged to safety continued to delay their attack.

All but one.

John Bell, who was in that first wave, did not hold back. John Bell saw Dooey Dolan. That was all he had to see. During that peculiar momentary truce, he went charging across the cornfield, his bayonet ready. Then he was standing at Dooey's back, trembling with rage, yet holding it in long enough to demand:

"Face me, you son of a bitch!"

Dooey slowly raised his head and turned to face whoever it was. He saw it was John Bell. "Hello, Johnny," he said. "Where've you been keeping yourself?"

John stared at the man at his feet. Dooey's eyes were vacant. He had an odd little smile at the corners of his mouth that came out with his seeing John, but there were tears running down his face that he seemed oblivious to. Then John recognized the girl he had in his arms, watched Dooey smoothing the dark hair against the dead cheek.

All his desire for vengeance went out of him. He stood there a moment, bewildered. "Dooey . . . ? What have you done to yourself?"

Dooey shook his head. "I don't know, John. I—maybe you could tell me. . . . ?"

John roused himself, looked around, saw where he was, spoke sharply. "Dooey, get out of here. Run—

anywhere! Just get out of here. There's still time. If you're not shot now, Scott'll hang you later."

Dooey said flatly, "Let him."

John looked at him a moment longer and recognized how useless further argument would be. He gritted his teeth, angry now with a friend he suddenly saw as having betrayed not him so much or his country, but only himself.

"You're on your own, Dooey," he said. He turned and ran back to his lines.

Dooey watched him go, but with eyes that no longer saw. He had the dead Maria in his arms and he felt himself to be dead with her. Mechanically, he released her, let her body lie where it was. He got up, walked back to his position, got belly-flat and picked up his rifle.

The shooting started again.

Little remained of the war now.

In the action at Churubusco, the Mexican forces were routed and all 67 San Patricios were taken prisoner—with them, Dooey Dolan.

Ex-U.S. Sergeants John Riley and William Ryan, along with eleven others who had deserted before the outbreak of the war were let off by General Scott with "D" brandings on both cheeks. The others were sentenced to hang.

While Dooey was under guard at Churubusco, where the American army would remain for nearly a month of renewed peace negotiations, John came to visit him several times.

To John, Dooey didn't seem to be at peace with himself, even though he had more than once claimed to be.

"Are you going to marry Sally?" Dooey asked quietly during one such visit.

"I hope to, if she'll have me," John replied.

Dooey nodded. "That's good."

That visit had been awkward for John. He hadn't told Dooey, now so obviously a broken man, of the vengeful feelings he had carried for so long, he hadn't told him about Sally. He had let Dooey think he had become enraged with him on the battlefield because he had seen him as a San Patricio, a traitor to his country. If Sally would have it, John was planning to marry her and adopt Dooey's baby. But he hadn't told Dooey anything about that.

What he had told him was: "I just saw red when I saw you in that Mexican uniform. I mean, you and I, we came down as buddies, and then to see you fighting *against* me! Well I—"

"I understand," Dooey had soothed him.

"I—I didn't know how—how you felt about that girl, Dooey. I just didn't know . . . how I would find you."

"It's all right, John," Dooey had said, his manner abstracted. "Everything's all right."

Which had gotten John to see that everything was not all right, that something was worrying Dooey.

It came out on another visit when John, buoyed up by more hope than he had reason to feel, had said, "Dooey, I think Scott's going to commute your sentence. He has to. There's too much anti-war sentiment back home for him to put Americans to death."

"He's not going to commute it," Dooey said. He frowned. "John, there's something you can do for me."

"If I can, I will, Dooey."

"There's a village called Huatexco up in the Sierra Madres, about a hundred miles north of San Luis Potosi. It's where I lived for a while. I want you to go there after the war. Find an Indian named Carlos

Alvarez. He's a wise man, John; you'll like him." Dooey gave him a wry, crooked smile. "Carlos and I, we were going to talk about this, that and the other thing after the war, but mostly about freedom and slavery. We're all slaves, John. . . ." Dooey bit his lip. "Anyway, tell Carlos I won't be able to make it, but that I hope he will find others interested enough to keep on talking. Maybe you'll be one of them, John."

John remained silent.

Dooey had more to say and he said it straight out: "Maria and I had a baby, John. A little girl. I'm pretty sure Carlos has her, because I think Maria would have given her to him before she came running to me. What I want is for you and Sally to take the baby. Take her back to the States. Let her be an American. Only, do what you can to let her grow up free, with a mind of her own. That's all, John."

John protested. "Dooey, you'll be able to do that yourself. You'll—"

"Goodbye, John."

In mid-September, John Bell went on to participate in the Battle of Chapultepec, while Dooey Dolan and the other doomed San Patricios were placed on a scaffold to watch the action from a short distance away.

It so happened that the castle atop Chapultepec had been in use as a military academy and was being defended in part by the academy's two dozen or so boy cadets—all between the ages of thirteen and fifteen. Though most of the Mexican army had withdrawn to other positions in and surrounding Mexico City, these boys had volunteered to remain and defend Chapultepec to the end.

Nine boys would die that day from American bullets and bayonets. They would be celebrated in history as *Los Niños Heroicos*, and monuments would be erected in their honor along the balustrade of the walk just below the tower that flew the Mexican flag they tried to keep out of American hands.

From where he sat on his horse, Dooey could see the action plainly. It lasted a day and a night, but in the end a valiant American infantry managed, under heavy fire, to reach the top of the two hundred-foot-high hill and make a dash for the tower from which the Mexican flag flew.

Now Dooey saw one of the boys climb the tower and come down with the flag wrapped around his chest. From the way he was darting about, it appeared that he wanted to run away with the flag, but he was quickly surrounded by charging Americans. The boy had no place to run.

Dooey saw a black volunteer stab the boy through the chest with his bayonet. He saw the boy pull the blade out and run to the balustrade, from which, the flag still wrapped around him, he dashed himself to death on the rocks below.

The three American flag bearers, who were past their own climbing days, had some trouble getting the American flag to the top of the tower. They had to pass it up window to window from the outside.

But they got the job done.

The Stars and Stripes waved high.

The next moment, Dooey Dolan was dead.

THE END

Historical Note: General Winfield Scott entered Mexico City in triumph a few days after the battle of Chapultepec. Five more months of negotiations followed. By the terms of Treaty of Guadalupe Hidalgo, finally ratified by the Mexican senate on May 30, 1848, the United States made a $15,000,000 payment to Mexico and agreed to assume private American claims against that country. In return, the United States acquired Mexican lands that have since become the states of California, Nevada, Utah and Arizona, and parts of the states of New Mexico, Colorado and Wyoming, as well as all of the area of Texas that had been in dispute.

FREEDOM FIGHTERS #7

The Turning of the Tide

by Jonathan Scofield

The Union forces under General Grant were reeling, their officer corps decimated by fire from the gray-clad Confederate ranks, when an unlikely hero came forward to lead them to a stunning victory. Fighting under the name of Lawrence DeWitt Dahlgren—a name that was not even his own—this mere corporal held the key to the turning of the tide against the Cause of the South.

Meantime, up North on the home-front, Laura, the lovely young heiress of the DeWitt clan, was caught up in the swirling, poisonous winds of treachery—as the fanatical Fremont Hunter schemed at her betrayal and a monstrous assassination plot against the gaunt, hard-beset man in the White House.

LOOK FOR
THE TURNING OF THE TIDE—
COMING IN SEPTEMBER
FROM DELL/BRYANS